LOST & HOUND

LOST & HOUND

A NOVEL

RITA MAE BROWN

ILLUSTRATED BY LEE GILDEA

BALLANTINE BOOKS

NEW YORK

Copyright © 2023 by American Artists, Inc.
Illustrations copyright © 2023 by Lee Gildea, Jr.

Published in the United States by Ballantine Books, an imprint of Random House, a division of Penguin Random House LLC, New York.

BALLANTINE and the HOUSE colophon are registered trademarks of Penguin Random House LLC.

Library of Congress Cataloging-in-Publication Data
Names: Brown, Rita Mae, author. | Gildea, Lee, Jr., illustrator.
Title: Lost & hound: a novel / Rita Mae Brown; illustrated by Lee Gildea.
Other titles: Lost and hound
Description: First edition. | New York: Ballantine Books, [2023] | Series: Sister Jane; 15 |
Identifiers: LCCN 2023003067 (print) | LCCN 2023003068 (ebook) |
ISBN 9780593357576 (hardback) | ISBN 9780593357583 (ebook)
Subjects: LCSH: Arnold, Jane (Fictitious character)—Fiction. |
LCGFT: Detective and mystery fiction. | Novels.
Classification: LCC PS3552.R698 L67 2023 (print) | LCC PS3552.R698 (ebook) |
DDC 813/.54—dc23/eng/20230203
LC record available at https://lccn.loc.gov/2023003067
LC ebook record available at https://lccn.loc.gov/2023003068

Printed in the United States of America on acid-free paper

randomhousebooks.com

2 4 6 8 9 7 5 3 1

First Edition

Dedicated to
my wonderful, vivid neighbors
Jim and Joan Klemic.
Damn the torpedoes. Full speed ahead!

CAST OF CHARACTERS

THE HUMANS

Jane Arnold, MFH, "Sister," has been a Master of Foxhounds for the Jefferson Hunt since her late thirties. Now in her middle seventies she is still going strong. Hunting three days a week during the Season keeps her fit mentally and physically. She is married to Gray Lorillard, choosing not to take his last name, which is fine with him.

Gray Lorillard isn't cautious on the hunt field but he is prudent off of it. Now retired, he was a partner in one of Washington, D.C.'s most prestigious accounting firms. Often called back for consulting, he knows how "creative" accounting really works. Handsome, kind, and smart, he has dealt with decades of racism. Doesn't stop him.

Betty Franklin has whipped-in for Jefferson Hunt for decades. Her task is to assist the huntsman, which she ably does. In her mid-fifties and Sister's best friend, she can be bold on the field and sometimes off. Everyone loves Betty.

Bobby Franklin especially loves Betty; he's her husband. They own a small printing press, work they enjoy. Bobby is a good business-man. He leads Second Flight, those people who don't jump but might clear a log or two.

Sam Lorillard is Gray's younger brother. A natural horseman, he works for Crawford Howard, who has a farmer pack of hounds. After hitting the skids he finally overcame his alcoholism with Gray's help. He is a bright man and a good one.

Daniella Laprade is Gray and Sam's aunt. Somewhere in her nineties, she can be outrageous. Stunningly beautiful, she even now looks good considering her years. No one in Jefferson Hunt has known life without her. Having three rich husbands helped her live comfortably. As to her numerous affairs, she was discreet.

Wesley Blackford, "Weevil," hunts hounds for Sister. He loves his work, and being young is learning, soaking up everything. Aunt Daniella had an affair with his grandfather, whom he greatly resem-bles. He is in love with Anne Harris.

Anne Harris, "Tootie," is another natural horseman. She whips-in to Weevil. Betty is her idol, as Betty exhibits incredible instincts in the hunt field. Tootie left Princeton to hunt with Jefferson Hunt. She is almost finished at the University of Virginia. She looks very much like her famous mother.

Yvonne Harris was one of the first black models. She and her detested ex-husband built a black media empire. Divorcing him, she moved to Albemarle County to be near Tootie in hopes of repairing that relationship. She wasn't a bad mother, but unwittingly neglect-ful. She can't understand that Tootie has little interest in racial poli-tics. Tootie is the product of her parents' success. She has no idea about earlier struggles.

Crawford Howard is best described by Aunt Daniella, who com-mented, "There's a lot to be said about being noveau riche and Crawford means to say it all." Given his ego, large as a blimp, he learned about Virginia and hunting the hard way. He made his first fortune in Indiana. They may have been irritated by him, but the Hoosiers were used to him. He is restoring Old Paradise, a great estate built with funds stolen from the British during the War of 1812.

Marty Howard, married to Crawford, patiently guided him to less bombast. She has a passion for environmental projects and the funds to pursue them.

Walter Lungren, MD, jt-MFH, practices cardiology. He has hunted with Sister since his childhood. He is the late Raymond Arnold's outside son. His father accepted his wife's indiscretion, raising Walter as his own. It wasn't discussed and still isn't. He and Sister have a warm relationship.

Ronnie Haslip is the hunt's treasurer, indefatigable in raising funds. He was the best friend of RayRay, Sister's late son. He is a good rider, loved by his chihuahua, Atlas.

Raymond Arnold, Jr., "RayRay," died in a farm accident in 1974. Loved and remembered by Sister, Ronnie, and others who knew him, they sometimes feel his spirit. He was a good athlete and a good kid.

Kasmir Barbhaiya, born and raised in India, was educated in England, like so many upper-class Indians. He foxhunts with gusto and rides well. When his wife died he left India to come to Virginia to be near an Oxford classmate and his now fiancée. He fit right in. He is a man with broad vision, knowing the world in different ways than an American.

Alida Dalzell brought Kasmir back to life and happiness. They met on the hunt field. She adored him but never made a move out of respect for his late wife. Ultimately, Kasmir realized his beloved wife would have wanted him to be happy. These two are made for each other.

Edward and Tedi Bancroft are stalwarts of the hunt. After All, their property, abuts Roughneck Farm, Sister and Gray's farm. Now in their eighties, the Bancrofts are slowing down a bit but fighting it every step of the way.

Ben Sidell is the county sheriff. He got the job coming from Columbus, Ohio, which was good training, as that is a university town. In Virginia, towns and rural areas have separate political structures, so Ben is not responsible for policing the university. There's enough to do in the county. He rides Nonni, a saint. Sister found the mare for him and told him to learn to hunt. It's the easiest way to understand Virginia, which is not like Ohio.

Cynthia Skiff Cane hunts Crawford's pack. She gets along with him. He went through three huntsmen before her. She also gets along with Jefferson Hunt.

Shaker Crown hunted Jefferson hounds for decades. A bad accident ended his hard riding. He fell for Skiff and helping her helped him, as he was lost without the horn. Hunting hounds was his life and he loved it.

Freddie Thomas hunts First Flight. She rarely talks about her profession, which is accounting. She, Gray, and Ronnie are all accountants, which sometimes amuses them. She is Alida Dalzell's best friend.

Kathleen Sixt Dunbar owns 1780 House, a high-end antiques store. Her husband left it to her even though they rarely saw each other, living hundreds of miles apart. They never bothered to get divorced. She drives Aunt Daniella around to follow the hunt. She absorbs so much about the hunt plus everything else. Aunt Daniella is a fount of information.

Rev. Sally Taliaferro is an Episcopal priest who hunts. She is always there if a parishioner or anyone else needs her.

Father Mancusco is the priest at St. Mary's. He's fairly new, only being there three years. He and Sally get along, both more than happy to give people's prayers in the hunt field.

Cameron Aldron owns a small airplane service. He will fly you or cargo anywhere within the United States. Being between D.C. and Charlotte international airports brings him a lot of business. He takes people to any East Coast city and will also go inland if need be. Business is good. He owns four airplanes and all are busy. People are sick of the big commercial airlines.

Barry Harper and Cameron were classmates together at Georgia. After graduating, Barry wound up in Atlanta defending rich criminals. He made a lot of money. Crime pays. He retired after two decades of law. He started a foundation to rescue amphibians and reptiles, which few Americans focus on.

Edward Clark, Jr., started and leads the Wildlife Center of Virginia, which is a hospital for wildlife and conservation medicine. He lectures worldwide. He hunts with Jefferson Hunt on Happy Hour, his gelding. As to this team, sometimes Sister wonders who is the monkey and who is the organ grinder?

THE AMERICAN FOXHOUNDS

Lighter than the English foxhound, with a somewhat slimmer head, they have formidable powers of endurance and remarkable noses.

Cora is the head female. What she says goes.

Asa is the oldest hunting male hound, and he is wise.

Diana is steady, in the prime of her life, and brilliant. There's no other word for her but *brilliant.*

Dasher, Diana's littermate, is often overshadowed by his sister, but he sticks to business and is coming into his own.

Dragon is also a littermate of the above "D" hounds. He is arrogant, can lose his concentration, and tries to lord his intelligence over other hounds.

Dreamboat is of the same breeding as Diana, Dasher, and Dragon, but a few years younger.

Hounds take the first initial of their mother's name. Following are hounds ordered from older to younger. No unentered hounds are included in this list. An unentered hound is not yet on the Master of Foxhounds stud books and not yet hunting with the pack. They are in essence kindergartners. **Trinity, Tinsel, Trident, Ardent, Thimble, Twist, Tootsie, Trooper, Taz, Tattoo, Parker, Pickens, Zane, Zorro, Zandy, Giorgio, Pookah, Pansy, Audrey, Aero, Angle, Aces** are young but entered. The "B" line and the "J" line have been just entered, are just learning the ropes.

THE HORSES

Keepsake, TB/QH, Bay; **Lafayette,** TB, gray; **Rickyroo,** TB, Bay; **Aztec,** TB, Chestnut; **Matador,** TB, Flea-bitten gray. All are Sister's geldings.

Showboat, Hojo, Gunpowder, and **Kilowatt,** all TBs, are Weevil's horses.

Outlaw, QH, Buckskin, and **Magellan,** TB, Dark Bay (which is really black), are Betty's horses.

Wolsey, TB, Flaming Chestnut, is Gray's horse. His red coat gave him his name, for Cardinal Wolsey.

Iota, TB, Bay, is Tootie's horse.

Matchplay and **Midshipman** are young Thoroughbreds of Sister's that are being brought along. It takes good time to make a solid foxhunter. Sister never hurries a horse or a hound in its schooling.

Trocadero is young, smart, being trained by Sam Lorillard.

Old Buster has become a babysitter. Like **Trocadero,** he is owned by Crawford Howard. Sam uses him for Yvonne Harris.

THE FOXES

Reds

Aunt Netty, older, lives at Pattypan Forge. She is overly tidy and likes to give orders.

Uncle Yancy is Aunt Netty's husband but he can't stand her anymore. He lives at the Lorillard farm, has all manner of dens and cubbyholes, as well as a place in the mudroom.

Charlene lives at After All Farm. She comes and goes.

Target is Charlene's mate but he stays at After All. The food supply is steady and he likes the other animals.

Earl has the restored stone stables at Old Paradise all to himself. He has a den in a stall but also makes use of the tack room. He likes the smell of the leather.

Sarge is young. He found a den in big boulders at Old Paradise thanks to help from a doe. It's cozy with straw, old clothing bits, and even a few toys.

James lives behind the mill at Mill Ruins. He is not very social but from time to time will give the hounds a good run.

Ewald is a youngster who was directed to a den in an outbuilding during a hunt. Poor fellow didn't know where he was. The outbuilding at Mill Ruins will be a wonderful home as long as he steers clear of James.

Mr. Nash, young, lives at Close Shave, a farm about six miles from Chapel Cross. Given the housing possibilities and the good food, he is drawn to Old Paradise, which is being restored by Crawford Howard.

Grays

Comet knows everybody and everything. He lives in the old stone foundation part of the rebuilt log-and-frame cottage at Roughneck Farm.

Inky is so dark she's black and she lives in the apple orchard across from the above cottage. She knows the hunt schedule and rarely gives hounds a run. They can just chase someone else.

Georgia moved to the old schoolhouse at Foxglove Farm.

Grenville lives at Mill Ruins, in the back in a big storage shed. This part of the estate is called Shootrough.

Gris lives at Tollbooth Farm in the Chapel Cross area. He's very clever and can slip hounds in the batting of an eye.

Hortensia also lives at Mill Ruins. She's in another outbuilding. All are well constructed and all but the big hay sheds have doors that close, which is wonderful in bad weather.

Vi, young, is the mate of Gris, also young. They live at Tollbooth Farm in pleasant circumstances.

THE BIRDS

Athena, the great horned owl, is two and a half feet tall with a four-foot wingspan. She has many places where she will hole up but her true nest is in Pattypan Forge. It really beats being in a tree hollow. She's gotten spoiled.

Bitsy is eight and a half inches tall with a twenty-inch wingspan. Her considerable lungs make up for her tiny size as she is a screech owl, aptly named. Like Athena, she'll never live in a tree again, because she's living in the rafters of Sister's stable. Mice come in to eat the fallen grain. Bitsy feels like she's living in a supermarket.

St. Just, a foot and a half in height with a surprising wingspan of three feet, is a jet-black crow. He hates foxes but is usually sociable with other birds.

Raleigh, a sleek, highly intelligent Doberma
He gets along with the hounds, walks out w
along with the cat, but she's such a snob.

Rooster is a Harrier bequeathed to Si
likes riding in the car, walking out with hou
and everything. The cat drives him crazy.

Golliwog, or "Golly," is a long-haired
are lower life-forms. She knows Sister does
Queen of All She Surveys.

Atlas, a chihuahua, stays with Sister
owner, is injured.

J. Edgar, a young box turtle with a be
Roughneck Farm. Golliwog, the cat, is app

USEFUL TERMS

Away. A fox has gone away when he has left the covert. Hounds are away when they have left the covert on the line of the fox.

Brush. The fox's tail.

Burning scent. Scent so strong or hot that hounds pursue the line without hesitation.

Bye day. A day not regularly on the fixture card.

Cap. The fee nonmembers pay to hunt for that day's sport.

Carry a good head. When hounds run well together to a good scent, a scent spread wide enough for the whole pack to feel it.

Carry a line. When hounds follow the scent. This is also called working a line.

Cast. Hounds spread out in search of scent. They may cast themselves or be cast by the huntsman.

Charlie. A term for a fox. A fox may also be called **Reynard.**

Check. When hounds lose the scent and stop. The field must wait quietly while the hounds search for the scent.

Colors. A distinguishing color, usually worn on the collar but sometimes on the facings of a coat, that identifies a hunt. Colors can be awarded only by the Master and can be worn only in the field.

Coop. A jump resembling a chicken coop.

Couple straps. Two-strap hound collars connected by a swivel link. Some members of staff will carry these on the right rear of the saddle. Since the days of the pharaohs in ancient Egypt, hounds have been brought to the meets coupled. Hounds are always spoken of and counted in couples. Today, hounds walk or are driven to the meets. Rarely, if ever, are they coupled, but a whipper-in still carries couple straps should a hound need assistance.

Covert. A patch of woods or bushes where a fox might hide. Pronounced "cover."

Cry. How one hound tells another what is happening. The sound will differ according to the various stages of the chase. It's also called giving tongue and should occur when a hound is working a line.

Cub hunting. The informal hunting of young foxes in the late summer and early fall, before formal hunting. The main purpose is to enter young hounds into the pack. Until recently only the most knowledgeable members were invited to cub hunt, since they would not interfere with young hounds.

Dog fox. The male fox.

Dog hound. The male hound.

Double. A series of short, sharp notes blown on the horn to alert all that a fox is afoot. The gone away series of notes is a form of doubling the horn.

Draft. To acquire hounds from another hunt is to accept a draft.

Draw. The plan by which a fox is hunted or searched for in a certain area, such as a covert.

Draw over the fox. Hounds go through a covert where the fox is but cannot pick up its scent. The only creature that understands how this is possible is the fox.

Drive. The desire to push the fox, to get up with the line. It's a very desirable trait in hounds, so long as they remain obedient.

Dually. A one-ton pickup truck with double wheels in back.

Dwell. To hunt without getting forward. A hound that dwells is a bit of a putterer.

Enter. Hounds are entered into the pack when they first hunt, usually during cubbing season.

Field. The group of people riding to hounds, exclusive of the Master and hunt staff.

Field Master. The person appointed by the Master to control the field. Often it is the Master him- or herself.

Fixture. A card sent to all dues-paying members, stating when and where the hounds will meet. A fixture card properly received is an invitation to hunt. This means the card would be mailed or handed to a member by the Master.

Flea-bitten. A gray horse with spots or ticking that can be black or chestnut.

Gone away. The call on the horn when the fox leaves the covert.

Gone to ground. A fox that has ducked into its den, or some other refuge, has gone to ground.

Good night. The traditional farewell to the Master after the hunt, regardless of the time of day.

Gyp. The female hound.

Hilltopper. A rider who follows the hunt but does not jump. Hilltoppers are also called the Second Flight. The jumpers are called the First Flight.

Hoick. The huntsman's cheer to the hounds. It is derived from the Latin *hic haec hoc*, which means "here."

Hold hard. To stop immediately.

Huntsman. The person in charge of the hounds, in the field and in the kennel.

Kennelman. A hunt staff member who feeds the hounds and

cleans the kennels. In wealthy hunts there may be a number of kennelmen. In hunts with a modest budget, the huntsman or even the Master cleans the kennels and feeds the hounds.

Lark. To jump fences unnecessarily when hounds aren't running. Masters frown on this, since it is often an invitation to an accident.

Lieu in. Norman term for "go in."

Lift. To take the hounds from a lost scent in the hopes of finding a better scent farther on.

Line. The scent trail of the fox.

Livery. The uniform worn by the professional members of the hunt staff. Usually it is scarlet, but blue, yellow, brown, and gray are also used. The recent dominance of scarlet has to do with people buying coats off the rack as opposed to having tailors cut them. (When anything is mass-produced, the choices usually dwindle, and such is the case with livery.)

Mask. The fox's head.

Meet. The site where the day's hunting begins.

MFH. The Master of Foxhounds; the individual in charge of the hunt: hiring, firing, landowner relations, opening territory (in large hunts this is the job of the hunt secretary), developing the pack of hounds, and determining the first cast of each meet. As in any leadership position, the Master is also the lightning rod for criticism. The Master may hunt the hounds, although this is usually done by a professional huntsman, who is also responsible for the hounds in the field and at the kennels. A long relationship between a Master and a huntsman allows the hunt to develop and grow.

Nose. The scenting ability of a hound.

Override. To press hounds too closely.

Overrun. When hounds shoot past the line of a scent. Often the scent has been diverted or foiled by a clever fox.

Ratcatcher. Informal dress worn during cubbing season and bye days.

Stern. A hound's tail.

Stiff-necked fox. One that runs in a straight line.

Strike hounds. Those hounds that, through keenness, nose, and often higher intelligence, find the scent first and press it.

Tail hounds. Those hounds running at the rear of the pack. This is not necessarily because they aren't keen; they may be older hounds.

Tally-ho. The cheer when the fox is viewed. Derived from the Norman *ty a hillaut,* thus coming into the English language in 1066.

Tongue. To vocally pursue a fox.

View halloo (halloa). The cry given by a staff member who sees a fox. Staff may also say tally-ho or, should the fox turn back, tally-back. One reason a different cry may be used by staff, especially in territory where the huntsman can't see the staff, is that the field in their enthusiasm may cheer something other than a fox.

Vixen. The female fox.

Walk. Puppies are walked out in the summer and fall of their first year. It's part of their education and a delight for both puppies and staff.

Whippers-in. Also called whips, these are the staff members who assist the huntsman, who make sure the hounds "do right."

LOST & HOUND

CHAPTER 1

September 23, 2022, Friday

The long slanting rays before sunset illuminated the dancing milkweed seeds, silver white, turning them gold, then scarlet, and finally a rich lavender. Jane Arnold, Sister to all, stood in her twenty-acre wildflower field watching the rising, falling, twirling milkweeds. The temperature cooled as the sun set. She hugged her old cashmere sweater, thin but warm, tighter to her as she walked back toward the farm road.

The field contained black-eyed Susans announcing fall had truly arrived. Jerusalem artichokes, coneflowers, their blue contrasting with the yellows; towering above all were the Joe Pye weeds. Sister never considered Joe Pye a weed but that was the title. Underfoot were the remains of lavender.

The light faltered. As it did so, the electric lights came on in the original log cabin of Roughneck Farm, built back in the early seventeen hundreds. Later, money rolling in, the owners added a clapboard addition, all of this settling on a stout stone foundation.

Breathing the cool air, Sister felt a tug of melancholy. Today was the day after the autumnal equinox. She always paused, as she felt the equinoxes gave us stillness, a time to reflect; look back and look forward. And she did.

Stepping onto the red clay farm road, some ruts deepening, she noted the apple orchard across from the log cabin. Over the generations it had been tended, pruned, restored, new trees planted when the old finally produced their last fruits, always with a flourish. One knew it was the end. She wondered was this the same for humans. How could one know?

A black fox, Inky, kept a large, tidy den in the apple orchard. Comet, another fox, gray, lived under the log cabin in cozy quarters. Not only did the warmth somewhat radiate downward, but Comet had also stolen every old coat, scarf, and saddle pad left unwatched. Target, a red male, who floated between two dens, and two farms, the other being After All due to his vixen who refused to live near the Jefferson Hunt Kennels, often bunked up with Comet. Target flirted with thievery, occasionally dragging off a pillow left on an outside chair or, better yet, the tattered remains of a hard-used blanket.

Inky, while not lacking for comforts, could not match the clever paws of the two boys. Were they human, they would have been called light-fingered.

The farm road, hard, as it hadn't rained for a week, crunched underfoot as Sister turned right to go toward her house, called the Big House, built during the glory days of Monroe's presidency. By that time, three generations of bold souls who had originally left the old country, England, had lived here. The third generation riding high after the war debts had been paid off, thanks to Hamilton's hard work and brainpower, had made enough to build a large, gracious, yet simple home, adorned with enormous chimneys. Virginia winters get cold, especially by the Blue Ridge Mountains. Inky watched the tall silver-haired woman pass by. Inky missed very little, noticing a twilight opossum meandering her way. Inky liked the creature but that girl could talk.

Sister carefully walked past the foxhound kennel so as not to disturb anyone. They knew she was near. Human scent is strong and Sister always wore the same cologne, Green Irish Tweed by Creed. If it was good enough for Marlene Dietrich and Cary Grant, it was good enough for her.

Reaching the herringbone brick walkway, she briskly stepped into the mudroom, peeled off the ancient sweater, folding it on a shelf, then opened the door to the kitchen.

"Why didn't you take us?" her Doberman, Raleigh, cried.

Rooster, the Harrier, looked on with mournful eyes.

The cat, an impressive long hair, would not lower herself to join the dogs. Sister clicked on the kitchen light, the overhead one above the round table.

"All right." She put two scoops of crunchies in the dog bowl. Then she peeled open a small expensive cat food container, dumping it in Golliwog's dish, using a table knife to get all of it.

Golly rubbed against her in thanks. Twilight lingered outside. The changing seasons altered the winds, the light softened, and twilight lingered, coating everything in a silvered dark blue until night finally took over.

She sat down at the table, her cellphone and a cup of hot chocolate on top of the old oak surface. Never pass up the opportunity to drink hot chocolate unless it's blistering hot.

She dialed her best friend.

Betty picked up. "Saw your number. Ready for tomorrow?"

"Am. Are you?"

"I am. Should be cool for an hour or two. Starting at seven-thirty helps. Of course, a lot of people aren't going to get out of bed at four or five. Still, we know who the diehards are."

"That we do," Sister agreed. "I love those foggy fall mornings. Sometimes scent lays down for you and sometimes it doesn't, but the early days of cubbing excite me. Tempers that autumn melancholy."

"Funny how it gets you. I love the coolness, the color of the trees, the wildlife getting ready for winter. So much activity. And yet there is that twinge. The flowers will soon be gone. The winds will pick up from the northwest and sometimes that can cut you to the bone."

"I am convinced those winds keep our complexions clean. Doesn't do a damn thing for the wrinkles though."

"Well, that's what plastic surgeons are for. You'd think plastic surgeons would be foxhunters. Think of the customers both from accidents and vanity," Betty declared.

"Ha. Well, who doesn't want to look younger?"

"Oh, Sister, put on a few pounds, it fills the wrinkles. I don't know how you do it. How long have I known you? As a friend, not just an acquaintance. Forty years?"

"You aren't sixty yet. Do your math."

"Okay. Thirty years. Bobby and I started seriously hunting when I was twenty-five. We thought it would be good for business and it sure was."

"You do excellent work. The wedding invitations are classic, as are special announcements, people's stationery. And you know even though people can print on their computers, nothing, nothing looks like expensive paper beautifully colored with the choice of script, or block actually, cut into the paper. I'm not using correct terminology."

"I love looking at typeface." Betty used the correct term. "Well, we nearly went under but we did bounce back after close to a decade. No one really wants a run-off wedding invitation. That is the recipient's first clue as to what kind of wedding it will really be."

"Now there are gay weddings. More business."

"Thank heavens. To change the subject, how many hounds are you taking tomorrow?"

"Fifteen couple. I like to take two youngsters at a time until mid-October. Then, as you know, I'll bump it up. Don't like overwhelming them. Absorbing the new people on horseback takes some adjustment as well. But thirty hounds, that's plenty."

"Tie, colored stock, or bow tie? I'm wearing my tie. Well, Bobby's tie. He has a zillion."

"One of my Ben Silver ties."

"Does this count as drag? For women?"

A pause followed this. "Why not? Next we could start a TV show. Drag in reverse."

"Good idea." Betty actually liked snitching her husband's ties.

"After hunting tomorrow, if you have time, I'll take you to the wildflower field. The butterfly flowers I put in I hope have paid off. You'll see."

"We might ride through them. Anyways, I'd love to see and hear your plans for planting and replanting. One of the things I really like about the younger generation is how environmentally conscious they are," Betty said.

"Me too. See you tomorrow."

Sister clicked off the phone. What a hopeful phrase, "See you tomorrow."

CHAPTER 2

September 24, 2022, Saturday

Thick fog stubbornly refused to rise. Usually it began to lift after sunup. Sometimes the fog would linger for a half hour, thick, beginning to thin then lift, a pure white, finally dissipating after an hour or hour and a half. At eight, the clinging fog didn't budge. Riding through it you felt it sticking to your skin.

At least that's how Sister felt. Hounds had not picked up anything . . . which she also felt was unusual . . . because of the saturated air, the dew on the grass. If that weren't enough, the temperature, low fifties, felt colder. Fortunately, she'd pulled on a cotton T-shirt under her light blue shirt; a navy stock tie, small red polka dots, kept her neck warm. The thin deerskin gloves felt good on her hands.

By now, pushing through the wildflower field, the small group walked toward the bridge at After All Farm, owned by the Bancrofts. If she hadn't recognized an odd sycamore tree, Sister would have had no idea where she was. Nor did she know where the hounds were, as no one was speaking. She could hear a clop clop behind her as the small field of thirteen people followed her as best they could, which meant they were too close because they couldn't see either.

The fog kept people home. Country roads are winding, dangerous. Her field consisted of the Bancrofts themselves . . . Tedi and Edward . . . both in their eighties, tough as nails. Behind them rode Gray Lorillard, Sister's husband, and his brother, Sam, as well as her joint master, Dr. Walter Lungren; Ronnie Haslip, the club treasurer; along with Kasmir Barbhaiya and his fiancée, Alida Dalzell. Bobby Franklin, field master of Second Flight, also known as the hilltoppers, had four people, one being Elise Sabatini. As this was her first day, Sister hoped the conditions wouldn't deter her. The Sabatinis owned Showoff Stables, a former hunt fixture. The other three, Ed Clark, president of the Wildlife Center of Virginia; Cameron Aldron, a pilot; and Barry Harper, president of a small amphibian and reptile foundation, cheered her on. Bobby did his best to see the rear of Clemson, Walter's horse.

Betty Franklin rode as whipper-in on the right and Tootie Harris, in her last year at University of Virginia, rode on the left. No one could see anyone.

Sister listened intently to hear her whipper-ins.

She could hear Weevil Blackford, her Huntsman, and the hounds. The occasional toot on the horn proved a big help.

Hounds, Diana in the lead, noses down, pressed on. Fifteen couple hunted today, two of whom were first-year entries, literally first graders. Fifteen couple meant thirty hounds, for hounds are always measured in couples, having been so since the days of the pharaohs, keen hunters.

The silence unnerved Sister. She relied on bird calls, the sound of deer tiptoeing away or running. During fall, squirrels could be crabby, throwing acorns at anyone who disturbed them. Most animals, preparing for winter, ignored the hounds. They knew them.

The older ones . . . raccoons, possums, and rabbits . . . informed their children as to the habits of hounds, adding that domesticated animals were spoiled and weak. The hounds ignored the rude calls. A few foxes were not above insults when by their den. Otherwise they kept their mouths shut.

Gunpowder's reverberating hooves made Sister realize they were closer than she thought to the covered bridge. A second set of hooves echoed. Maybe that was Betty following Weevil, on Outlaw, her rock-steady horse. One never knows what's going on out there. Seeing helps. She didn't want to run across a deer trail only to collide with a downed tree.

The bridge appeared, ghostly, before Sister.

The fog thinned enough that she could make out the bridge's opening plus she could just see the dark red color on the sides by the opening. Keepsake, her Thoroughbred–Quarter horse cross, readily strode forward.

On the other side of the bridge, she turned left, staying on the wide farm road. Much as she wanted the hounds to hunt a bit, she was glad of the slow pace. A hot run in these conditions would be dangerous. What's the point of starting the Season with injury?

A low hoot indicated a barn owl. No answering hoot was forthcoming. Sister knew to the right was the large home, After All, Georgian architecture but made of fieldstone, unusual. After All often appeared in architectural books focused on eighteenth-century Virginia homes. After All barely made it, the original portion built in 1790, the wings following when the money rolled in. Money was unpredictable then as now. Onward they moved in a northeasterly direction. Trees lining the road, their upward limbs reaching out, tips visible as they dipped.

Trinity, coming into his prime, stopped. *"Aunt Netty, has to be Aunt Netty."*

His littermate, Twist, came over. *"Is. She's such a pain."*

Trinity called out, *"Aunt Netty."*

Diana, older, knew the somewhat younger hound was reliable. She didn't check the spot. Soon all hounds were running, the sound oddly muffled.

Sister kept on the road, thinking Betty and Tootie must be having one bitch of a time on the narrow side trails. This territory, while gently rolling, boasted thick woods. You needed to see where you were going.

Sure enough, hounds veered left toward old Pattypan Forge, a large structure used for two centuries before more forges were built, especially after World War I once the economy recovered. Pattypan was in use nearly thirty years after that, finally shutting down in the 1950s. Fewer and fewer people were metal workers. No one was left to manage the forge.

Although hounds were running, Sister kept it to a trot. She was determined not to lose anyone, including herself, on this trail. Some limbs hung down more than they had at the trail clearing late August. There'd been enough wind since then for unwelcome surprises. She heard hooves behind her.

Hounds stopped. So did she. She called back to the small field. "No heroics today."

"Good," Edward Bancroft replied.

Hoofbeats came toward her, hounds slithered by her.

Sister backed off the trail, not so easy as her Huntsman came by.

"Madam." Weevil slowed. "I'll head for the Lorillard home place. Has to be better than this." He tapped his crop to his cap, adding, "Put that old crab to ground in the forge."

Then he slowly cantered, the field happy when he passed, as everyone was wedged in.

Sister followed Weevil and each rider freed herself or himself from the brush as she passed. You never impede the Huntsman, the whippers-in, or the Master.

Soon they were back out on the road, the atmosphere feeling even more clammy. The farm road, firm and wide, usually free of all traffic, gave everyone a breather. Not that they ran hard, but vigilance can be tiring.

Nearing the tidy white clapboard home, not in view, Sister checked her cinch. This area was home to one sturdy male fox plus the odd visitor.

Keepsake shied and snorted. Since Keepsake was a steady horse, Sister thought a bear might be in the vicinity. Often, even a human can smell bear. She didn't catch the scent but something was affecting Keepsake. Sister thought she saw something on her right. Looked like a shadowy figure but low. Had to be an illusion.

Hounds opened. She did, too. The road was wide and safe, fog or no fog. A brisk seven-minute gallop brought them to the lovely home, somewhat visible. Hounds, staff, and field were close. A bit of fog thinned by the house but it remained unusually heavy elsewhere. The hounds dug under the front porch.

Weevil dismounted, handing his reins to Tootie, who had ridden up.

Kneeling down he peered under the porch through the slats. Fog hung there, too. But he could smell the fox, Uncle Yancy.

Uncle Yancy, Aunt Netty's reluctant spouse, had zipped in there to fool hounds then zipped out. He was successful, as he already stretched himself out on the shelf above the mudroom door to the kitchen. Piles of folded towels, old sweaters allowed him to snuggle behind them. The heat from the kitchen kept the mudroom warmer than outside, but not as warm as the kitchen. It was a cozy home, easy to get into, and easy to get out of. Hounds continued to dig at the front porch while Uncle Yancy dozed off, in the rear of the house.

Weevil mounted up.

Sister rode up to him. "Let's lift. The weather isn't getting any better. I don't trust it."

"Yes, Madam." He nodded as he agreed.

Betty and Tootie fell into their positions on either side of the pack. On the way back to the covered bridge and then across the wildflower field to the kennels, people's trailers, Sister felt a dropping northeast wind at her back. Usually the winds came from the northwest.

Once there, hounds in, horses up, the other horses tied to the trailers with feed bags, a few inside the trailers, the small group gathered inside Sister's house.

Gray made coffee, Betty made tea, and a bottle of sherry sat on the kitchen table. No one was interested in alcohol at this hour.

Walter helped put out butter, muffins, scrambled eggs, and bacon, as hunts often finished with a breakfast even in the afternoon.

Kasmir and Alida guided Elise to the food.

"Should I be first?" she wondered, still full of energy from her first hunt.

"Of course." Alida smiled. "This was your maiden hunt."

"Even though I couldn't see a thing it was exciting when the hounds started barking."

No one corrected her to say "speaking." Why? She'd figure it out in good time.

People filled plates then sat at the large dining room table while Gray, who had filled the samovar, brought people coffee. Finally, he sat down.

"Here's to a steaming hunt season."

They lifted their coffee. "Hear. Hear."

Then Sister tapped her glass, raised it. "Three cheers for Elise Sabatini's first hunt."

Happy cheers, hand claps, and hands thumping the table followed.

Elise was thrilled.

Everyone felt that surge that accompanies a good time. Maybe it wasn't much of a hunt, but they were outside, together, hounds spoke a bit, and no one parted company with their mount. Betty sat next to Sister, not at the head of the table, which she deferred to Gray. She liked seeing him be the host. Gray and Sam resembled each other. Each man was light-skinned, handsome, very masculine. Gray sported a military moustache, while Sam remained clean-shaven. Gray, being older, had salt-and-pepper hair. Sam's was still mostly black.

Betty, next to Sister on one side, Alida on the other, caught up on their predictions for the football season.

"Giants. They'll come back," Alida predicted.

"No way." Betty sniffed good-naturedly. "Now the comeback will be the Miami Dolphins."

"Ha." Sister laughed.

"They will. You just watch. You never got over the Dallas Cowboys."

"That's not fair." Sister bit into her croissant. "Teams go up and down."

Elise joined the conversation. "My husband would sit here and go on and on about the Kansas City Chiefs."

"Pittsburgh." Bobby finished his scrambled eggs, rising to get more. "Anyone need anything?"

"No thanks" came the chorus.

"Barry, saw a brief interview with you on my cellphone wildlife app. You were convincing," Sam complimented the middle-aged man.

"Cameron put me up to it." He nodded across the table. "Said there are now so many video shows, blogs, podcasts, I should really work media. Of course I can't hold a candle to Ed Clark."

Ed, next to Ronnie, leaned forward. "You need a big mouth."

Everyone laughed, including Barry.

Ed and Ronnie returned to their discussion about fundraising for the Wildlife Center of Virginia as well as the Jefferson Hunt Club.

Both men enjoyed kicking around how to raise money, as neither organization was for profit.

Ronnie, scribbling on a napkin, said, "Fundraising is the second oldest profession."

Ed thought a moment. "Would we get anywhere using the first?"

"As two men of a certain age, Ed, I don't think we'd make a dime. Plus you don't incline that way."

Laughing, Ed replied, "I know, but there are times when I wonder how low could I go to keep the Center flourishing?"

Sister observed the two poking each other, laughing. She believed Jefferson Hunt brought people together. Riding in the hunt field overcomes barriers. The fox doesn't care about your color, religion, social status, or income. He'll make a fool out of you if he can. Usually he can. Foxhunting is a great equalizer. You can stay on your horse or you can't. Eventually everyone hits the dirt. If one is going to be sensible about it, take up canasta.

Cameron was still encouraging Barry about media.

"Barry, sit with an iguana. People will love it."

Betty giggled. "But would the iguana?"

Turning to face Betty and Sister, Barry confided, "Reptiles and amphibians are my focus, as you know. If I sat with a raccoon, more people would be interested."

"True." Edward Bancroft joined the conversation. "But if you give people an interesting fact, most people do get intrigued."

Sam teased Cameron. "You can fly Barry to interviews. That would impress people, an airborne limo."

"Hear that, Barry?" Cameron prodded his friend. "Your foundation is small. You need to grow. You might not raise as much money as the Wildlife Center of Virginia but good things will happen. People trying to save animals are compelling."

"Even people who try to save trees can be compelling." Alida had a deep interest in arboretums, green spaces.

"They can be so beautiful." Betty enjoyed visiting botanical gardens, arboretums. She wanted to see where Virginia Tech was growing American chestnut hybrids. The Department of Forest Resources and Environmental Conservation had a great interest in Tech's program, as did everyone interested in overcoming virus damage to plants, trees.

"Auburn," Sam named a rival university, "does a lot of interesting stuff."

Gray called out to his brother, "Don't start. There are enough Tech graduates here to jump on you."

Sister smiled at Sam. "At least you didn't say Harvard, your alma mater."

Cameron, a bit newer to the club, looked at Sam. "Harvard. Well, I graduated from Georgia, the Harvard of the South."

"I drank myself out of Harvard." Sam was frank. "Don't worry. I'm not embarrassed. Everyone here knows I failed. But I cleaned up. I have work I love."

Everyone started talking at once. Betty told Cameron, "Don't worry. You haven't stirred up an old pain."

"Whew," he said.

Barry, observing all this, piped up. "Well, I, too, graduated from Georgia, where I barely made it."

The talk switched back to college football, as opposed to the pros.

Riotous challenges followed. Laughter, bets, and money waved in the air, created a lively gathering.

The breakfast broke up. Tootie and Weevil came in late but they, too, enjoyed the group. Weevil, being Canadian, was more interested in hockey, but football was okay.

As the people left, Betty, Tootie, and Weevil helped clear plus put the food away.

"You two take some of this. My handsome husband made too much food. He usually does," Betty urged.

Walking into the kitchen, Gray said, "You can never make a mistake overfeeding people."

"That's the truth." Betty smiled. "Say, did anyone notice an odd apparition in the fog?"

Sister stopped washing the dishes for a moment. "Like what?"

"I was on the right, following the farm road. Anyways, trying to stay with hounds, I couldn't really see. It looked like someone, a man, sitting in a chair, facing the farm road. Fuzzy. Doubt there was anything there. Fog can fool you. That's why you don't fly in it."

"Remember the Big Bopper?" Bobby put a plastic cap on a food container. "Buddy Holly, Ritchie Valens, and J. P. Richardson were killed in 1959."

"Bad weather, fog or not. Ugh." Betty put away the clean cups as Golliwog sauntered into the room.

"Where was she? And where are the dogs?" Betty wondered.

"Golly was under the sideboard, praying for dropped food. The dogs were in the bedroom with cookies and toys. I didn't want Elise's first breakfast to be with the dogs," Sister answered. "She likes animals but perhaps not at a breakfast."

"So back to the apparition." Betty returned to her subject. "It startled me. But I couldn't swear to really seeing anything. We were moving on, fog thick. Had to be something like a branch, logs piled in an odd way."

"Funny. Keepsake shied. Thought I saw something large by the road, too, but I doubt it. We haven't been back there since the latest windstorm."

"All right. Almost done." Gray, tall, reached up to put away more cups handed to him by Betty, who stepped off the library stool.

"Here. You do it better than I do."

As the last of the group dispersed, Sister ran upstairs, let Raleigh and Rooster out.

"Thank God." Rooster barked.

"I hate being in the bedroom when there are people downstairs." Raleigh, the Doberman, put his nose in Sister's hand.

Gray, now in the library, smiled as he heard Sister and a pair of dogs coming down the back steps.

Golly, on the back of the sofa, ignored them when they padded into the room.

Gray clicked on the TV. He loved college football. Sitting down next to Sister, he draped his arm over her shoulders.

"Isn't it funny that both Betty and I thought we saw something in the fog?"

"Fog really can distort objects," he replied.

It was no distortion.

CHAPTER 3

September 25, 2022, Sunday

The African Methodist Church had an early service. Sam and Gray usually took their aunt Daniella to the eight AM service. Occasionally, Gray would go with Sister to Emmanuel Episcopal.

A light mist covered the trees, tombstones, and tarmac. Not as heavy as yesterday's fog, but Sam still drove slowly away from the home place. He'd pick up his aunt on the way to Charlottesville. Gray would meet them at the church, the one they had attended as children. Aunt Daniella had been a member for over ninety years. She and her sister, Graziella, were taken there at four and six. Aunt Dan admitted to being ninety-four, so the timeline shifted at will. She was in no hurry to be precise.

As Sam drove his clean truck, he slowed, then stopped with shock. Opening the door to the truck, he was hit by a brush of colder air, along with a faint odor of death. Not old death but the beginnings of the process of decomposition.

He stared at one sightless eye as two vultures flew off the corpse's shoulders to watch Sam from the tree branches. The birds had eaten some of his face. One eye was missing. Blood pooled in the man's hands. Rigor mortis had passed. Sam, like most country people, knew the rough stages of decay based on the season. Whoever this was had recently come out of rigor. The fog was so thick yesterday, he'd noticed nothing on his way to the Old Home Place. Others called it the Lorillard-Laprade place.

Hopping back in his truck, Sam called his brother.

"Gray, go pick up Aunt Dan. I found a dead man. Need to call Sheriff Sidell and wait for him."

"On the way to church?" Gray was astonished.

"If fog hadn't been so thick yesterday, we all might have seen this guy. White. Well dressed. Blood leaking out of his ears. Dried-up blood. Don't know how he was killed. Anyway, go. I've got to call Ben."

"Right. Aunt Dan, Sister, and I will come to the house after church. I'll call Sister. You're okay if she comes over?"

"Yes, of course." Sam, like Gray, had known Sister since his childhood, admiring her for her fairness and horsemanship.

Sam sat in the car, shaken. No one wants to find a dead body but this fellow had been here long enough for the birds to have pecked out one eye, and to tear flesh. Something had chewed on those swollen hands. Another twenty-four hours and he would have been really chewed up. Protein attracts all meat eaters, especially those who eat carrion.

Twenty minutes later, Ben Sidell drove up in the squad car, accompanied by Jude, a young officer. Behind them followed the ambulance with the forensic team.

Sam stepped down as Ben got out. Both men knew each other well, as both hunted.

Ben walked to the corpse. "Sitting straight up."

Sam pointed to the dark thin rope tying the body to the chair, a simple wooden chair, high-backed.

"Right. Marsha." He called to the woman heading the forensic team. "Get the pictures, close-up of his hands, too." He turned to Sam. "Someone had a nibble."

While not exactly gallows humor, law enforcement people become accustomed to corpses.

Jude walked behind the body. "No signs of battering."

"Hmm. Fortyish. Well dressed. White. No rings. No watch." He paused. "Could have been stolen." He backed away. "Over to you."

Marsha and two others examined the corpse. They wore thin plastic gloves. Photographs were taken as they inspected.

Ben, Jude, and Sam leaned against the back of Sam's truck.

"Sheriff, the fog was so thick yesterday, we must have passed the body. He's a little way off the road but not all that much."

"Was a punishing fog. Nothing but accidents. Of course, on my one weekend off work," Ben remarked.

The department scheduled one weekend off each for officers and staff and headquarters per month. In a crisis everyone had to work though.

"If he'd been here before the fog, I would've seen him. So what do you think, a day and a half?" Sam asked.

"Sheriff. Could be he was killed somewhere else then brought here. Given the condition of the body, he's been dead close to two days," Jude, sharp-eyed, said.

"You might be right. The cool nights helped. Be in worse condition if this were July." Ben looked at the body again. "He doesn't look like he was on food stamps."

"Maybe that's why he was killed," Jude shrewdly noted.

"We've gone this entire year with three murders in the county. Now four." Ben rubbed his chin. "The other three, the perp was right there. Drugs, domestic violence. Emotional. No planning. This was planned."

Sam asked, "Would you like to take a picture to show Aunt Dan? She knows more people than I do."

"No. Let's not disturb her Sunday. She doesn't need to see this. As there are no signs of struggle, I will work from the direction that he was killed then moved. He is sitting in the chair here for some reason. The killer or killers wanted him to be seen."

Sam frowned. "And once you establish the time of death, he could have been moved here Friday night. So maybe the fog spoiled the killer's plans."

"Why?" Jude, late twenties, liked law enforcement a great deal because he was working with Ben, who was willing to explain things.

"Maybe whoever did this wanted someone in the hunt club to see," Ben replied.

Sam blinked. "Or me."

"You're in the hunt club."

Sam nodded. "Are these cases more exciting than, say, domestic violence?"

"They are, but I'll tell you, Sam, domestic violence is a lot more dangerous for us." He nodded toward Jude. "People are screaming at one another. Blood is spilled often and it's usually a battered woman's. The man might have a gun; we've gone in once or twice when a child has a gun. Or a teenager. You never know. And what drives me crazy is, sometimes the battered woman, you drag off her man, and she starts screaming at you to leave him alone. He didn't mean it."

"It's hard to understand." Sam drew in a deep breath. "As you know, I was a falling-down drunk, living on the streets. I can sort of understand if there is alcohol involved. You have no judgment. But still, if you've been called to a domestic violence scene, chances are it's not the first time."

"Right."

Jude, who didn't know Sam's history, looked at Sam, and Sam said to him, "Blew a scholarship to Harvard. One of the first black undergraduates taken. Just blew it. Drank myself right out of Harvard and anywhere else. My brother saved me, as did Aunt Dan and my cousin Mercer, whom you didn't know. He died about seven years ago. But even with bad judgment, I don't know what provokes a person to kill. Maybe you've had that same argument for years and . . ." He snapped his fingers.

"Happens," Ben agreed, watching the forensic team being precise. "About done?"

"Another ten minutes. We have to carefully move him." Marsha put her hands on her hips. "I'll call the medical examiner in Richmond, unless you have another plan."

"No. The sooner we get an autopsy the better." Ben flipped his notebook, writing the time, the place, Sam's testimony.

"Anything I can do?" Sam asked.

"No. I'm glad you found him." Ben turned as Marsha was stripping off her gloves. "Nothing in his pockets?"

"A pack of Life Savers," she said.

"Guess they didn't work." Ben shrugged. "Sam, sooner or later reporters will get to you."

"Yeah. Yeah. I'll call my boss in case they go there. Crawford probably won't like it." Sam named his extremely wealthy boss, who was spending a fortune restoring a grand old estate named Old Paradise. "Can I go home?"

"Sure. By the way, how was the hunt?"

"Slow. One little run. Couldn't see and Sister took that into account," Sam replied.

"If you see her today, give her my regards. Tell her I'll be out next Saturday," Ben said.

"Will do."

Aunt Daniella, Gray, Sister, and Yvonne Harris, Tootie's mother, came to the house, where Sam had already started lunch by making his famous chicken corn soup.

The old kitchen, crowded, bubbled with talk. Aunt Daniella sipped her glass of bourbon, a necessity after church. She swore the bourbon helped her find the deeper messages in the sermon. No one believed her, but so what?

Gray held up his scotch, looking at Sister. "To my oxygen thief."

The others clinked glasses.

Sister was slightly blushing, her voice lifting up a touch. "Where do you come up with this stuff?"

"You do take my breath away." He beamed at her.

"You two are lucky," Yvonne simply stated.

"The secret is keep talking. We talk about everything and we don't always agree. So we agree to disagree, but I can talk to Gray about anything. If it's boring, he doesn't say so."

"You know, honey, you're right. Haven't we all seen couples at dinner somewhere, not saying a word to each other?" Gray smiled, he loved her praise.

"We have," Aunt Daniella agreed.

Sam . . . besotted with Yvonne, his riding student, as she wanted to hunt . . . kept quiet.

Yvonne liked him, was confused, so she kept quiet. A wretched divorce now two years back made her feel wary and hopeless. She feared her wealth would attract men as much as her looks. Sam, not impressed with her money, nonetheless felt unworthy, as he had so little.

The others noticed so they changed the subject.

"How was Ben?" Sister asked Sam.

"Said he'd be out Saturday. Seeing him working, he's totally professional. As is the team. Then again, this is their job. Although thankfully we aren't suffering the murder rate that Richmond has," Sam filled her in.

"Isn't it shocking how many children have been killed in Richmond? Children caught in crossfire. It doesn't appear to be slowing down," Yvonne noted.

"When people don't fear consequences, society decays." Aunt Daniella spoke forcefully. "When I was a child, I did what Momma and Daddy told me and if I didn't, I got my nether regions swatted." She looked at her nephews. "Your sister rarely got a whopping but I majored in them. Rules were rules and I believe that discipline is what got me up and over, so to speak. As for you two, Graziella made you cut your own forsythia switches, because they sting the most."

"Yes, she did." Sam laughed. "Momma was sweet but you knew where the lines were."

"Now she'd be accused of child abuse." Gray leaned back in his chair, as the heat felt good and he was full. "If there's another way to teach a child that actions have consequences, I doubt it is as effective as a swat with a forsythia branch."

"I never believed that until I had Tootie. I finally realized as she reached two that you can't reason with a two-year-old. I don't know, as I never slapped her, but I sure sent her to her room." She thought a moment. "What are we going to do? She finishes this year and has applied to every vet school there is. She's praying for Cornell. Part of me wants to see her go. Part of me doesn't want life here upended. I mean, what if Weevil follows her?"

Silence followed. Again, Aunt Daniella broke it.

"Yvonne, they have to figure that out. It may be that she leaves. He stays, then they can't stand being apart and find another way to be close. I don't know. Ithaca is beautiful but it's a long way away. As for finding another huntsman, that will give Sister fits."

"You're right." Sister nodded. "I miss Shaker. We worked closely for decades. But there's no way he can risk jumping after his injury."

"You know, nothing really stays the same," Sam mused.

"With that thought, I'll clear." Yvonne stood up and Sister with her.

No one questioned it but they easily fell into the roles assigned them by sex, even if those roles were becoming outmoded.

Sam rose to help carry the bigger dishes while Gray built a fire in what used to be called the parlor. Once all that was accomplished they retired to the simple warm living room/parlor. The mantel bore an old Napoleon hat clock in the center.

They chatted, caught up, talked about the young entry hounds. Gray refreshed everyone's drinks.

As he sat down again, his brother remarked, "You know, Ben said something that made me wonder. He said maybe the body was put there for someone in the hunt club to see. As the fog was so thick, no one did."

"Both Betty and I thought we saw something but didn't think much of it. An illusion." Sister snuggled in the old wing chair.

"But to put a body out to scare someone? It's creepy." Sam lowered his voice. "Well, that's not to say that's what this is really about. That's Ben's job."

"But you're right, Sam. It is a creepy thought," Yvonne agreed with him.

CHAPTER 4

September 26, 2022, Monday

The wildflowers and weeds brushed against the small group, waist high. Sister, Betty, Gray, Yvonne, Freddie Thomas, along with Alida Dalzell and Kasmir Barbhaiya, stood in the middle of the colorful field. Seedpods were open.

"There are fourteen species of milkweed native to Virginia," Marty Howard, leader of the group, explained.

Marty, married to Crawford Howard, used some of their considerable fortune toward environmental projects while her husband focused on the restoration of Old Paradise.

"Is it true only monarch larvae eat milkweed?" Freddie asked.

"Yes. The butterflies will eat lots of nectar from flowers. They need as much energy as they can hold for their long migration. Here." She brushed a butterfly milkweed, almost two feet high. "The orange flowers bloom from June to September and attract many insects. The orange is a beacon."

"Butterfly bush?" Betty asked.

"A good one. Brings in butterflies, different species. Butterfly bush is easy to plant. Put a few around the house. What's out here," she pointed to the scattered bushes, "is a gift from the birds."

"What else can we plant apart from butterfly bush and those fourteen milkweeds?" Alida, hair brushed back in a becoming bun, wondered.

"Ironweed, Joe Pye . . . lots of Joe Pye . . . goldenrod." Marty paused. "I know. Bad for allergies. Cardinal flower. Lilies bring in some bees, as do many other flowers, wild or garden. Color is a big draw and we have to assume that insects can smell the nectar. Honeysuckle. If you bought an Audubon butterfly and moth book, the description of the various species usually mentions their habitat. As you know, our bee population as well as our butterfly population are diminishing. All those chemicals."

"The problem is, farming is much harder without weed killer." Gray mentioned an unfortunate fact.

"Yes, it can be, but we are beginning to learn more about plants that repel weeds. Our ancestors and the tribal peoples here knew so much. We don't give them credit and really we don't know the half of what has disappeared. But I have written a list for each of you as to what to plant. Some things need to go in now, early fall. Also, there is a list of selected books."

The group thanked her and they turned to walk back to Sister's house. Some pollen stuck to their clothing. Hitchhiker weed with its sticky burrs got everyone. They picked off the burrs as they walked toward the house, passing the kennels on their right and the stables on their left.

Diana, one of the hounds, turned to her brother, Dasher. *"Wonder what they're doing out there."*

He watched the small group, all of them foxhunters except for Yvonne, who was hoping to hunt. *"You never know with people."*

Comet, the fox under the cabin porch, also watched them through the latticework. No one carried food. A pity.

Target, a red who often bunked up with Comet, also observed. *"Sun feels good. How's the treats?"*

"Oh, Tootie and Weevil toss out the best stuff. They put the cans in the garbage cans but they leave me all manner of things."

"Sometimes, I can nip something off the back porch, but the Bancrofts don't feed foxes. Too bad. All the grilling. The smell drives me wild."

"Getting old, the Bancrofts. Humans stop when they get old."

As the foxes discussed food, aging, and the upcoming winter, the people filtered into the living room at the farm. Gray, who liked hosting, brought out small sandwiches, crackers, fresh vegetables with dip. Then he took drink orders. He and Kasmir carried in the orders. No one wanted anything stronger than sweet tea.

"Thank you, Marty. You've done so much research." Sister was grateful.

"I love it. I truly believe if we work together, we can save many species and reduce the harm we do to wildlife."

"Like city lights at night," Alida chimed in.

"Apart from baffling birds, it adds to the amount of power we waste. Billions of dollars for, what, a neon sign advertising a car?" Freddie munched a carrot.

"Or underarm deodorant." Betty grinned.

"Now, Betty, I'm for that," Yvonne teased her.

They talked a bit, then Freddie asked Gray, "Your brother found a body?"

Marty put a little more sugar in her tea, stirring the cold liquid. "He told us when he came to work today. We'd seen a brief news report. Brief because it was late. But Sam said he made the gruesome discovery on the way to church."

"He did." Gray affirmed her information. "It didn't make the noon news. Don't know why. But it did make the six o'clock news, and again at eleven, I assume."

"That's where I saw it." Kasmir crossed one leg over the other, which always relaxed him. "Sounded most unpleasant."

"Was. Sam said whoever it is or was, he didn't recognize him. The body was out of rigor mortis. Vultures had at him."

"Rigor mortis is awful enough." Freddie leaned forward. "In the fog. I didn't hunt Saturday, trying to get ready for the mid-October IRS filing. I would have missed it like everyone else, I'm sure."

"Why put a body in a chair . . . tied to a chair, according to the news," Marty said, coming back into the conversation. "Off to the side of the road but not into the trees? So no one would hit it. Obviously. But sit someone in a chair?"

"Do we know the cause of death?" Alida asked.

"No. Sam said that Ben ordered the body to be sent directly to the medical examiner's in Richmond. Should know soon enough. The summer murder sprees are winding down."

Gray was appalled at the rise of crime, not just in Richmond but in many major cities.

"We wondered about that when we met at Gray and Sam's place. Aunt Daniella thought it strange. Said she never heard of anything quite like it."

"That's a testimony." Betty smiled, knowing Aunt Dan's age more or less.

"What startled me was the idea that whoever killed this person wanted us to see him. *Us* as in those of us who hunt here."

"Or the Bancrofts, who live down the road . . . or even you, who lives up the road," Freddie declared.

"Well, none of us did see him," Alida stated the obvious.

"Honey, how was the killer to know there'd be a heavy fog?" Kasmir uncrossed his legs. "My idea is, whatever this person wanted us to see, he didn't get what he wanted."

"Why us?" Yvonne hadn't thought about plans being spoiled.

"If we knew that we'd probably know what this is about," Sister added.

"It can't be a message for the hunt club. We don't have anything anyone wants." Alida put her drink on the coaster. "Sure, it would have scared us, but why?"

"Money? Revenge?" Betty thought out loud.

"The club pays its bills. That's it," Gray stated, as he often went over figures with the club's treasurer, Ronnie Haslip.

"Revenge." Betty pronounced *revenge* in a louder tone.

"I hope not." Kasmir rubbed his knee. "Because if the killer didn't get what he wanted, then maybe he'll be back."

"Don't say that." Alida grabbed his sore knee. "Sorry."

That night, sitting in bed, Golliwog on her lap, the dogs on the floor, Sister turned to Gray during a commercial. "Awful thought. Just crossed my mind again. Kasmir saying whoever this is might not be finished."

He replied consolingly. "That has to have occurred to our sheriff. Ben will tell us if we need to worry. Once he knows how the man was killed and who he is, assuming he will, more things will fall into place."

"Well, yes. I just hope no one else falls into place before that time. To kill another human being is a terrible thing."

He took her hand, kissed the back of it. "It is and it's done every day all over the world. We are a species that can be unbelievably cruel as well as kind. Nothing has changed over the millennia."

She kissed his hand. "I do think our ancestors dressed better than we do."

"I prefer you undressed."

"I thought you were watching the football game."

CHAPTER 5

September 27, 2022, Tuesday

"Lower your hands," Sam instructed Yvonne.

"Sorry." She patted Old Buster on the neck.

A slight six-mile-an-hour wind from the west made the day air-conditioned. The temperature was in the seventies, sun bright as the two walked toward the trail behind the sumptuous stables at Crawford and Marty Howard's home estate, Beasley Hall. Crawford built Beasley Hall ten years ago, so it was a new "old" estate. Crawford loved restoring Old Paradise, although he didn't think he and Marty should live there. In time, he would donate the five thousand acres plus the stunning estate to the Virginia Historical Society if they met his requirements. If not, he and Marty were considering creating a small college there with the emphasis on Virginia's early history, especially architecture.

"He is so kind." Yvonne patted Buster again.

"He is. Crawford bought him for Marty. She's worked hard on her riding but doesn't have as much time to ride since they bought Old Paradise. She goes out but not regularly like she did three years ago. Marty clears three six without batting an eye. Haven't put her over four-foot fences yet. She needs to ride more regularly."

"Are there four-foot fences?" Yvonne asked, a tremor in her modulated voice.

"In the old days on the weekends, hunt clubs often ran drags. The saying was you jumped forty by four, meaning you jumped four-foot fences. Forty of them. It was a different time. Everyone rode Thoroughbreds except for some landowners. Now there's Warm-bloods, Quarter horses, Appendix horses, Haflingers, cobs. Always had children on cobs when I was young, or elderly people, but it was different then. You never saw color in the hunt field."

"What do you mean?" The breeze brushed her cheek, those high cheekbones ever so lovely.

"Oh." He laughed. "No paints, never saw palominos, all you saw were bays, dark bays, chestnuts, and a few grays, as those are the colors for Thoroughbreds. Now anything goes and people aren't running as fast as they once did. Remember, Yvonne, when I was young, people had familiarity with country ways, even if city dwellers. People took the train from Richmond to Deep Run, which was close, but also they traveled to hunts farther away. So they only hunted on Saturdays and wanted to run and jump."

"Ah. Is that why Sister only rides Thoroughbreds?"

"Well, she does love them and she looks good on them. Has a great eye for a horse but she wouldn't be averse to saying she'll ride a cob when she's in her eighties. Keepsake is an Appendix, half Thoroughbred, half Quarter horse. Handsome horse but if you study him, you see his butt is a bit different than a Thoroughbred's. Just a bit bigger and rounder."

"Like Old Buster." She grinned.

"Buster does have a big engine back there. Actually, Marty is glad you're taking lessons on him. She says he's too good to sit and she's right. All right, Madam, let's pick up a little trot. Trail's wide enough. You stay right with me."

Both squeezed their horses. Sam rode Trocadero, a flashy young Thoroughbred that Crawford bought for himself. Crawford rode Czapka, a Warmblood; kind though the big fellow was, he was a bit much for Crawford, who was not a natural rider. As for Trocadero, Sam brought him along patiently but doubted the boss could ever handle a horse as quick as the gorgeous blood bay Thoroughbred. Sam suspected the real reason Crawford bought the young fellow is there are so few blood bays out there, flashy, a rare color. Crawford liked being the center of attention. Working for him involved propping him up with lots of praise, but you can either ride a horse or you can't.

Yvonne, exhilarated, urged Old Buster on, passing Sam as a challenge.

He laughed, thrilled to see her rising confidence, as she had been so timid when they started lessons nearly two years ago. He caught up with her and soon the two horses, in sync, looked like a pair, granted mismatched, but still a pair. Trocadero's trot was a long reach; Old Buster had to up it to a languid canter.

They fell back to a walk, Yvonne grinning. Sam smiling. She truly was the most beautiful woman he had ever seen. Younger men felt the same way about Tootie, her daughter, but a man forty or over could only stare at Yvonne and dream.

"I love this. Sam, you have been so patient and I was so scared."

"Well, you have a long leg. You are a balanced person. You try. As time has gone by, your leg has become so strong. You told me that when you were young, you were a dancer, and it shows."

"That helped me when I started on the runway. I wasn't scared but I knew being one of the first I would be given extra scrutiny." She waved her left hand dismissively. "Let them look."

He laughed at her. "Yvonne, they were doing that anyway."

"Oh, the women. All those rich, white women willing to pay thousands of dollars for dresses I would never wear unless paid to do so."

"Really?"

"Sam, fashion is a racket. Granted, there were and are a few great designers, those who want to make a woman look beautiful. Mainbocher was one of my favorites. Mother loved his work. Halston never got too crazy until the end. At least that's what I thought. You wouldn't believe how cheaply some of that stuff was made. Not Halston. I mean in general."

"Given that something had to fit you, didn't they sorta fiddle with it?"

"Sure."

"What were the other models like?"

"You know, Sam, they were terrific. One or two descended to ugly competitiveness but most of those girls really did understand I was under a certain type of pressure. I made some good friends. Still friends. Then other black models came along. A few wanted to be the star, most wanted the money. You make good money. I never, ever wanted to be a model."

"Having those men fall over you, you didn't like it?"

"I did not. They didn't want to know me. At least the women who fell over me, and a few did, actually wanted to know me. I've never been inclined that way but you would be surprised, or maybe not, how many women of great wealth have female lovers, not male."

"Why do you think?"

"Because the women listen to them. Men pretty much ignore you. Even my ex-detested-husband ignored me unless we talked about what he wanted to talk about. He didn't give a damn what I thought or felt. I'm the dumb one. I thought he cared. Building the

TV network was exciting, so I didn't think too much about my feelings. Then again, my feelings were wrapped up in the network. The focus was black life, culture, but that proved broader than we anticipated. Took years to refine it. And I still modeled for a few designers I liked. Only in Chicago. No more trips to Paris or New York. Have you been to Chicago?"

"'Ware branch." He held a branch so Trocadero could get by. It was hanging off a tree by the path. She paused, let it swing back, then joined him.

"Chicago?"

"Yes, I have. The lake is overwhelming. A lake with whitecaps." His smile showed such white teeth. "A big bustling city, but what surprised me more than anything was how flat the land is. A pancake."

"I had to make the opposite adjustment." Her leg touched his.

"Another trot? Say to the old stone ruins?"

"Sure." She followed his lead.

The trot, easy, felt terrific. A coop loomed ahead in a side fence. Sam popped over. She hesitated for a moment.

"Dammit, I can do this."

She did, too.

He stopped. "Good on you. You can jump. We've worked on this."

"You usually give me a warning when we're in the ring if we're riding together."

"You will take whatever shows up in the hunt field. Really, have you looked at some of the people out there? You can do this and I hope you do it soon. I'm tired of answering people's questions about when you will be out."

"Really?"

"Really." He took a breath. "People like you and most of them want to see you out when your daughter is whipping-in. Foxhunting families make people happy."

"Did you know Sister's first husband and son?"

"Sure. RayRay looked a lot like Sister but had his father's dark coloring. A good kid. The farm accident was horrible. Horrible." He closed his eyes for a moment. "In the old days, PTOs, the turning part at the back of the tractor, weren't covered. The shaft was exposed. Everyone knew that, but RayRay, fourteen, wore a baggy T-shirt, leaned over and it caught. He was choked to death in about a minute. So fast."

"Must have nearly destroyed Sister."

"She bore it. But I think it took years to achieve a kind of equilibrium. The one who fell apart was her husband. Sat comatose, cried then started drinking. She did what she could for him. Little did I know that once I was mature I'd turn into a drunk myself. He finally came out of it, but boy, there were some ugly years there. Totally unfaithful, too.

"She stood by him. Her support was the late Peter Wheeler. He owned Mill Ruins. The farm Walter has leased for ninety-nine years, like the English do."

"I had no idea. Tootie never mentioned it and you know Tootie looks up to Sister."

"Sister doesn't talk about her pains. She just goes forward. Aunt Daniella and Mom, still alive then, rallied round. Sister became devoted to them. We always were fairly close, we don't live far apart, but that created a bond. Suffering does. Aunt Dan lost one husband, others still lived." He laughed again. "My beloved aunt has lived quite a life. Mother, on the other hand, was satisfied with my father. Once he died, a massive stroke, she showed no interest in men."

"Perhaps Aunt Dan made up for it."

"God knows she did. Hey, see that stone fence. Come on." He pushed Trocadero into a nice trot.

Sam wanted the young horse to be able to trot to a jump as well as canter. Too often horses rushed the jumps and some of that was a response to the nervousness of their rider. If someone falls far behind they often forget their good sense, wanting to catch up any way they can. Then, too, some feared the jump.

Over he sailed, with Yvonne three strides behind him.

"I love this horse." She was jubilant.

"He is special. Long in the tooth but special. What a magical time of day. The late mornings. A good morning gets me working harder. You know, you'll get a lot done."

"I do. Sam, you don't have to say anything if it's too upsetting, but do you have any idea how that man was killed? That man in the chair?"

"No. Some dried blood out of his ears. One eye gone. Some flesh chewed off of his face. The vultures flew away when I stopped."

She grimaced.

"Think of them as nature's garbagemen. He was protein. He wasn't totally disgusting yet, but the body was getting there. Weird."

"Yes. Well, a better subject. Marty gave a concise, good lecture yesterday in the wildflower field about monarchs and other butterflies."

"She's a person who, once something appeals to her, she goes all out. She and Crawford are supporting this. Working with the National Wildlife Federation. I think the division they are working with is Garden for Wildlife."

"That's what she said. I'm going to do it. She said we can buy prepared seed packets, big packets."

"You can. Ronnie Haslip is selling them. The money goes to the organization. I was surprised he became involved."

"He'll keep organized books." Yvonne liked Ronnie. "I so love this horse. Do you think Crawford would sell him to me?"

"Let me work on that. Marty is the key. But he would be a perfect horse to start hunting with, just perfect. He knows the game. The horror in the hunt field; green horse, green rider." He grinned. "You'd have a made horse. No greenie."

The stable gleamed up ahead. White with royal blue trim, some thin gold stripes here and there. Crawford had wanted to use red but Marty, as they were building, convinced him it would be too flashy. She figured out flash doesn't work in Virginia. He still hadn't gotten the whole message but he was improving, thanks to his sensitive wife. Marty recognized an old Virginian, meaning an old family, could use red and gold. New, probably not. She paid attention at the foxhunts. When she first saw that Betty and Bobby Franklin's colors were hunter green and orange she knew there was latitude but only so much.

Sam, respected for his riding and teaching skills, felt he had nothing to offer Yvonne. He knew he was falling in love with her. Watching her overcome her fears, and who doesn't have them when coming to riding late, he grew to respect her. Seeing her learn to fit into a community she had harshly judged, hoping to repair her distant relationship with her daughter, he began to understand her. It wasn't as though she hadn't made mistakes or suffered hard knocks, but the woman was worth millions, maybe more. He had nothing to offer.

Of course, he did. He loved her for herself. How often does that happen to a spectacularly beautiful woman?

As for her, she swore after her divorce there would be no more men in her life. Never, never. Never, but Sam was so kind to her, to her daughter, to animals. Then again, he was divinely masculine.

Did they belong together? They did. They'd have to figure it out or, like so many, realize years later what they missed. Love has no rules. The hell with class, race, even gender. The magic is there or it isn't.

"Yvonne, did you really not like modeling?"

"No. I know a Virginia girl wouldn't say this, but Sam, I loathed swinging my tits over the runway."

He laughed so hard, he lurched forward onto Trocadero's neck, which the fellow took as a pedal-to-the-metal sign. The horse shot forward, Sam now having his arms around its neck.

Old Buster, good boy that he was, did not take off after him.

Sam finally got Trocadero under control before plunging into the stable.

Old Buster, now at a canter, came up, stopped.

"Sam, are you all right?"

"Yvonne, do you eat with that mouth?"

They both dissolved laughing.

CHAPTER 6

September 28, 2022, Wednesday

Ben Sidell rubbed his eyes. Staring at a computer screen made his eyes water. He leaned back in his chair. Usually he kept the door to his office open, but reading the medical examiner's report, he closed it for full concentration.

Returning to the screen he again read cause of death, probable time of death, the details only a terrific medical examiner's department can give law enforcement. Virginia had one of the best in the country. Of course, Ben thought it was the best. He got the job as sheriff of the county after coming from Columbus, Ohio. Born and raised in Ohio, he loved his native state while recognizing it lacked the coherence, social, cultural . . . take your pick . . . of Virginia, a state that remained remarkably true to itself in both good and bad ways. There really was a Virginia Way.

Having served in a city with a huge university helped get him the job in Albemarle County. The University of Virginia was in the jurisdiction of the city of Charlottesville. In Virginia, cities and counties boasted separate councils, law enforcement departments, parks, etc. This could be confusing but the division reflected the needs and concerns of citizens far better than a county where city and the rural areas were lumped together politically. City people and country people do not think alike. How can they? They face distinctly different realities.

The reality Ben was facing was murder. The county fortunately confronted few murders and those often sprang from domestic violence, usually the woman being killed by her boyfriend or husband. If not that, a blowup at a bar could provoke a killing, as well the odd incident of road rage. Ben thought the Covid crisis . . . media confusion if not false statements . . . added to underlying tension, which could and did explode into anger. Even during the mask-wearing demands, people would attend city council meetings or county meetings to scream at one another through masks. This was un-Virginia; Virginians rarely screamed at one another, especially in public. It is a cherished state belief that revenge is a dish best served cold.

Well, whoever killed the still unidentified man may have served it cold, but serve it he or she did.

A knock on the door lifted his head from the blue light. "Yes."

"Sheriff, it's Jackie."

"Come in."

She opened the door, a young officer whose father had been a cop.

"Sit down. You have that look on your face." He liked her, as she was so keen to learn.

"Lamar Bly is hammering away. He wants a statement from you concerning Owensville Road, where it meets Route 250. More complaints about sightlines while waiting to turn east or west onto 250."

"Give me his email. I'll send him a statement. Very simple. It's lousy."

The corners of her mouth turned up. "I'm sure he'll print that."

Ben leaned back in his old chair. "I'll buff the statement and suggest state funding. As he's one of our county commissioners, state funding is music to his ears. Means the county won't be asked for money."

She rose and handed over a sheet of paper from her clipboard. An organized person, she had written down almost verbatim Lamar's conversation plus his email. She sat back down then stood up again.

"Sorry. I know you're busy."

"We all are, Officer. We are overworked and underpaid and we are supposed to solve problems for which there is no solution." He paused. "Like mental illness. Well, while you're up, do bring Jude in here."

She left. He could have buzzed Jude but this gave him time to go to the bathroom. Sometimes he would almost forget. Fortunately, his office had its own bathroom, a small luxury, especially if he had to shave. Ben needed to shave twice a day.

As he exited the bathroom, closing the door behind him, the two young officers came in.

"Sit down."

They did.

He took his seat behind his desk, printed off the medical examiner's report. As it was printing he came around to pull up a chair closer to them. The whirr of the printer accentuated his report.

"The medical examiner concluded it was murder. Just got the report. There wasn't much doubt, and to their great credit, they were fast. Granted, suspected murder is important. You'll note when you read the report that the damage to the body was caused by vultures."

"How did he die?" Jude wondered, as he had seen the body.

"Interesting. Heroin. Pure heroin. No fentanyl. No lacing. No arsenic, which as you know is still used. Pure heroin."

"Strange. Can you still buy pure heroin?" Jackie knew what was in the street was anything but pure.

"Unlikely." Ben folded his hands, then rose as the printing

stopped. He squared off the papers, putting them on his desk. "I'll sort them through for you in a minute. Back to cause of death. Since it was pure, give me your thoughts."

"Maybe the victim was a chemist or maybe the killer was a chemist," Jude posited.

"Or the killer is a doctor who can get pure heroin."

"That thought crossed my mind. Would a smart killer use something that law enforcement officers recognize is hard to come by?" Ben noted.

"Maybe he's making a statement," Jude spoke.

"He or she made a few statements. The victim's ears had been punctured, the eardrums, and here's one, his tongue had been slit down the middle."

Both of their eyes opened wide.

"The message . . ." Jude trailed off.

"Is that the victim can give no message." Jackie finished the thought. "A forked tongue."

"Yes." Ben was back in his chair. "Our victim knew something, or so it seems."

"This looks like a planned murder . . . cool, calm, and collected." Jude then mentioned, "But seeing the body, the murder planned, yes, but why was the body tied to a chair off the road? We are supposed to look?"

"Good thinking. The fog messed with that plan." Ben stared up at the ceiling then back down. "And our victim died in their car or at another location, but he didn't die on the After All farm road. Time of death indicated that he had been dead for some hours before being placed where he was. He had gone into rigor mortis and was probably coming out of it when tied. The boys," he looked at Jackie, "and girls down there in Richmond are so sharp."

"You can drink heroin, right?" Jackie questioned.

"I don't see why not, but shooting it in a vein is better and when you read the report you will see he did indeed have a needle mark on the inside of his left arm, right below the elbow."

"So he shot himself up?" Jude asked.

"I would think, but it could be that the killer held a gun on him and he had to shoot up, or the killer shot him up when he was tied."

This thought disturbed Jackie, because she hadn't considered that.

"Let's review this." Ben first got up, put his papers in order, handing them to his young team. This gave them some time to think.

"Well, we can start from the fact that this was premeditated." Jude then added, "And well thought out, at least the killing part."

"He had been dead for roughly twenty-four hours before being placed in the chair. Hard to move a body in rigor, so whoever did this did not move the body immediately after death. He had to hide it and wait for darkness." Ben was sure about that.

"Was dark. The fog didn't come up until early morning." Jackie, an early riser, paid attention to the weather.

"Hence the fouled plan." Jude opened his hands as if in supplication. "What can be served by an unknown man sitting in a chair to be seen? By foxhunters?"

"It's possible the killer didn't know the hunt club cubbing schedule." Jackie knew her hunting terms. As Albemarle County was horsey, many people did.

"Possible." Ben nodded.

"Well, who else would see it? The Lorillard brothers. Maybe the Bancrofts, although chances are they wouldn't be heading to the Lorillards'. Not that they don't visit, but a killer couldn't depend on it."

"Yeah, well, how can the killer depend on the hunt club members seeing the body?"

"Ah." Ben smiled. "What if he or she laid down scent?"

This shut up both Jude and Jackie, who not being hunters never considered such a thing, didn't know it could be done.

"You can do that? How?" Jackie wanted to know.

"Soak a rag in fox urine, tie it to a rope, and drag the line of scent where you want. So my idea is that the body was tied, placed in the darkness, and the killer left a line that would go by the body, along the road, or by the side of the road."

"Well, then what happens?" Jude was puzzled.

"Hounds follow the line to the body. However, hounds actually picked up a fox despite the fog . . . or who knows, because of the fog. The air was heavy, clammy. Scent was rising. It rises with the heat, but there had to be vestiges of scent, yet they got a more recent scent line. If any of the drag scent was there, they ignored it for the hotter line, which ended at the Lorillard house."

"No kidding." Jude rubbed his chin. "So everyone, including the hounds, would go past the body and not know?"

"Hounds probably smelled the body but their job is to chase foxes. They wouldn't veer off. For one thing, this pack is too well trained. Even the youngsters out for the first time wouldn't veer off if the older hounds were speaking, which they were."

"Do you think our killer knows what happened?" Jackie found this fascinating; it was why she got into this business in the first place.

"Probably. Remember," Ben came back to the body, "this man was to have been seen by foxhunters. There is really no other reason he would be placed where he was. If this was some kind of broader warning, why not put him alongside 64?" He named the interstate.

Jude and Jackie held the papers they had been handed and Ben remained standing.

"I'll read this," Jackie affirmed.

"Me too."

"Think of this. We don't know who that victim is. But I am willing to believe someone in the hunt field knows him."

As the two left Ben's office, this disquieting thought in their minds, Jackie turned to Jude, a fit young fellow with a warm smile. "Someone knows him?"

"That doesn't mean whoever knows him killed him. The body is probably a warning."

Jackie stopped, looked up at the tall fellow. "Oh Jude. That means this is close to home."

CHAPTER 7

September 29, 2022, Thursday

U.S. Geological Survey maps, lined up on Betty Franklin's long table at her home, held everyone's attention. Jefferson Hunt Club held a board meeting once a month during hunt season, once every other month in the off-season. Members served a three-year term. Meetings were hosted by individual members, as Jefferson Hunt had no clubhouse. A plus and a minus. The plus was no building and upkeep expense. The minus was no gathering place available to all.

At least two members had to be hunt staff. Sister and Walter, as joint masters, were in attendance. They only voted if there was a tie.

"Okay, you can see where we are gaining territory and where we are losing." Ronnie Haslip, the treasurer for over twenty years, pointed. "To the east, we are losing. To the west and the south, gaining. Obviously, the development is in the east toward Richmond."

"Sure didn't used to be that way." Sam stood up to get a closer look at the maps.

Ronnie had outlined each fixture, a task taking days. His commitment to the club was solid. He was generous with his time.

Freddie, elected to the board last year, said, "Granted, the territory is rougher out this way but that's better than dealing with someone who paid over a million dollars for a McMansion on five acres."

Ronnie laughed. "And they still have to buy riding mowers, Weedwackers, maybe even a backhoe. Crazy, really. You might as well buy more land."

"Well, no crazier than paying ten thousand dollars a month for a decent, not even fabulous, apartment in Manhattan," Alida Dalzell remarked.

Alida and Freddie were old friends from when they met in Raleigh, North Carolina, years ago, right out of college. Freddie invited Alida to come up and hunt with her. They hunted together in North Carolina then Freddie moved to Charlottesville to start her own small accounting firm, a success. The real success was when Alida met Kasmir. The visits became more frequent. Kasmir, who had lost his wife back in Mumbai, had moved to Virginia to be close to a childhood friend and his wife. He attended Oxford as a young man, so Virginia didn't seem foreign to him in language or in culture, in some ways.

Ronnie put his finger on Showoff. "The Sabatinis have agreed to let us hunt their property, so now we have a straight line between Welsh Harp and the farm on the other side of Showoff. But that's not why I've put surveys out."

Everyone looked at him. Ronnie was obsessive about details so they wondered what was coming. He had spent too much time on this for it just to be about a new fixture in the west losing land on the east.

"Okay. Sister, you had a few of our people to Marty Howard's lecture in your wildflower field," Ronnie said.

"Did."

"And it went well?"

Looking up at Ronnie, standing, Sister nodded.

Betty piped up. "Sorry you couldn't be there. Marty really gave us so much information."

"She enjoyed it, too. Most especially when people promised to order seed packets. I drove over there to talk to Crawford about PVC pipes, which is when I saw Marty. Crawford's rebuilding the bridges over creek crossings. Thought I would tell him what my experience has been. He really doesn't need to tear out the clay pipes, but that's another issue. Crawford likes everything to be the best. As your treasurer, I want to save money. Clay pipes can last one hundred years."

Bobby, serving drinks, spoke, although not a board member. "True, Ronnie, but clay pipes can attract roots. You sure don't want a willow tree near them."

This group knew one another so well, no one was offended by Bobby's interjection. Even in disagreement they got along well, respected one another's opinions.

"That's the truth." Sister had dealt with willows. "But if the pipes are free of roots, or major cracks, I have to go along with Ronnie. Save money."

Ronnie was not an accountant for nothing. "True, but the real question for all of us, not just as a hunt club, is, What will the costs be in the future? Look what happened to gas prices."

"Boy, is that ugly." Walter, a cardiologist, moaned as he drove to the hospital five days a week, as gas spiraled ever upward.

"Okay. Back to these maps." Ronnie swept his hand over the carefully placed colored maps. "You all know the old fixtures. We are learning some of the new ones. There are places on each of these farms where wildlife habitat could be improved, be it mammals or monarch butterflies."

"Have you been talking to Ed Clark again?" Alida named the founder and president of the Wildlife Center of Virginia.

"Have, and if no one objects, I'll talk to him about the ideas we discussed here. He is so good at fundraising. He might see something we missed."

The Wildlife Center, one of the world's leading teaching and research hospitals for wildlife, was right over the mountain from Jefferson Hunt Country. A show about it, *Untamed,* was on PBS's LearningMedia. While many members watched it, most all knew Ed personally, having visited the Center.

"Okay," Ronnie spoke again. "Here is my idea. As foxhunters, we are outside more than most Americans these days. We see the effects of weather, we see human impact on wildlife and plants. Not much of it has been good. And like most hunt clubs, our base has changed."

"You mean people don't grow up with knowledge of the country anymore?" Sister tried to push him, as Ronnie could rattle along.

"Exactly. When I was a kid," he looked at the woman who had known him since childhood, he being the best friend of her son, "people understood hunting, fishing. Many took a train from the city, or as roads improved, drove to hunt or fish. Most people had a rudimentary understanding of country life. Now someone in a subdivision sees a bear and they panic. Know what I mean?"

"Well, we do. Not everyone panics, but people have no idea of the life cycles of wildlife, food needs, really basic stuff. Then add in the coyotes, who have made it from the West and are now part of our lives." Bobby could see no good coming from the coyote invasion.

"And they are so much heavier and bigger than, say, in Idaho." Freddie traveled a lot in the West, loving the distance between herself and Washington, D.C.

"More to eat and easier to catch here," Sam interjected.

"Ronnie." Sister simply said his name in a tone Ronnie had heard for most of his life.

It meant, get on with it.

"Okay. Here is my idea, finally." He laughed at himself. "Why don't we create seed bags, say fifty-pound bags? We give ten percent of our profits to either the Gardens for Wildlife or to the Wildlife Center, if people become interested in mammals. We can also deliver food for raptors, bears, you name it. We give ten percent and we keep the rest. After all, we are delivering the goods and we can help with some of the work."

A silence followed this as the small group absorbed it.

"Where can we get the seeds?" Sam asked.

"Sabatini's. She has put in over one hundred acres in butterfly plants, etc. Had no idea until I had the chance to talk to her. She, like Marty, is passionate about this."

"And Marty Howard?" Freddie asked.

"She also has set aside acres for this, as well as sunflowers, acres and acres of all manner of berries, the plant and fruit foods of mammals. Our very own foxes love berries. She intends to harvest and sell these things and she has the workforce to do it. Elise may need a workforce larger than she imagines. Right now she thinks she can do it all by herself. We can buy from both of them. Anyway, we support the people who support us and we support wildlife and monarchs. We have to do something."

"We do, Ronnie. We really do, but we are all caught up in daily life. You know from hunting how much there is to do to keep our territory open. Build jumps, fix broken jumps. Again, so many people work full time, we are shorthanded." Sister keenly felt the workload. "In the old days, many foxhunters enjoyed inherited wealth. We have a few people with strong resources, but not like the old days. People work. They don't have the time."

"Yeah, that's really true. But even when I was young and you could hire day workers, it took many hands," Bobby chimed in.

"Well, you can't hire them now." Alida threw up her hands. "No one wants to get their hands dirty."

"That's not exactly true." Walter stepped in, not wanting an argument. "But even someone who, say, isn't college educated may not have practical skills. There are fewer and fewer schools for electricians, plumbers, cabinetmakers. All of those jobs take training. You might say, What skills do we need out there? Ronnie, you drove over to talk to Crawford, about drainpipes. Who knows about drainpipes today? Who knows how to put them in? A few specialized contractors, but even thirty years ago more people knew more handy knowledge, for lack of a better word."

"I know." Ronnie sat down. "But if Elise becomes overwhelmed, we can help. She'll give us a bigger discount. The Sabatinis are shrewd, good businesspeople. Marty needs no help on that issue. Crawford will bus people in if he has to do so. But Marty will truly appreciate what we are doing and let us not forget we all need to stay on good terms. It was Marty," Ronnie nodded to Sister, "who finally got Crawford to become a farmer pack, registered by the MFHA after creating havoc for years."

Crawford formed his own foxhunting pack in a fury because Sister did not pick him to be her joint master. She realized she needed one. He was sure he should be that person. He had recently moved to Albemarle County, threw a lot of money around, bullied people. He would have been a disaster as a master. Yes, the money would have helped enormously but they would have lost most every landowner they had, including the Bancrofts, old money, old blood. No way would they tolerate that behavior. When Crawford started his own pack, his hounds rioted. He blew through three huntsmen, all of whom left in a huff or were fired when they tried to tell him what hounds really needed. Then, too, if a member of a recognized club hunts with an unrecognized club, there really can be hell to pay with the MFHA. The national organization couldn't stop him from hunting on his own land but they could stop others from hunting with him. Undemocratic as that might seem, it ensures clubs adhere to the national standards. Given the ever thundering march of people knowing nothing about hunting and assuming the worst, this is not a superficial approach. Then again, it had worked since 1907, the founding year of the Master of Foxhounds Association. Crawford would have none of it, creating hardship, mostly for Sister.

A few years of being ostracized, except by merchants, slowly forced him to realize his approach was not what would be described as the Virginia Way. Marty got it instantly. She would say to him, "We aren't in Indiana." Their home state had people who didn't appreciate the Howard approach either but there he was a known quantity.

"It's a great idea," Walter weighed in. "It will take a lot of work on our part and we need to make sure our members not only like the idea but are enthusiastic."

"If we could get media coverage for our work to help wildlife and butterflies, that won't hurt either." Alida had a sound appreciation of media power. "We always have to overcome the stain of once being a blood sport. People won't let that go."

"Because we are terrible at promoting ourselves." Freddie reached for her iced tea.

"I know. I know." Sister nodded. "But Freddie, I am a lot older than you and I was taught your name only appears in the newspaper when you are born, when you marry, and when you die. I know times have changed, but self-promotion is hard for me and many of my generation. I'm not even a golden oldie. I'm a platinum oldie," she joked.

Sam, like Ronnie, who had loved her since childhood, spoke up. "Sister, the old ways pushed a lot under the rug, but that kept a kind of harmony. And before I forget, can you imagine what a splash Yvonne would be if she signed up, so to speak?"

"Smash." Betty loved the idea. "Think she might?"

"Her first hunt will be this Saturday. I leave it to you."

"Thanks." Betty smiled. "Why would she listen to me?"

"Oh, Betty, Yvonne has changed. She came here with so many misinterpretations plus a horrible divorce, all in the news. But everyone takes her as she is, which I think was a big surprise, and she has mended her relationship with Tootie. She might be glad to help. She knows how to handle the media." Sam tried not to sound too enthusiastic.

"Yvonne can handle anything," Walter added.

"What about a nonprofit?" Freddie asked. "Hunt clubs can't be for-profit organizations. It's against the Master of Foxhounds Association rules."

"Yes," Walter agreed. "But let's save this issue for another day. We will need a 501(c)(3) organization." He noted the designation of many nonprofit organizations.

"Freddie, you, Gray, and I are all accountants. This club is top heavy with accountants. I say we all get together and figure this out," Ronnie said.

"Okay," she agreed.

They talked, decided who would talk to whom, what to put into the big seed bags, who could take photographs to show how to plant things. It was a busy, full meeting, after which they were all thrilled to sit and gossip. Actually, share the news. No one was willing to admit to gossip.

Walter and Bobby sat next to each other arguing about football. Then Alida sat down and asked them about the World Series. A lively discussion followed as to who just missed making the Series, when it would be held, etc.

Sister, talking to Ronnie, leaned over as Freddie sat on his other side. "Ronnie, you never fail to delight me. Now, here is my idea, which has nothing to do with the treasury. We vote on board members the week after Opening Hunt. And Sam's term is up. We have to convince him to run for a second term. And here's my other idea: Ben Sidell on the board."

"Can he do that while he's a public servant?" Bobby asked.

Sister's face froze for a moment. "Good Lord. I never thought of that, but Bobby, public servants do have private lives."

"He's right, though, Sister. I'll check into it," Ronnie volunteered.

"He's got a case on his hands," Alida said. "Still no ID yet on the murdered man."

"It's too weird." Freddie ran her finger under the back of her flats, feeling a little rub.

"What I have learned is never to say, 'What next?'" Sister laughed.

CHAPTER 8

September 30, 2022, Friday

"When did you get that?" Betty noted Sister's sherpa jacket as they walked hounds early in the morning.

"Last week. My leather jacket is worn out, plus it's too heavy for these mornings. By mid-October I'll be back to the leather. Then again, I should probably fork out for a new one. What I love about leather is the wind can't cut you. Wear a couple of layers underneath and you're fine."

"You are, except the more layers, the more you feel like the Michelin tire man. Layer after layer."

"If they had fur, this would be no problem," Tootsie said as she walked next to her littermate Taz.

"They don't know the difference," Dragon butted in.

The two T's stopped talking. They didn't like Dragon . . . but then, no one did. Arrogant, terrific speed and nose, he would lord it over the others except for his littermates, who were also gifted.

Tootie and Weevil walked up front, a brisk pace. Apart from finally becoming lovers, they worked well together. Hunt clubs with partners and family members as staff so often worked with an advantage, because these people could anticipate one another. Tootie could read Weevil. Betty, thanks to years of whipping-in, could read Shaker, the Huntsman who had retired due to his injuries. She adjusted to Weevil but had to remember he would push forward sometimes too quickly. A little patience goes a long way.

"We haven't had time to catch up since last night. What do you think of Ronnie's idea?" Betty asked.

"It's terrific, hits all the bases, but it's a big undertaking, complicated, will need a mailing center as well as storage. Sure has media possibilities and we need to demonstrate our commitment to wildlife, the environment. But it will take more than a year."

"We are dependent on Mother Nature cooperating."

"For everything." Sister noticed Giorgio, her most handsome dog hound. "Betty, I really should breed him. He turned out to be a better hunter than I thought he would."

"Take him to the shows?"

"It's so much work. But I think it would make Weevil happy. And he would love to be in the pack class."

Sister mentioned the final class of any foxhound show where the huntsman and two whippers-in walked hounds over a prescribed course. Winning it was the cherry on the sundae for the whole show.

Betty observed the flashy hound. "His nose is good."

"Yes. He matured slowly. But time has erased my doubts. He's four now."

"They're talking about you." Pookah listened.

"Yeah." Giorgio liked the younger dog hound. *"I am a little slow. Not like you, Pookah. You get everything so fast but when I do get it, I never forget it."*

Sister eyed the hill they were about to climb. "You know, as long as we do this we will never get old."

"Doesn't mean we won't feel old," Betty replied.

They both laughed.

"Ronnie is such a brick. He has thought about this and it could work but we need something to bring in some extra cash between now and then. We can't always rely on cap fees and contributions. Kasmir has been unbelievably generous but I'd like—I don't know."

A monarch butterfly flew in front of them. One of the last, leaving for Mexico. "Your field helped. Gorgeous creatures." Betty's eyes followed the orange creature, wings outlined in black with white dots.

"That's why Ronnie's plan is so good. We truly will be doing something. The rub is no hunt club can be for profit."

"Ah, the 1907 rules. Well, those rules were made by white men with oodles of money. And they were good rules. If clubs with money rented land, poor clubs would be out in the cold. Relying on landowners allowing you to hunt, no money, no rents, evened the playing field. Plus they divided up territory. It has worked since 1907."

"Yes, it has, but our country has changed so much. How many clubs can rely on rich members anymore? And how many people even know about hunting as we do it? They think we're out here shooting foxes."

"They don't seem to notice that we are shooting one another." Betty breathed a bit heavier halfway up the steep farm road.

"People obviously like to kill one another."

"Like the man in the chair." Betty shook her head. "Too strange. Well, back to money. Bobby, who is smart . . . after all, he married me." She giggled. "He says let Gray, Ronnie, and Freddie figure it out."

"Right." Sister was glad they reached the top of Hangman's Ridge, where criminals were hanged in the eighteenth and early nineteenth centuries. Weevil stopped, allowing hounds to play.

"We can wait it out?" Betty said.

"What?"

"That 501(c)(3). I give Ronnie's plan two years to get established."

"It just seems like there ought to be some small thing we could do to bring in some extra cash now."

"There's always a horse show. The old hunt club fairgrounds are still standing."

"Barely. We need the money to fix them up. They are so pretty, though, those stands under the big trees. Would take thousands to bring it back. Then would we make money?"

"We'd make money. The question is, how big a show, and would you have small shows as well as one big blowout? Bet you could pay back rehabbing costs in two years. Three at the most. You could keep part of the entry fees for running the club now. Put the other part toward construction costs."

"God, Betty, the work."

"True, but shows make money. Hunter jumper shows do if they are well run and the prices are good."

"Okay, babies. Let's go." Weevil called the hounds to him as he started back to the kennel. Going down the hill would be easier than going up.

Wind picked up. Always did on the ridge. A bracing twelve mile an hour wind, or close to it, had everyone zipping up their jackets.

"Keeping out the wind?" Betty asked.

"No, but the fleece is still keeping me warm. What I need to find is a leather jacket lined in fleece that won't cost me a fat check."

"Be at least five hundred dollars." Betty put her hands in her pockets.

"Ugh. Back to money. Should we ask people about shows? Then bring it up at the next board meeting?"

"Meaning as the stalwarts?"

"Yes."

"You know the obvious way to make money is illegal. Drink, drugs, driving cigarettes up to New Jersey and New York."

"While you're at it, Betty, prostitution."

"Now, there's a good one. For men and women."

"I never thought of that." Sister laughed.

"It's not called the oldest profession for nothing." Betty laughed with her.

"Funny, I expect we are surrounded by illegal activities. Now there's bitcoin. Must be opportunities to steal there, too. Really, we must be surrounded and we don't have a clue."

"Do we want to find out?"

"No."

Time would answer that, as it always does.

CHAPTER 9

October 1, 2022, Saturday

"Lift your leg."

"I'm not a dog." Yvonne lifted her leg out of the stirrup.

Sam, shaking his head, tethered her girth then placed her left foot back in the stirrup iron.

The gathering, twenty strong on this slightly cooler morning, gathered at Cindy Chandler's Foxglove Farm. Everyone fussed with last-minute preparations. Checking stirrup length, trying to get their collar to lie flat in the back, pulling on gloves. Finally, the humans mounted up, they walked toward the fenced pastures on the east side of the well-kept farm.

As this was Yvonne's first hunt, people complimented her turnout . . . perfect, naturally. She was a bit nervous but felt the support. Everyone wished her well.

Aunt Daniella, driven by Kathleen Sixt Dunbar, as Yvonne usually drove to the meets, was there to cheer on someone she had learned to care for, enjoy.

Aunt Daniella turned to Kathleen. "Give the girl credit. Learning to ride takes guts at fifty."

"Aunt Dan, I expect it takes guts at seven."

"Maybe, but the ground is closer then." The old lady laughed.

Sister, on Rickyroo, called out, "Gather round."

As they did she noticed Cameron, Barry, Ed Clark, and even Buddy Cadwalder down from Philadelphia. The regulars flocked nearby.

Nonni, Ben Sidell's kind mare, noticed Rickyroo, impatient, as always.

"Ricky, this won't get you going any faster."

"Why do people have to talk? Why can't they just mount up and go?" the handsome Thoroughbred complained as Sister patted his shiny neck.

"Humans have to talk. They can't help it. It's like going to the bathroom. Have to do it." Nonni's nicker was loud enough for the other horses to hear, so nickers filled the air.

"Wonderful to see you all on this first day of October," Sister greeted them. "If anyone needs to come back early, I expect one of you with colors to be the navigator." She reminded those with colors of one of their duties, rarely needed.

A foxhunter earns their hunt button first in many hunts, which means they've been a regular, learning territory, etc. A hunter who takes the fences after a number of years is often awarded the hunt's colors. Some hunts, such as Orange, a fabulous Northern Virginia hunt, do not award colors. But most do. If someone does run into trouble, a member with colors is expected to offer assistance. You are also expected to know the territory, and if worse comes to worst, be cool in a crisis. That is more difficult to ascertain as, fortunately, few crises occur, such as a broken arm or your horse pulls up lame. But when they do, they must be fixed; an ambulance may need to be called, maybe not. Sister and Walter, like most masters, realized you never know until the crisis occurs who has a cool head and who doesn't.

Sister continued. "This is Yvonne Harris's first hunt with us, so we wish you well, Yvonne, and I think you'll bring us luck. Maiden riders often do."

Elise Sabatini whispered to Freddie, "I didn't."

"No one could have. The day was one of a kind," Freddie replied. "So consider this your first hunt."

Tootie, standing on one side of the hounds waiting as patiently as the horses, gave her mother a thumbs-up. Weevil winked.

"Hounds, please." Sister gave the traditional marching order to Weevil.

"All right, my beauties," he called in a higher voice, which excited them, then he gave a toodle on the horn.

Glowering in their specially reinforced paddock, Clytemnestra, a huge cow and her even bigger son, Orestes, looked menacing.

"Is that the biggest, fattest cow you have ever seen?" Angle, a second-year hound, spoke low to Trinity.

"I have seen her tear apart a paddock and Orestes follows. He's bigger but stupid. She is mean as snake shit." Trinity offered a harsh but true opinion.

Sally Taliaferro, an Episcopal priest, rode up next to Yvonne. "God bless."

Father Manusco, next to her, on the other side of her horse, remarked, "Sally, she's Catholic." He then looked at Yvonne with a big smile. "Bless you, my child."

Yvonne laughed. Sister thought of these two in young middle-age as her two divines. They shared so much in common and if dogma motivated them, they certainly didn't show it.

Hounds trotted up the slight rise to the two ponds, one higher than the other, feeding into the lower. The sound of falling water sounded restful to many. Cindy had a lot of water running under her farm as well as one narrow but fast creek on the western side, smack up against the beginning of the Blue Ridge Mountains.

Dreamboat, one of the D's, stopped, tail feathering rapidly. He didn't open immediately but followed this line between the ponds, as there was a path, then he moved faster.

Diana, his sister, joined him.

Together they opened. *"Fox. Fresh."*

Everyone rushed to them, including Jethro and Jerry, two young entries on their first hunt, like Yvonne.

"Fox," Jethro squeaked, his voice not completely changed.

Sister, proud that he spoke out, laughed to herself, as he sounded like a bird at the moment.

The trot opened to a canter, now up the hill. They passed the perfect old schoolhouse, so well maintained by Cindy, and a home for Georgia, a gray vixen, whom Cindy shamefully spoiled by feeding her. Naturally, Georgia had put on weight, feeling no need to scrounge for food. Also she liked living in the schoolhouse, as she had a dog bed, blankets, and toys. Cindy was shameless.

Hounds picked up Georgia's scent as they blew past the schoolhouse but they were on someone else, a fox unknown to them and a fox that was now running due east.

What a glorious way to start October. Weevil pointed Kilowatt toward a tiger trap jump marking the end of Foxglove on the east. Logs, upright forming a coop, while not formidable, might cause a horse not accustomed to the jump to look or balk. One of Jefferson Hunt's good features was, Sister and Walter built different types of jumps. Sister wanted her people to have seen and jumped everything, so if they went to, say, Kentucky, where there are stone fence jumps, they'd be fine.

Kilowatt floated over the tiger trap, followed by Sister and then the entire First Flight, including Yvonne. Old Buster was gold plated. Those made horses, perhaps a year or two older, are hard to find.

Sam watched as he took the jump behind Yvonne on Trocadero.

He thought to himself, "That horse is worth more than Trocadero. Gorgeous and talented as this boy is. If everyone had an Old Buster when beginning, we'd all be in better shape."

Sam had seen enough people, some with riding ability, get overmounted. It was never pretty.

By now, the canter shot up a gear. They were flying. Tears ran from Yvonne's eyes as the wind hit them but her leg was tight as a tick. She had never felt such raw animal exhilaration.

Tootie, on the left, had cleared a simple four-log jump farther down the fence line, whereas Betty had to take the tiger trap before Weevil to keep up with hounds. He needed to stay behind his hounds. The whippers-in needed to be up on the sides. Whipping-in is not for the fainthearted. You sit on a hill freezing your ass off and then, bam, you are running so hard you can barely breathe. And you never know when it will happen.

Sister hadn't heard any large oomph's or rubs on the jump. Everyone made it. Before her stretched a relatively flat pasture filled with large round hay bales dotting the green grass. Pressing on, they stopped at a row of hay bales neatly stacked against a post and rail fence. Hounds moved around the hay, some crawling under the bottom rail of the fence. Giorgio, Dreamboat, and Pansy leapt up on the large hay bales. Without a moment's hesitation, the two youngsters, Jethro and Jerry, effortlessly leapt up. The fox had barreled to the hay bales, dropping down between them to a den he had in the bales.

Seeing her two J's up there made Sister happy. Her J's had such athletic ability. They followed the big kids.

As Sister pulled up, sat there at a slight distance, Weevil dismounted and blew "Gone to Ground."

"How do we get him?" Jethro peered down into the narrow spaces between the bales, too narrow for even a squirrel to slide through. The narrow alley between the bales, side by side in a row, allowed the fox to drop down, wiggle to his den. Clever, but then again, they usually are.

Dreamboat replied, *"We don't. He's safe in his den."*

"What do we do now?" Jerry was a bit confused.

Pansy, who liked the young hound, said, *"We find another fox."*

The field, happy to catch their breath, watched the hounds. Alida slipped her phone from her inside jacket pocket to take a picture of the four hounds on top of the hay bales. She then slid the phone back in place. She felt naked without her phone, as do so many people, but the good thing about a few people in the field carrying phones is, if need be, they can call for help. If major help is needed, that decision had to be made on the spot. It's best if the field master can make that decision, but sometimes the field master is way ahead. Sister did not chide Alida for carrying the phone, but then Alida knew protocol. You never had to worry that she would do something to make things more difficult simply by not knowing how problems are handled. Again, that's why people get their colors. You need to know things, like never mouth off to a landowner. Basic, but could be forgotten or committed by someone who had a short fuse.

Back in the saddle, Weevil blew a few notes, turned back toward Foxglove, as they had covered more territory than they realized while running flat out. No point in going miles away from the main fixture this early in the Season. As the cool weather held, cool as in low fifties, he felt confident they would pick up another fox.

They did.

Again, this was not a fox they knew. Hounds could identify individual scents, as they could identify people's individual scents. Foxes could identify humans from their looks and scent as well as hounds. Comet, over at Roughneck Farm, knew where Golliwog had been and the cat knew Comet's capers. He had a naughty streak.

This fox had headed toward Foxglove but the scent faded quickly, so the field vaulted back over the tiger trap jump while Weevil, up ahead, veered right toward the thick woods.

The fast-running creek provided enough moisture near its banks for a whiff.

"What is this?" Jerry flared his nostrils.

"Bear."

Aero confirmed the scent.

No sooner had this younger hound said "bear" than the large, glossy brown bear charged out of the thicket.

This stopped the field, as horses snorted, some shied.

Rickyroo snorted but held his ground.

"We'll die!" a green horse cried, giving her rider a real handful.

"Shut up, Nitwit," Nonni commanded. *"He doesn't want to see you any more than you want to see him."*

The bear turned out to be a she who had been investigating whether she wanted to winter in the woods or if she preferred the grounds on the other side of the schoolhouse, which might provide more shelter from the winds from a bear's point of view.

Lumbering on, faster than those people who had no familiarity with bear could have imagined, the large creature turned her head, calling to the pack. *"Assholes."*

"How rude!" Diana shot back, continuing her verbal abuse.

No point lingering with all that bear scent around, plus the sight of a large animal hurrying back into the woods. Sister clucked to Rickyroo. He trotted forward, horses behind following. A few horses balked at the sight of the retreating bear. Not that the bear considered going back into the woods a retreat. Finally, with urging from riders, the entire field passed the woods, emerging on cut pasture, still a few round bales remaining to be moved.

This good pasture rolled up toward the schoolhouse. Weevil called to his hounds as he headed down toward the ponds, hoping for scent near the water. Hounds found, circled the area, then roared up toward the farm road near the schoolhouse.

Once up there, footing good, hounds ran down the road, passed the stables and barn, trailers all parked about, keeping on the farm road.

Once on the other side of the buildings, as well as Clytemnestra and Orestes, hounds paused. Audrey and Aero, younger, dawdled. Weevil was just about to tell them to move along when Aero stopped, Audrey alongside.

"*Comet.*" He named the gray fox from their farm.

She put her nose down. "*Is.*"

They sang out, the pack came to them, now all speaking.

If the humans had known what was going on they might have assumed they would soon be crossing Soldier Road and plunging into the wildflower field on that side of the road, only to climb the slippery steep slope up to Hangman's Ridge. But Comet had headed toward the very west end of Foxglove Farm.

The western part of the farm, terrain rougher, ended at the edge of an old farm abandoned but now for sale. Its history, like that of so many farms, covered centuries and generations, often ending in a line literally dying out. The hope was the property would be bought by people interested in reclaiming an old farm right next to a lovely farm, a good investment.

Hounds swept through high grasses. The grass swaying indicated where they were because you couldn't see a thing.

Whoosh, whoosh, whoosh could be heard as the drying-out grass and weeds brushed legs and horses. So did the hitchhikers, now sticking to pants and horses' legs. Along with the stickers that itched as they pierced clothing came all those tiny little green flat hitchhikers that had to be pulled off or peeled off with duct tape.

Yvonne was getting a real hunting baptism.

But on they pushed; Comet, about a quarter of a mile ahead,

swerved back toward Foxglove, but low so he now approached the creek, which passed through most of the lands abutting Soldier Road on the east. On the west side ran another creek, Broad Creek. One of the pluses of this part of the county was all the running water heading for big rivers.

Now down by the creek, hounds could move more easily, as the grass had thinned out.

"*He's close,*" Dasher, nose down, called out.

Everything stopped. No scent.

"*What?*" Jerry, totally confused, looked to Dreamboat, older and wiser.

Wiser he was, for the large hound peered into a huge log, an opening on top. "*I know where you are.*"

Comet, knowing the hounds, as he saw them daily, replied, "*I am here visiting a friend. If you look around you'll see all kinds of entrances.*"

Diana, next to her littermate, put her nose in the opening. "*Comet, you dragged us along. Who is down there?*"

"*No one you know. Now, come on. Leave us alone.*"

All the hounds surrounded the huge old log. A few stood at other den openings. Foxes, clever, might disguise an opening, use a log, or use a high creek bed, not always so smart. But multiple entrances and exits were not uncommon.

Weevil dismounted, horn in hand. He peered down into the log opening, inhaling a whiff of fresh fox. Blinking, he blew "Gone to Ground."

Betty held Kilowatt's reins. No fool, Weevil stood on the log and mounted up. He could mount from the ground but if help was nearby, why not use it?

"I've never been down here," Weevil said to Betty.

"It gets rougher, more ravines, a few flattish pastures should someone rehab them, but if we head straight west, we'll be right at the base of the mountains in fifteen minutes."

"Ah." He looked west, pastures shrouded in growth and saplings.

This place would take a lot of work.

Weevil turned east as a clean worn deer path was easy to see.

"Find your fox."

Hounds dutifully tried as the field touched low trenches, for that path worked better for deer than people.

Sister headed up toward the way they came. The broom sage was high, but all the riders had beaten down a serviceable path.

Betty noticed Sister wave her crop at the whipper-in. Betty took this as a sign Sister was going to stay behind the hounds if possible.

Hitchhikers still stuck to people once they reached higher ground but it was better.

Hounds started speaking. Sister followed the sound but did not go back down into the thick undergrowth. Filled with vines and trees fallen over the years in high winds, it was complicated getting through down there.

Picking up a trot, she reached the edge of Foxglove. Once into the back pasture, she stopped, for the sound was now coming straight at the people.

The D hounds blasted out of the heavy undergrowth, followed by the bulk of the pack.

"Hold hard," Sister ordered.

Hounds threaded through the horses.

Old Buster, stock still, observed with interest. Trocadero pranced. So did a few other horses.

Weevil, now up at the rear of his hounds, had the wisdom not to slide though the nervous horses and people. He raced to the front of the field, crossing by Sister and Rickyroo. He quickly caught up with the pack, now roaring.

Sister fell in thirty yards behind him. The made horses, those with experience and solid temperaments, followed.

The shaken riders turned for the trailers about a mile ahead, Ronnie Haslip leading them.

Sam, Trocadero under control, followed Yvonne; Old Buster moved up close to Sister as so many people left.

Hounds, screaming, blasted across the farm road into Cindy's wildflower field. Everyone could see Soldier Road. If hounds crossed they would face a hard climb on tired horses, plus a long walk back.

More people turned in.

Sister moved up into the center.

Hounds raced into the middle of Jerusalem artichoke, ragweed, goldenrod, a few pansies, compliments of birds over the years as well as a few odd sunflowers. Purple fountain grass, some having migrated from Cindy Chandler's tended flower beds, swayed in a higher breeze.

Hounds stopped. The scent vanished. Casting themselves, searching; Weevil quietly watched.

Jethro asked Taz, *"How can that happen?"*

"No one really knows." The older hound slowly sniffed, head down.

"Foxes can turn it off and on, I swear." Dragon told the truth, so no one complained.

Weevil slowly walked back up to the road. One by one, hounds followed. He could see people at their trailers in the distance.

Sister smiled at him, riding toward him. "An odd day."

"I'll say." He watched Zandy keep pushing. "The Z's have a great work ethic."

She smiled. "Wish we could give it to people. Well, Huntsman, let's go to the breakfast. The field is already there. May not be anything left."

"Yes, Madam." He called to the hounds, "Come along."

Sister looked behind her. Kasmir, Alida, Gray, Freddie, Ben, Sam, and Yvonne were all that was left.

Fortunately, there was still food by the time they got inside. Everyone was hungry.

Sister, a deviled egg in hand, complimented Yvonne. "You stuck it out."

"Love it." Yvonne did, too.

Tootie, next to her mother in line, was putting hot little sausages on her plate as Cindy brought more out from the kitchen. "You did great, Mom."

"Let's give Old Buster credit." Yvonne felt she could eat everything on the table.

"Mom, you need to buy that horse."

Sam, behind the ladies, piped up. "I'm trying to convince Marty."

"We'll have to come up with a Purchase Posse," Sister promised.

Cameron Aldron, Barry Harper, and Ben Sidell crowded around Weevil.

"Was the fox in that log?" Cameron had been close enough to see.

"He was, but he had to know the den. He ran for it. Sometimes in a pinch, a fox will jump into a gopher hole, which you can hear."

Barry grinned. "Animal cussing."

"Yeah, but no one is coming out surrounded by hounds." Weevil was famished.

Gray saved him. "Gentlemen, let the man eat."

"Oh, sorry." Cameron realized Weevil hadn't a plate.

Barry said to Ben, "That's a sensible horse."

"She is."

"Where did you find her?"

"Sister Jane. When I came here to take up the sheriff post, I more or less fell into foxhunting." Ben drank his stiff rye garnished with an orange peel.

"How do you more or less fall into foxhunting?" Cameron

laughed as he took Ben's empty plate from him, tossing it in a receptacle in the big dining room.

"Working on my first case I met Sister. She told me if I wanted to get along, I should foxhunt. I'd meet people, learn Virginia ways. Eventually some people would trust me."

"Where are you from?" Barry asked.

"Columbus, Ohio."

"Ah." Cameron smiled. "She was taking care of you. She liked you. She found you a terrific horse."

"She did."

"My bride has an eye for horses. If I ride a horse, I know if I like it or not, but she has the eye," Gray bragged on Sister.

"She helped me." Ben admired the older woman.

"Speaking of help, any news on the murdered man?" Barry sipped his drink, hot tea with a splash of bourbon.

"No. We've sent out information. I keep thinking some department somewhere will get back to us."

"Strange situation," Barry remarked.

"A touch macabre." Cameron frowned.

"I'm getting the signal. Excuse me." Gray saw Sister waving to him.

Walking over, she grabbed his hand. "Quiet, everyone. Let's toast Yvonne."

Gray clapped his hands. Sam, seeing his brother ask for quiet, whistled.

People did stop talking.

"Foxhunters. Last week Elise Sabatini had her first hunt and today was Yvonne Harris's first hunt. She stuck it out to the end. Three cheers!"

They all raised their glasses. Yvonne, accustomed to being the center of attention, nonetheless was surprised. Aunt Dan, who had watched with Kathleen Sixt Dunbar, cheered loudly.

Yvonne held up her own glass and said, to everyone's delight, "To the Hounds." Then Sister toasted Elise, explaining Elise's first day was tepid. Betty asked Yvonne if she would help them develop a media presence. Yvonne said she would love to do that.

Once home, Nonni happy at the Franklin stable, where he rented a stall, Ben took a hot shower. He turned on his computer. Had there been an emergency, his staff knew how to reach him, so this was more curiosity than business.

His eyes focused. The murder victim had been identified. He was Timothy Snavely, caucasian, thirty-nine. President of Snavely Import-Exports. Successful in his business. Single. Apparently no family. From Charlotte, North Carolina.

CHAPTER 10

October 2, 2022, Sunday

Sister stood in front of the refrigerator staring at items placed on it with magnets. Golly, Raleigh, and Rooster slept in their beds on the kitchen floor by the back stairway. The sound of the steps announced Gray was coming down from upstairs.

She turned to see him in a new jacket. "That looks good on you."

"Thanks. Cool, so thought I would try it." He walked over to her. "It's two quilted fabrics, fairly thin material with a thin layer of down in between. Thought I'd go outside and give it a test run. What are you doing? Transfixed by the refrigerator?"

"Trying to figure out our October schedule."

"Filling up."

"Closes out with the Waynesboro Symphony Orchestra on October 28. At the Paramount." She named the restored 1931 theater on the mall in downtown Charlottesville.

"Should be terrific. I noticed the theme this year is 'An Evening on the American Frontier.' Remember the first time you saw the West?" he asked.

"After graduating high school. Mom, Dad, and I drove across to Oregon, then down the coast and drove back through the middle of the country. I never imagined the United States was so big. Looking at a map isn't the same as actually seeing it. Roads weren't so good then, so it took us seven days each way, plus Dad had to stop and take pictures. Leica cheered the day my father was born."

He laughed. "It's a dad thing."

She leaned on him for a moment. "Did you remember to send in our contribution to sponsor a chair?"

"I did. I rarely forget anything with a dollar sign in front of it."

She smiled. "Sorry. I know that. But you haven't told me which chair you sponsored."

"The tuba."

"What?" Her eyebrows raised.

"I did. Tuba players rarely get the spotlight. And I love the sound. The other day I was driving back from Middleburg and Sirius classical played a symphony . . . wait, maybe it was a concerto, for the tuba by Wynton Marsalis."

"Well, if it's Wynton Marsalis it has to be good, but you never cease to surprise me."

"Good." He kissed her on the cheek. "I'm going out to check the gardens around the house. Want to see if they need mulch or even leaves on them for winter. Come with me."

"Okay." They went into the mudroom, chillier than the kitchen; she pulled a Carhartt off the hook, fished in the pocket as the dogs joined them. "Aha. Have it."

"Have what?"

"My list for winter plants. I'm on a plant kick. Have all my butterfly and bee plants in the big wildflower field. This is my house garden list."

Stepping outside, the air was cool, maybe low fifties.

They walked to the back of the house, dogs in tow. In the near distance was the hound graveyard, bound by wrought iron with a life-like statue of a hound, Archie, in the middle.

She stopped, pointing to the garden along the back of the house, late autumn flowers giving up the ghost. "We need winter flowers. We're good on spring, summer, and fall, but we need true winter flowers."

"Aunt Dan has those beautiful camellias by the back door."

"She does. Red. Maybe I should buy her some red twig dogwood for back there." Pointing, Sister said, "Beautyberry shrub. Right here. It's that purple that catches your eye and the birds love the berries. They remain on all winter. And here, next to that, blue holly. Have to have a male and a female."

"That sounds good." He liked it when she was enthusiastic, so full of ideas.

"Right." She grinned up at him. "We need color but the various heights of plants make a difference. So," she rubbed her chin with her gloved hand, "we need something lower, mounding sort of. Thinking about winter heath. It blooms in later winter. You know, I really should hire a landscape gardener. I pull stuff out of the air, plant it, then live with it. They are a lot more organized. You know, somebody like Jon Carloftis. But I don't think we could afford him. He's such a big star."

"Honey, I don't know much about landscape gardening or the people in it but I do remember when we visited Winterthur. The plants, trees, and gardens were so beautiful. It was hard to take it all in. Plus the place is huge."

"Fortunately, we are on a different scale."

They both laughed, walking along the back of the house while she threw out ideas then explained the shrubs and plants to him.

"You know what, I'll show you pictures in my garden books. But no matter what, we have to have hellebore, Lenten roses. We can put those in the front of the house. Have to have them."

"Whatever you say."

"He's such a pushover." Rooster bumped Raleigh in play.

"He loves her." Raleigh felt he understood humans, which he did.

"Is gardening a lady thing?" Rooster wondered.

"No. Men do it, too. Crawford will spend a fortune on Old Paradise. But gardeners get obsessed. Think how Mom has been with her monarch butterfly field. That's what I call it." Raleigh paused. *"Golly hides under the stuff around the house. She jumps out and thinks she scares me but she doesn't. I know she's there."*

Rooster sniffed. *"She puts her claws out, too."*

"They are sharp," Raleigh acknowledged.

While Sister and Gray walked around the house, Ben Sidell sat at Ed Clark's kitchen table, notebook opened.

"Thanks for calling, Ed. It's Sunday. I'll be as brief as I can."

"No problem. I would think time is important."

"For any crime, but murder captures people's imagination. It also unnerves them." He clicked his ballpoint pen. "What was your business with Timothy Snavely?"

"I had no business with him but I recognized him from the drawing on the news and the one in the paper. I happened to be at the Charlotte airport in North Carolina coming back from Denver. Gave a speech about six months ago. There was a commotion at the next gate. Reporters, cameras. A delegation from Namibia was disembarking. The mayor was there, the usual group of politicos. But the first person out of the chute was Timothy Snavely. He paused, photographs. Then came the Namibians, a group of various bankers, politicians, and businessmen. Later, reading the next day's paper, I saw Timothy Snavely was identified as a president of an import-export business."

"So you never spoke to him?"

"No."

Ben tapped his pen on his notebook. "Perhaps a man with a finger in every pie."

"Lots of uranium in Namibia. I go to South Africa at least once a year. Namibia used to be part of South Africa. Full of wildlife like the springbok, an antelope. There are over two hundred species of reptiles. Lions, elephants, Kirk's dik-dik."

"I beg your pardon?" Ben's eyebrows raised.

"A small antelope. Ten pounds. Maybe ten pounds."

"I see. That was it. Unless the paper identified Snavely's purpose."

"The paper did. He was heading a North Carolina group, hoping to open up trade with Namibia. The politicians were followed up by trade representatives. I only know that as it, too, was in the newspaper. I left, as I had to get to another runway to catch a plane home."

"If you think of anything else, Ed, call me."

"I will. Does anyone have any idea what an importer-exporter would be doing here?"

Ben sighed. "No. It's a fresh case. There's lots of homework."

CHAPTER 11

October 4, 2022, Tuesday

A simple three-rail fence loomed ahead, the three rails stacked together, no airy space showing between. The footing was decent. Sister trotted toward it, Lafayette ready to go, when out of a thicket on her right shot a young male deer . . . a spike, which is a young male with his antlers small and sticking straight up. As he aged, the antlers would grow to become formidable. Confused, he ran straight for Sister, who stopped as the young animal, frightened, veered away from Lafayette at the last minute.

Sister patted her trusted friend on the neck then continued to the fence, maybe three feet, not much. She'd learned over time to never underestimate a fence. A smaller fence can damage you just as much as a whopper. Lafayette pushed off his hind end, easily closing the three feet.

Behind Sister, fourteen people rode, a number higher than usual for Tuesday during cubbing, but the weather, pleasant, encouraged people to enjoy it before the frosts closed in.

Warm at eight-thirty AM, maybe sixty degrees by nine-thirty AM; it would prove bad for scent. So Weevil and Sister wanted to make use of what cool temperature they had. Within two weeks at the most, the mornings would be brisk, but then the days would warm up. By mid-November, few warm days would occur, unless a brief visit of Indian Summer pleased everyone.

Hounds moved along, not much speaking but noses down. They moved in a straight line, one behind the other, and Weevil figured they were on something. If the line warmed up, the hounds would speak. If not, they'd push along to find another line, with luck.

Dragon, arrogant as always, screamed, *"Let's get him."*

Diana checked her impetuous brother. *"Coyote."*

Jethro turned to Thimble. *"Can we run a coyote?"*

"We can. Sister and Weevil prefer fox, but if we pick up coyote, it's okay. Boogie. The coyote will probably run in a line straight as a stick."

No time for questions, the pack with four youngsters all out today ran. Coyotes are fast. As Thimble said, the line was straight.

Coops in a three-board fence gave everyone a chance to jump, while Bobby Franklin took Second Flight to a gate. The Second Flight was falling far behind. Not much he could do about it.

Ten minutes of galloping brought the pack to a deer trail winding up a steep grade. Up they ran, full cry. At the top of the grade a flat small meadow allowed a view of the quarry.

Hounds poured over the edge of the flat meadow then stopped. Somehow the coyote evaded them, when a few moments ago he was in plain view.

Noses down, hounds cast themselves to pick up the line.

"Ever notice coyotes are picking up fox's tricks?" Pookah said to Aero.

"Maybe." Aero moved with deliberation.

"Living around people makes life easy for them."

Trinity chimed in. *"More to eat—including pets."*

"Ugh." Pookah lifted his head, his frustration apparent.

Weevil, also frustrated, watched as the field was joined by the Second Flight, who observed the frustration.

Betty, at the bottom of this hill, waited patiently.

"Dammit," Weevil whispered under his breath as he blew the pack back to him.

Jethro, Jeeter, Jinks, and Jerry took their cue from the older hounds as they turned and trotted back up the hill.

Weevil turned Showboat to retrace their steps. As they crossed the meadow, raindrops began to fall. The rain was light but as they walked down the other side, coming out by fenced pastures, it started to fall harder.

Sister rode up to Weevil. "Snakebit."

"Right." He pushed hounds to move a little faster.

Took them ten minutes to get back to the trailers, by which time water had slid down the back of their necks, found its way into where boots gapped. Gloves, too, became slippery.

Most of the jackets, a thick weave, kept riders dry. A downpour would have gotten through but this was a steady, medium rain. It dripped off the brim of their hunt caps.

Finally back at the trailers, people eagerly dismounted, walked their horses into the trailers. Some removed saddles, others didn't, but everyone threw a sheet or cotton woven covering over their horses.

Bridles came off. Faces were wiped. Hay hung up inside. Water buckets available.

Weevil and Tootie put up the hounds while Betty took care of their horses. This was a well-oiled routine.

A small, old, log cabin by the trailers provided refuge for the people. The owners allowed Jefferson Hunt to use the cozy place, provided they cleaned it.

People brought in deviled eggs, sandwiches, cheese and crackers, while Kasmir and Bobby carried a cooler each.

Betty grabbed a thermos.

The temperature began to drop.

Ronnie Haslip, feeling a slight shiver, put logs in the fireplace, crumpled paper underneath. Within minutes the crackle and glow promised warmth.

"Look at the temperature on your phone," Sister told Betty.

Pulling her glasses out of her coat pocket, Betty punched the weather app. "Dropped seven degrees. So now forty-seven degrees Fahrenheit."

"Any predictions?" Sister asked.

"To be forty-two degrees Fahrenheit by ten AM. And a light frost tonight."

Alida looked up from putting down a potato salad bowl. "What a switch."

"It's the beginning of fall." Ronnie walked over to the table. "You don't know from one day to the next."

Tootie was warming herself by the fire, as she wore a thin jacket. "That's the truth."

"Take your jacket off and hang it on the chair," Freddie suggested. "It'll dry out in no time."

Tootie took off her soaked jacket, returning to the fire. Weevil brought her a plate and a hot tea. Then he pulled a chair up for her so she could sit.

Everyone threw out ideas as to how the coyote vanished.

Sister gratefully dropped in a chair when Gray brought it for her.

Yvonne shivered, Sam placed his coat around her shoulders. "Cold came up fast."

"Sure did. And I borrowed Tootie's salt sack, thinking it would get hot. Don't you need a jacket?"

He smiled. "No. I pulled on an old long-sleeved undershirt."

"How smart is that?" She looked up at him.

"I checked three weather apps. All said it would rain, the mercury drop, but they forecast that to happen at noon. Anyway, I'm fine."

Barry Harper, next to Freddie Thomas, sighed. "Walked into the office yesterday. My lock had been picked."

Her fork stopped midair. "Damage?"

"No, not really. But whoever it was took my stamp collection."

Ronnie, overhearing, said, "That could be worth money."

"It's worth something, but mostly they were stamps I chose for the drawings and color and weren't rare. I'm not organized like most collectors. Whoever this was left all the old stamps, like the two-penny stamps, no artwork. Stamps can have beautiful artwork. I like wildlife stamps."

"That's puzzling." Freddie put her fork back in her mouth.

"Did you report this to Ben, the sheriff's department?" Ronnie pressed a little.

"I hesitated. It seems so small compared to what he's dealing with now, but finally I did," Barry answered.

"Do you have a list of what was stolen?" Ronnie was curious.

"I do. Only stamps from the last thirty-five years, ones with pretty drawings, wildlife . . . like salamanders . . . pretty coloring. Like I said, it's a small thing."

"Will you let us know?" Yvonne called out from the fireplace.

Gray, passing out drinks, reached Freddie, Barry, and Ronnie. "Could be some fascination with design or subject. People get obsessed with weird things. Like subject matter, colors. Stuff," Gray volunteered.

"I'd better go through my notes. I took pictures of all my stamps. Good that I did. And I am one of those weird collectors."

When he returned home, he pulled out his folder. He kept one in the office, one at home.

He had photos of every stamp in his collection.

CHAPTER 12

October 5, 2022, Wednesday

"Lenten roses." Aunt Daniella luxuriated in her plush rocking chair.

"She has that on her list."

"Good. Pretty. Well, will you remember this or do you need paper?"

Gray replied, "Have my notebook right here."

He pulled a reporter's notebook out of his pocket.

"Oh. Witch hazel. You never go wrong with witch hazel. Bottlebrush buckeye, white summerlong blooms. Chokeberry is bright red. Tough."

"Aunt Dan, why plant a summer bloomer. Buckeyes?"

"Oh. Forgot. Little tan pear-shaped fruit. I'm not so sure how it will do here but just popped into my mind. I'm sure she'll plant red twig dogwood."

"She's got that," he agreed.

"You know, next time you all leave from the kennels or After All, I'll have Yvonne, unless she's riding, take me to the house after the hunt, or Kathleen can take me. She'll still follow. We're Yvonne's support group."

He laughed. "Good. I think Yvonne has many supporters."

"Ha. They'll get nowhere. Of course, Alida's and Freddie's friendship mean a lot." She paused. "What about your brother?"

"What about my brother?" His eyebrows raised.

"Gray, don't you think he's fallen for Yvonne?"

Sam had not confided freely to his brother but Gray knew him well. He chose his words carefully.

"He's dedicated to teaching her how to ride. She did so well at Close Shave, not an easy fixture."

Her gray eyebrows narrowed. "That's not what I asked." Tapping the arm of the rocker. "If you're going to be difficult, get me a drink."

Rising from his own comfortable seat, he walked to the bar. Her ice machine produced large square cubes. He put two in an elegant cut-crystal glass. Then he added an overflowing jigger of Woodford Reserve. Pulled an orange from the small fridge, cut a thin slice, dipped it in the amber liquid, then secured it on the glass rim. He returned, handing her the potent libation.

"Thank you. One for yourself."

"A light one. Getting darker early. I need to be alert. People drive like fools." He returned to the den.

"They always have." She gratefully sipped her magic potion. "I do so love my early-evening drink."

He joined her with his scotch and water. "Back to Sam. He feels he has nothing to offer any woman but especially a woman like Yvonne."

"Nonsense." Her voice rose. "He is so good with a horse. He's honest. He's handsome. Well, our family is good-looking."

Gray nodded. "Thanks to you and my mother. Those Lorillard girls."

She sighed. "Oh Gray, if only Graziella were alive. Sam did pull himself together with your help. He's so intelligent. Just so intelligent. It makes me wonder if Carrie Nation wasn't right." She stared at her drink then knocked it back. "But only for a moment or two."

Gray laughed. "Aunt Dan, I believe some people are born with," he paused, "the affliction. Once the booze gets ahold of them, they go down. Drugs. All the same, I think."

"That beautiful Dorothy Dandridge, dead at forty-two. Drugs." She smiled. "Sorry, dear, she was before your time. A woman of surpassing talent and beauty. Hollywood."

"I've seen *Carmen Jones*," he remarked. "She was outstanding. And wasn't she friends with Ava Gardner?"

"Another great beauty. She didn't care about color. But she would certainly understand alcoholism. She drank. But you know, even at the end of her life she was something to look at."

"As are you." He held up his glass in tribute.

"You're my nephew. You have to be nice," she purred.

"The simple truth."

"But yes, Ava Gardner was friends with Dorothy. Apart from being wild as a rat, Ava hated racism. The studio would threaten her if she went to too many parties with Dorothy or Hattie McDaniel. Oh my, another bad girl." Aunt Daniella laughed with pleasure. "I think we all had more fun, dear. Or maybe I think that because I was young. Those were the movie stars I liked as a young woman. You know, Gray, it will never end."

"What?"

"Inequality. It changes for me. The subjects of hatred and dismissal might change but inequality is a fact of life throughout the world, throughout time."

"That doesn't mean we don't fight it."

She smiled slyly. "Of course, but there are many ways to fight. Tell your wife I'll look at her gardens."

"She'll be pleased." He crossed one leg over the other. "Do you still have Mercer's stamp collection?"

"What brought that on?"

He leaned forward. "A strange thing. Barry Harper, you know the fellow who's been with us for two years when he has time?" She nodded, so he continued. "His office was broken into over the weekend and his stamp collection was stolen, but not all of it."

"Stamps can be very valuable. Hundreds of thousands valuable."

"Yes, but the oddity is, according to Barry, whoever it was only stole stamps with pretty drawings of butterflies, maybe flowers. He emphasized good drawings. Little works of art. Nothing else."

"That is odd. Maybe it has something to do with his nonprofit organization. Amphibians. I don't really think of turtles or snakes but I guess some people like them." She sighed, feeling relaxed.

"There are so many small nonprofits."

"He didn't make his money saving turtles." She held up her glass while he got up to refill it.

"Lawyer. Made his bundle and walked away."

"Maybe he didn't walk away far enough."

"He made more money than Cameron. But Cameron is like a small FedEx. He flies packages everywhere. Has to be lucrative." She happily took her fresh drink. "Do you think Barry made a lot of money?"

"Enough to start a nonprofit. Funny, how you see people who make a great deal of money, when they quit, they often want to do good works. Athletes do it during their career. It's good publicity, but once their career is over, they often continue."

"People have to have a goal."

"Mercer's stamp collection," he prodded.

"Oh yes. I have it. It's in the safe. I have no idea of its value. It was important to him. I can't let it go."

"When we were kids he'd tell me about famous stamp collectors. There is a national organization, the American Philatelic Society. He joined at sixteen. I razzed him about it. He said there were good lectures. He'd go on about what a stamp can tell you. I'm sorry to admit it went in one ear and out the other."

She giggled. "Me too, but he just loved it."

"As long as it's safe."

"It is."

He put his feet up on the hassock. "Ah."

"Shoes tight?"

"At the end of the day, my feet are tired. Oh, before I forget, you know that you and Kathleen Sixt Dunbar are our guests at the Waynesboro Symphony Orchestra."

"I do. I so look forward to it. Who else is going?"

"Much of the hunt club. Sam asked Yvonne. She said yes."

A long sip, then the nonagenarian low voice said, "Tell him he has a lot to offer a woman, especially a woman like Yvonne. Forget the money. She's thrilled with her first foxhunt. Well, why not? Tell him to make her laugh. You know when she came here she had forgotten how to laugh. Little by little, she has moved on from that fractious divorce. She is close to her daughter. Really. Keep her laughing, help her with her goals. Underneath that gorgeous, somewhat bitter exterior with men is a truly beautiful woman. She needs love. She needs a real man. She needs to give love."

Startled at this outburst from his aunt Dan, Gray stuttered, "I will. I mean, I'll try. He's not always easy to talk to, Sam. I had no idea you were so close to Yvonne. I knew you all got along. I . . ." He thought, "I'll try."

"I have grown to love her. I understand her. Once I was that beautiful woman. You think life will be easier for such a woman. In some ways it is. In other ways, no. And I love Sam. And I love you. I don't want to leave this earth without seeing her and my dear beaten-up Sam happy. You are happy and I take comfort in that."

"Aunt Dan, you aren't sick, are you?" His face was stricken.

She laughed. "No. I'm having an emotional moment. I'm closing in on one hundred, Gray. I can't live forever."

"Aunt Dan, I can't imagine life without you."

"Oh, I'll be here. I simply won't be here in physical form." She smiled at him, a warm enveloping smile. "Help your brother."

"Yes, ma'am," he promised.

CHAPTER 13

October 6, 2022, Thursday

Driving back from the hunt, which was held at Skidby on South Chapel Cross Road, Sister and Betty didn't mind the slow pace.

Following six trailers, they weren't going anywhere fast. The field members left ahead of them, so staff trailers, Sister, Weevil, Tootie, and Bobby were in the rear. Yvonne and Sam drove behind Kasmir and Alida in the lead.

Once at the crossroads, the lovely chapel before them, everyone turned right toward the east. Kasmir and Alida turned right again into Tattenhall Station. Each truck and trailer passing honked. "Goodbye."

"Yvonne rides with Sam to Beasley Hall. You'd think she'd just go home to Beveridge Hundred," Betty noted.

This was the estate Yvonne had purchased from Cecil and Violet Van Dorn on Chapel Hill's South Road. The older couple had a life estate so they lived in the large clapboard house while Yvonne lived in the dependency, more than large enough for her. If the Van Dorns moved to assisted living, she'd take over. She had glorious plans for the interior of the Federal home built in 1832. Beveridge Hundred abutted Kasmir's Tattenhall Station.

"She says she wants to untack Buster, wash and dry him, check his hooves, and give him treats."

"Ah so." Betty sounded like a German.

"Back at you."

"You've visited Germany. You visited before Bobby and I went in 2022. Loved it."

"Ray and I first flew over in '90." She sighed. "Where did the time go?"

"I'm saying that more and more these days." Betty wiggled her toes in her brown boots, informal attire. "My feet got cold."

"Mine always do. Won't be too long before Opening Hunt. My black formal boots are bigger, so I can wear two pairs of socks. In my bye-day boots I can't." She mentioned the hunting term for informal days.

"You figured you'd only wear them during cubbing?"

"No. But my brown boots and those oxbloods that I love are pushing forty. Given the expense of bespoke boots and our tack, I take good care of things. But they can only last so long."

"We'll only last so long." Betty laughed.

"What a happy thought," Sister rejoined.

"Back to Yvonne cleaning Buster. I would have thought she'd pay Sam to do all that."

"Tootie says her mother wants to know about horses and Yvonne has fallen desperately in love with Buster. Sam is trying to get Marty to sell the golden child."

"That he is." Sister avoided a pothole. "If every new hunter rode a Buster, they'd learn so much faster and we wouldn't be holding our breath. Oh hey." Sister slowed then stopped. "There's a box turtle by the side of the road. He should be in his winter quarters."

"Don't get out. I'll get out." Betty knew Sister would pick up any animal looking as though it needed help or was lost.

"Rooster's towels are in the backseat."

"Right." Betty hopped out, opened the small door behind her door, grabbed the towel, which evidenced Rooster's chewing.

She put the towel around the creature, who ducked his head in. Then she got back in the truck, placing the turtle on the floor in the back, carefully removing the towel.

"Thanks."

"He won't stick his neck out and look at me."

Sister laughed. "I could be so hateful."

Betty having closed that door used the chrome rail between the doors to help hoist her in the front. "Damn, these trucks are too high. Glad you put the Jesus strap on."

"Even Gray has to use one, and he's six two. You buy a new truck, you need handrails on the outside, Jesus straps on the inside."

"Who can afford a new truck?" Betty sounded dolorous.

"That's the truth. This baby is 2006. Like my boots, I've taken care of it, but the day will come. Duallys, without a lot of goodies, cost, what, seventy-two thousand used? Load them up with goodies and you can go over ninety thousand. It's lunacy."

"It's inflation." Betty settled in the seat as Sister pulled back on the road. "I can smell the turtle."

Sister agreed. "They do have a distinctive odor. Is it male or female?"

"Damned if I know."

"I'll look when we get home. Better yet, I'll call Barry Harper to see if he'll take our passenger."

"You know, I should give something to his foundation. I give to the Wildlife Center of Virginia." Betty continued to hold on to the Jesus strap.

"Last year, Gray and I gave two hundred and fifty dollars. Neither of us is big on amphibians nor reptiles but we wanted to show support for all wildlife."

"Mmm. Wonder if Ben's found out anything about Timothy Snavely." Betty shivered slightly. "I don't know, gives me the willies."

"The corpse has been identified. That's a start. Snavely was in the import-export business. Now, there's a business ripe for crime." Sister turned off the two-lane state highway onto the long gravel road to her farm.

"Like drugs?"

"Yes. That's obvious. Or homemade liquor. But what about smuggling, say, some copper."

"Be heavy," Betty posited.

"They'd find a way to cover the weight. Like watermelons. I don't know, a thought?"

"Maybe not watermelons." Betty smiled.

"If we had criminal minds we'd figure this out. Well, my first priority after we take care of the horses is to get the turtle settled."

Betty replied, "What is that saying, 'Behold the turtle. He only makes progress when he sticks his neck out.'"

"Ending sentence with a preposition." Sister cut the motor.

"Don't start with me."

"Oh. I'll remember that, but 'Behold the turtle. He only makes progress when he sticks out his neck.'"

Grammatically correct or not, it was true.

CHAPTER 14

October 7, 2022, Friday

"This fellow is young." Barry examined the box turtle in the makeshift box where Sister had placed him with greens and a low pan of water.

"How can you tell?" Sister asked, while Golly sat on the kitchen counter, appalled that her human was focused on a turtle.

"This isn't perfect but you count the rings on the shell and divide by two. So he's about three. Box turtles mature at about five."

"I've always liked the design of their shells."

"Turtles and tortoises can be beautiful. This guy seems healthy. He may have gotten confused, it's beginning to get cold, or he may have wanted to cross the road, thinking food and shelter would be better on the other side. But I'll take him with me and have my vet look at him to be sure. There are vets specializing in amphibians and reptiles. I use Audrey Simpson." Barry looked down at the young turtle, who was looking up at him. "In time they know who you are."

"One doesn't think of a turtle coming to your call." Sister felt a bit of affection for the young fellow.

"They know you bring them cantaloupe, grapes, oranges, vegetables. And in time, if you put him on the floor for extra exercise, he might follow you."

Rooster, curled in his sherpa bed in the corner, announced, *"Sister, Golly doesn't come to your call."*

"Peon." Golly sniffed.

"Do they like attention?" Sister asked.

"Not so much. You can brush their shell or gently rub the top of their head, but turtles are loners mostly."

"Barry, how did you get interested in amphibians and reptiles?"

"As a kid, snakes never frightened me. I read about them, learned to recognize how a poisonous snake's head is different, more triangular than a regular snake's. Then as I learned about amphibians I became fascinated with creatures living on land and water, being adept at both."

"It is a good survival mechanism, I would think."

"Indeed." He smiled. "If you'll allow me, I'll take this fellow to the compound, what I call the compound. He is male. Has red eyes, his shell underside is a little concave."

Sister waited then spoke. "Only if you don't give him away."

Barry blinked, surprised. "No. Of course not."

"I get very attached to animals. I even had a pet possum as a child. Drove my parents crazy, but I watched him eat. The turtle has crawled under the small branches I've put in this makeshift box. And he's dug in the dirt I put in, too."

Barry beamed. "They like cool nights, not cold. Say low sixties. They'll dig a shallow little spot or wedge under a log. They can't take harsh cold."

"Deeper or better insulated dens? Is *den* the right word?" She, too, was becoming fascinated.

"They'll find warmth. Even human outbuildings can provide protection. You'd be surprised at how they can tuck themselves away."

He smiled. "I'll talk all day. This is my passion and I thank you and Gray for your contributions to my nonprofit."

"It's a small amount, but when we both learned of your organization's name, we just had to." She laughed.

"Oh. Stick Your Neck Out. Thought it would get attention. And when classes come from the grade school, it attracts the children, a bit different. The kids will stick their heads up then down. Now, not all the kids like the snakes but most all like the turtles." He brought a large carrier with towels, some food, and a tiny drinking fountain that he could press if the turtle looked parched.

He didn't.

"Good." Golly sat up, the tip of her tail flicking.

"If you jumped in the box, I'd hope the turtle would pee on you," Rooster unchivalrously said.

"Turtles don't pee on others." Raleigh's deep voice always sounded authoritative.

"How do you know?" Rooster challenged.

"Because while you were talking, Mom asked the same thing when he picked up the turtle to put him in the carrying case."

"Oh." Rooster had been looking forward to an argument.

"Why don't you come to see my place. I'd love to show you around. I have turtles older than we are. Some can live past one hundred." Barry carefully placed the turtle, now head shut in his shell, inside the carrying case. "This fellow should easily make it to thirty-five."

"I will come and I'll bring Betty." She picked up the turtle. "Maybe Ronnie. He likes learning about animals."

"When you all set your schedules, call or text me."

As Barry walked to the door with the turtle, Sister walked with him. "Any news on your stamps?"

He stopped. "No. Such a small collection. I must be the odd duck in the hunt club, turtles and stamps."

She laughed. "Barry, if you only knew."

CHAPTER 15

October 8, 2022, Saturday

Cubbing weather excelled at variety. One day the temperature would just make the mid-fifties, warmish but not bad. The next day at ten the thermometer climbed to the mid-seventies. Big temperature bounces diminished the chances for a good hunt. Everyone had a theory as to why but no one really knew. The second day after the temperature bounce often turned out good. Then again, it snowed briefly a few days ago, a few twirling flakes. That was central Virginia.

This Saturday was the second day after a drop. However, the winds picked up.

Hounds moved through the wildflower field, what was one year of milkweed pods finally blown to bits.

Weevil cast hounds crosswind, moved northwest, the usual direction of wind. Members of the field tucked their heads down, as the wind made their eyes water.

Buddy Cadwalder, visiting from Philadelphia, pulled his cap down, hoping the brim would deflect the wind. Didn't work. He had been visiting Jefferson Hunt for a year now when he could manage the time. From the City of Brotherly Love, the trip took about five hours. Wisely, he rented a stall at the Bancrofts'. His hope was to see Kathleen Sixt Dunbar on a regular basis. She enjoyed his company, he felt hopeful. But she could only enjoy his company if he made the trip.

Kathleen, wearing a hunter green turtleneck, which set off her auburn hair, drove her BMW X5 with Aunt Daniella in the passenger seat.

"Think I should head for the Bancrofts'?"

Aunt Daniella answered, "Sit tight for a little bit. They could head back this way."

"It's windy. Sister says wind is a form of torture."

Aunt Daniella rubbed her hands together. "It is unless it's blowing scent right to them."

"If your hands are cold, turn up the heat on your side." She pointed to a knob. "Right there. Your temperature now is seventy degrees Fahrenheit."

"Think I will, seventy-four degrees Fahrenheit." She turned the knob to the right. "Cars are so complicated now. Oh, that feels warm already."

Motor running, Kathleen popped the SUV into gear, slowly driving toward the main road as the field took the hog's back jump into the Bancrofts' property.

"Weevil decided to get out of the wind. Once he's in the woods, there will be some protection." Kathleen crawled along.

"You have been listening when we drive," Aunt Daniella remarked. "Let's see, three years now."

"Has it been that long?" Kathleen wondered.

Abdul, her Welsh terrier, sat in the backseat, alert. Human concern over time baffled him. You only have the moment you're in. Why dredge up the past or worry about the future?

Reaching the state road, Kathleen turned left, drove the mile and a half to the entrance to the Bancrofts' farm. She slowed halfway down the drive, not knowing if hounds and horses would appear.

"The horn sounds distant." Aunt Daniella put her window down. "Like he's staying in the woods but heading north. I think you can go through the covered bridge. If they come out behind you, you can pull off the road."

Kathleen motored to the bridge.

The rumble intensified against the walls. She had her window down now as well.

"Hmm."

Kathleen replied, "Quiet out there."

The silence was due to hounds trying to pick up a line. They were still on the other side by the creek, the west side.

Cameron Aldron flipped his tweed collar up, as did Walter Lungren behind him. No one spoke but if they did they would have noted the temperature was dropping. Usually the temperature would rise as the morning progressed. Not today. A cold front was moving in.

Weevil blew encouraging toots on his horn, which belonged to a huntsman from the 1960s. The sound, rich and mellow, captured human and hound attention.

"Find your fox."

"Stuff is blowing up my nose." Ardent sneezed.

"Me too," Parker, a year older, commiserated.

Skinny Jinks, still filling out, called, *"Maybe. Think I've got something."*

Dreamboat trotted over. *"Faint but he's right."*

All the hounds scrambled over as branches swayed overhead. With deliberation, tails feathering, the pack moved toward the farm road, yet stayed in the woods. They veered due north. The pace picked up to a slow trot.

Sister, knowing the only wide trail was the farm road once over the creek, headed for it. Kathleen and Aunt Daniella saw her up ahead. Soon the field was behind her, followed by Bobby Franklin and Second Flight.

The wind smacked everyone on the face, but hounds were speaking so all kicked on. Kathleen followed seventy yards behind the last person.

"What's Barry Harper doing in the rear? He's usually First Flight," Kathleen wondered. "Maybe letting the other riders block the wind."

"Hell no, Kathleen. He wants to be by Elise Sabatini. She's a looker."

"Oh." Kathleen hadn't thought of that.

"Speaking of men looking at women. How's Buddy Cadwalder?"

Kathleen didn't answer at first, moving a bit faster, as in twenty miles per hour. "Ah. Quiet again. Buddy? I like him. He's thoughtful."

"Good." Aunt Daniella pulled her scarf high around her throat. "Even a crack, a little opening and I feel the dropping temperatures."

"I do, too."

Hounds moved on the same line, which heated up. Then they turned, heading due west again. Sister had to turn back to find a decent east-west path. Kathleen pulled over to the side of the road, cutting the engine. The minute Elise and Barry trotted by, Kathleen turned on the motor.

"Ah." Aunt Daniella held her hands to the vent.

"It's getting hateful. Yvonne's tough, being out there, and winter will be colder than this." Kathleen turned around.

"She's having a wonderful time. She says she'll never have to go to the gym again."

"I believe it."

Out they drove, reached the bridge. Windows down again.

"Moving fast. They're heading straight for the fence line." Aunt Daniella, having lived ninety plus years in the county, knew her territory intimately. "Go through the bridge, then stop. We might be able to see up to the fence line."

Kathleen did. They focused to their right. Aunt Daniella, on that side, had her window down a bit.

"Hounds are speaking. The field has to take the hog's back jump. Yep. There go the hounds over it. Next Weevil."

Sister followed in three minutes. The narrow cleared path allowed riders to gallop in single file. Everyone kept up.

The fox, Comet, shot for his den under Tootie's cabin. He reached it, ducking in under the porch, sliding into his spacious den.

Hounds reached the porch five minutes later.

"Come out," Thimble hollered.

"Yeah." Twist couldn't think of anything more original.

Weevil arrived, dismounted, blew "Gone to Ground." He also knew Comet, so this was the end of the run.

A blast of air made some tree branches scratch the cottage's windows, an eerie sound.

Another blast turned cheeks cold.

Sister turned her collar up. "Weevil, pull them up. We've been at it for two hours. This weather isn't going to get any better."

"Come on. Come along."

Comet came out of his den to peer through the latticework. The wind, not as bad as higher off the ground, rustled his gray fur. Back to the den.

Jeeter, a first-year entry, asked Zorro, *"Does a fox ever come out of his den?"*

"I've never seen one. Once they reach it, that's it. Kind of like our kennels. You get back, it's warmer, you got food," Zorro replied.

"He has food in there?"

"Sure. He can come out and find stuff from the cottage or he can go to the stables. Humans leave food around."

"They never eat it all?" Jeeter was surprised.

"They make too much. Seems like that to me. Sister, Gray, Tootie, and Weevil fill up their garbage cans." Zorro happily marched to the kennel.

He'd had enough of the wind, too.

Betty took Midshipman, a young Thoroughbred Sister was now hunting a bit.

"He did pretty good in the wind." Sister handed the reins to Betty. "Young but a good mind."

"They all need time on the target. I'll throw a blanket over him and Outlaw. After the breakfast, I'll come out and clean them and the tack."

"I'll be with you. See you at the house."

The breakfast was a potluck, always a delight. People brought their favorite dishes or tried a new one on the group.

Gray, who didn't hunt today, had the coffee and tea ready, along with ham biscuits.

Once everyone was inside, the kitchen table was full. People grabbed food. Few people eat a big breakfast before hunting. Everyone is starved. They filled their plates, carried them to the long dining room table, and sat down. It's so much easier to eat if you don't have to balance a plate on your lap.

"Bet it gets into the twenties tonight," Kasmir predicted.

Buddy came in late, plate in hand. "Put on Liberty's heavy blanket."

Blankets became a discussion.

"Is everyone getting ready for the midterms?" Cameron asked.

"Are you trying to make us sick?" Freddie teased him.

"A waste of time and money," Betty said with firmness. "Think what all that money the parties spend on ads could do for each state."

"That's the truth," Elise piped up. "But the media is how people pick up information. It isn't cheap."

"Hey, speaking of cheap . . . sorry, that's the wrong way to put it. Barry, did you ever find out what your stolen stamps are worth?" Bobby asked.

"Sort of. I contacted the Philatelic Society in New York. There's one outside Philadelphia, too, but I have friends in New York. They put me in contact with a fellow in Tennessee. Sent him the list I had and some pictures. He said he couldn't give me an exact figure but he estimated about seven thousand dollars," Barry answered. "Most of the stamps are from 1987."

"No kidding," Ronnie Haslip remarked. "I wouldn't mind that for our treasury. We'll never be able to rehabilitate our fairgrounds without cash."

"We know. We'll focus on fundraising after Christmas." Freddie didn't want to hear about the fairgrounds.

"There are stamp collections worth fortunes. Mine is a modest amount. That doesn't mean I wanted to lose those stamps," Barry grumbled.

"Funny they are from 1987." Ronnie looked at Barry.

Cameron, who had joined the group, full plate in hand, shrugged. "Maybe they were easy to grab."

Ronnie added, "Maybe 1987 means something. Barry, investigate the year."

"Well, maybe it means you should investigate your security." Cameron pointed his fork at Barry.

"New subject." Gray tapped his cup of tea. "Does everyone have their tickets for the Waynesboro Symphony Orchestra?"

A chorus of yesses and some raised hands.

"I need two," Buddy volunteered. "For the balcony."

"Me too." Alida called out, finally warming up. "Make it four. We're expanding."

"Gray, are you taking Aunt Dan?" Sam asked.

"Yes."

They chatted on. Warm, fed, and happy. Finally, when the group left around noon, Sister and Betty walked out to the barn. They checked the horses, took off the blankets, brushing the horses down, then putting the blankets back on.

"Glad they didn't get too sweaty," Sister said.

"Me too. Don't like washing horses in the cold. They dry out with a sheet in their stall then we put on the blanket, but it's one more step."

"Is." Sister put a treat in the palm of her hand for Midshipman to delicately lift off. "Before we do the tack, let's go to the cottage for a minute."

They pulled heavier coats back on, passing the kennels, where Weevil and Tootie were finishing up their chores. The hounds were already asleep on their raised beds or in the condos stuffed with straw. A smaller swinging door allowed the hounds to go in and out without letting too much cold air in.

Kneeling down, side by side, Betty following Sister's lead; a pair of luminous eyes stared back at them, as Comet heard the approach.

"You outrun us every time." Sister had seen the guy around her farm for years.

"I can run fast, forty-two miles an hour." Comet told the truth.

"That little devil yipped." Betty laughed.

Sister laughed as well. "Wouldn't it be fabulous for one day, just one day, to be a fox and feel what it's like to run on four feet, to have that acute hearing and sense of smell?"

"I guess." Betty smiled at the fox, eight feet away.

"Maybe at sunset I'll bring him some leftovers from the breakfast," Sister thought.

"Good idea." Comet popped back in his den.

CHAPTER 16

October 9, 2022, Sunday

"The collars are three hundred dollars apiece." Ronnie grimaced.

"Dear Lord, we can't afford sixty tracking collars." Sister blanched.

Gray, also sitting in Ronnie's living room, placed the papers on the modern glass coffee table. "We don't need a collar for every hound in the kennel. We only need ones for those hunting. There are always hounds left back because they're in season, have a cracked foot pad, stuff like that."

"You're right, honey. It's so expensive. I know you're right. But if twenty hounds are out, that's twenty collars."

Ronnie, who had hunted with Sister since he was ten and who was one of her late son's best friends, scanned his figures again. "Why can't you put tracking collars on the young entries and some on steady hounds like Dasher? You wouldn't need a tracking collar for every hound out there. If you had, say, eight collars and twenty hounds, the wheel whip will know where hounds are."

A silence followed this.

Sister folded her hands together. "We can try."

"Next question." Ronnie ran his right hand through his thinning sandy hair. "Who will or can be a wheel whip?"

No hesitation, Sister piped up. "Shaker."

Shaker was the long-term huntsman of Jefferson Hunt who had to retire due to a serious injury. He could still ride, but not hard. Despite the doctors' best efforts, his thigh bone had healed a bit off center. The real problem was his concussion. He forgot everything about the accident and once recovered he had memory lapses. He had fought it but finally handed the horn to Weevil.

"Do you think he would do it?" Ronnie liked Shaker, understood his pride.

"I do. He'd be back with the pack. He knows the territory, so he would know where to drive, where to sit. And we would pay him," Gray said.

"How much?" Ever the treasurer, Ronnie sat straight up.

"What is more fair? An annual stipend or by the hour?" Sister asked.

Gray folded Ronnie's copy for him lengthwise. "My suggestion is start the season . . . well, the formal Season, we're almost there . . . with an hourly rate. We'll see what the sum comes to. Remember, Shaker probably can't be at every hunt."

"Why?" Sister looked at Gray.

"Skiff." He named Cynthia Skiff Cane, who hunted Crawford's now registered farmer pack.

She shook her head. "Of course. I never thought of that. I still think of him as our huntsman, in a way. All those years together." She sighed.

Gray, sensitive to the situation, suggested, "Offer him the job. He'll talk it over with Skiff. She hunts on Saturday and so do we. My hunch is he'll help her on Saturdays."

Ronnie interjected, "Well, he can't ride but he can help her with the draw."

He meant the hounds selected to hunt that day.

Gray spoke again. "He knows the territory, both Crawford's and ours. So let's take Saturday."

"It's our biggest day," Sister said, raising her voice.

"Yes, it is." Ronnie's mind was turning . . . well, spinning.

"Look, if we can find someone soon, they can ride with Shaker and eventually take Saturdays."

"Great. Two salaries." Ronnie slapped his hand on his knee, which made his ferocious chihuahua bark. "Atlas, that's enough."

"No." Gray laughed as the little dog ran in the room and gave everyone the evil eye.

Then he jumped in Ronnie's lap.

"Give everyone twenty dollars an hour?"

Sister said, "Would be the same as one salary. Mmm. Five to six hours each hunt day, depending on the fixture."

"Not even that much. The wheel whip wouldn't need to help at the kennels. I figure three hours per hunt, four at most." Gray could come up with numbers in an instant. "So figuring four hours, sixty dollars per day. Three days. One hundred eighty."

"Reasonable." Ronnie nodded.

"Do you know, Ronnie Haslip, that is the first time I have ever heard you agree to a sum without a fight." Sister smiled.

"Well, mark this day on your calendar and we can celebrate it." He laughed with her. "But as your treasurer it's my job to control costs."

"You do a great job, Ronnie. You have for years, but with all this inflation, we'd better raise money just in case. I don't see prices falling. In fact, I would bet on a recession," Gray stated forcefully.

"Don't say that out loud, honey. People know all that work you did and still do in Washington. You'll scare the bejesus out of them."

He had a tight smile. "Better we scare the bejesus out of Washington."

Ronnie kissed Atlas's head. "Gray, no one ever learns. It's an endless cycle. Okay. Back to the budget. What do we do about raising money for eight collars? A ten-inch screen on the wheel whip's truck, which will be your work truck, costs $1,499.99. Eight-inch costs $1,299.99."

Sister threw up her hands. "My old truck. It will probably die on the first hunt."

Gray laughed at the thought. "Sam and I will take care of the truck. Bragging, but we're good with engines. The truck will make it."

Ronnie laughed with them. "Whoever is driving it will look country."

"Chewing tobacco should complete the picture." Sister smiled. "I'll start thinking about a Saturday wheel whip."

"Hey, what about Kathleen Sixt Dunbar? Aunt Dan will do it for free. They're usually following anyway. This time they'll be right in the middle of it." Gray brightened.

"Fundraiser?" Ronnie loved the thought of a ninety-four-year-old wheel whip, who could wheedle funds from a new standpoint.

Aunt Daniella had held steady at ninety-four for the last two years. Even Gray didn't know his aunt's real age. His late mother had lived with her and for her. This was the generation that believed a woman who tells her age will tell anything. Aunt Dan didn't need to tell her age to revel in gossip, old or new.

"Do you want to call, or shall I?" Gray wondered.

"Let's do it together. The one-two punch." Sister grinned.

Ronnie returned to money. "We need a fundraiser."

"The Waynesboro Symphony Orchestra is October 28. That might make enough. You have your tickets?" Gray looked at Ronnie.

"Two." Ronnie fidgeted with Atlas's collar. "I don't have a date."

"There's got to be someone. Maybe not in our hunt club, but we're surrounded by other clubs. There has to be someone," Sister encouraged him.

"Doesn't have to be a foxhunter," Gray added.

"This is such a problem," Ronnie moaned.

CHAPTER 17

October 10, 2022, Monday

Marty Howard stood next to Sister in what she now called Sister's monarch field.

Looking across the acres, spots of the color from the black-eyed Susans here and there, Marty noticed a sycamore far at the edge of the field. "I don't remember that tree."

Sister replied, "More dramatic now. More bark is off."

"They're usually near water."

"It is. That little creek near it feeds into Broad Creek, dries up usually, but this was a rainy spring and summer. Made everything wet."

"Yes, it did. I thought I could catch and store rainwater in those large lined wooden tubs. I did, but Crawford says they are period pieces. We have to use what Sophie used in the first quarter of the nineteenth century. Showed me what was used."

"It's the everyday stuff that gets lost. For instance, did Athenians, ancient Greeks, use colanders?"

Marty laughed. "Who would have thought of that?"

Sister tapped the ground lightly with her right foot. "Exactly."

"Well, maybe Sophie did use large tubs. They wouldn't be tin. Too expensive."

"Right. Wooden tubs bound by metal hoops is a good idea. And if the planks were grooved so one fit slightly into the other, they would be tight."

"That was my mistake. I should have thought of grooving the wood. I lined the tubs with tin."

Sister slowly walked forward, Marty in tow. "That was possible for her, as she was ultra-rich."

"That she was, but you know, Sister, working on Old Paradise, the big main home, the outbuildings, I learned she used the best materials. Not for show, but because they would last. She knew what she was doing."

"Here. Step over this log." Sister pointed down at the fallen trunk of a tree. "Got the branches cleared but not the trunk. Here we are."

Both women leaned over the fence as they looked at the small tributary to Broad Creek. The flow was medium, not gushingly strong but moving along.

"What do you think? A week from high color?" Marty asked.

"Yes. All my milkweeds opened. They're ready for winter. The odd flower hangs on. The frogs and toads . . . snakes, too . . . all in their winter quarters. Swallows gone. Some robins have stayed. Most birds are gone."

"Gets quieter. Wanted to see how your field was going and I wanted to ask if I could give a big party, invite your club, and I would speak to them about the monarchs. I have a good film to show off their journey." Marty squinted to focus on a blabby blue jay in the distance.

"Of course. We have to find a date. Fall gets jammed up. Old Paradise or Beasley Hall?" Sister inquired.

"Beasley Hall, I think. I remain overwhelmed by Old Paradise."

The two women turned to walk on the narrow path.

"You have the outbuildings housing workers. I imagine they like those wonderful old buildings. Charlotte Abruzza has that stone two-story near the main barn."

Charlotte Abruzza handled research. She did a lot alone but organized teams when necessary.

"Near being a quarter of a mile." Marty laughed. "Everything at Old Paradise is on a big scale."

Back at the house, Sister made hot chocolate for both of them. It was cold outside but not bitter cold. Still, it was a toast to fall.

"That cat has your scarf in her A-frame," Marty noticed.

"I gave up."

"Who built the A-frame? It's, well, spacious."

"It has to be. Golly is fat." Sister laughed.

"I am not," came the indignant reply.

"Ha." Rooster, reposing in his sherpa-lined bed, snorted.

"Gray built the A-frame."

A car came down the road, parked by the house. The dogs knew it was Betty's Bronco. The humans only knew it was a car.

"Me!" Betty called, opening the mudroom door, then the door into the kitchen. "Ed Clark has been released from questioning."

"What are you talking about?" Sister pointed to the hot cocoa on the stove.

"Oh, hello, Marty." Betty walked to pour herself a cup. "He was taken in for questioning."

"Will you start at the beginning!"

"Right," Betty answered Sister as she sat down.

"Ben Sidell received a call to inspect Ed's horse trailer. The caller would not identify himself. Ben properly got a search warrant, drove to Ed's house. Oh, the caller hinted this might have something to do with the theft of the stamps."

Marty reached for another napkin.

"We all adore Ed. I'm not telling you anything you don't know. Anyway, they get there. He asks Ed to open the door. Ed does.

" 'Anything look out of place?' Ben supposedly asked."

"How do you know this?" Marty hung on every word.

"Betty, what happened in the trailer?" Sister tried not to be impatient.

"Ben searched the pockets of Ed's hanging coats. Nothing in the right, but a pocketknife filled out the other pocket. A cotton handkerchief and rawhide strips, should the stirrup straps break. Nothing unusual.

"Ben looked up in the nose of the trailer. The carpet was flat. He didn't pull it up. Then he pulled up the boot keeper. That ever-so-useful covered step in all our trailers for our boots or anything. There in the step box was an old sweater, a beat-up vest, and a box. Ed immediately said the vest was his. But the box was not.

"Ben opened the box. It was Barry Harper's stolen stamps."

"Why would Ed steal stamps?" Marty found all this absurd.

"He said he'd never seen them before."

"I believe that." Sister was getting an uneasy feeling.

Betty took a long sip. "Ben is having the box fingerprinted."

"Well, Ben held and opened the box," Marty added.

"That will show, but maybe other fingerprints will, too." Betty looked at Sister then at Marty. "Why would someone do this to Ed, of all people?"

"An old grudge?" Marty shrugged.

"Two reasons." Sister spoke with confidence. "To throw Ben off, waste his time. Or as a warning. And remember, Ed is leading a campaign fund to expand the wildlife center. Maybe it has to do with money or jealousy."

"Ed doesn't know anything," Betty said with a raised voice.

Sister tapped her fingers on the table. "Ed is known internationally. His work is legendary. We know he would never steal. Ronnie works with Ed on the campaign fund. Maybe Ed's work is costing someone money. Like poachers in South Africa."

Betty gulped. "Sister, don't say that. Those people kill. Rhino horns, elephant tusks, millions of dollars."

Marty thought. "Ed isn't a coward. He's faced down people who are cruel to animals or harm habitat."

"Let's hope these damn stamps are someone's idea of a joke." Sister shook her head. "Stupid. Like to stamp out Ed and tree huggers or raccoon huggers, I don't know."

Betty listened to her dear friend. "Possibly, but this can't be good."

CHAPTER 18

October 11, 2022, Tuesday

A red-shouldered hawk sat high in the branch of a white oak. Below, hounds spread out, noses down. The humans, mounted, waited. A meadow mowed a week ago surrounded the first Catholic church in the county. As people began to move west after the Revolutionary War, a few more Catholics arrived.

In time, there were enough to build a small church in Charlottesville. Over time Bishop's Court was abandoned but even over the generations a few Catholics kept the place tidy. The Church owned the land, as it passed to no individual. Yvonne Harris, raised Catholic in Chicago, took an interest in it as she began to be enchanted by the architecture and history of central Virginia. Once she purchased Beveridge Hundred, she turned her interest to this simple, charming church. Although religious freedom was enshrined in the First Amendment, that didn't mean Catholics were treated equally. Little by little she talked to those people she met at St. Mary's in Charlottesville. Some became interested.

Watching hounds, Yvonne's imagination drifted. What did the first parishioners look like? Were they denied public office, as they had been in England?

Yvonne was keenly aware of mistreatment, thanks to her color, which even though light identified her as black. Like Aunt Daniella, her features were WASP sharp. That proved some advantage, especially on the runway, but any form of institutionalized oppression grated on her nerves, nibbled at the edges of her well-being. It was wrong. Such pettiness had no place in the United States.

As she mused on those long-gone members, the red-shouldered hawk waited for hounds to move her way. Surely they'd scare up some tasty little mice or even a rabbit.

The early-morning rays caught the steeple, cross on top. Bishop's Court looked so peaceful. Hounds opened. The quiet vanished in a thrilling roar.

Old Buster's ears flicked forward, he stepped out behind Czapka, the big warmblood that Crawford rode. Sam rode the fellow to keep him fit. Glancing over his shoulder he saw Yvonne ready. They all took off almost on cue.

Sister knew this territory intimately. Bishop's Court didn't remain flat for long. The pasture and small graveyard soon gave way to a drop then a climb up the Blue Ridge. She knew once a horse climbed the steep grade on the first wave of the mountain chain, best not to go down if you could help it. If you rode back down, stay down.

Or ride the high trail even if hounds turned and ran low. She'd give them five minutes. If the fox didn't turn back, then she'd find a way down. Hunting in mountainous terrain proved different than hunting on undulating or flat terrain. You used some different muscles than a gallop on flat land.

Hounds screamed. The hawk lifted off, staying above them. They circled behind the church, stopped.

"Find your fox," Weevil encouraged them.

"He's not far." Dreamboat encouraged the pack. *"Little wind's back here, little wind devils. Keep pushing."*

Aztec, Sister's Thoroughbred, trotted behind the hounds circling the church. They burst out on the front side, charging into the woods, then followed on the church road as hounds remained close in view.

Betty threaded her way along an old deer trail. Tootie was already out on Chapel Cross Road South, which ended at the Bishop's Gate Driveway, a two-lane dirt road.

Across the Chapel Cross Road, hounds roared. Weevil ran close behind. Sister stopped a moment once out on the state road. The woods on the other side of the road were a timber tract. Mostly old loblolly pines. She moved onto a timber trail but hounds veered far from it, now running though the timber. They were perhaps five miles from the actual Chapel Crossroads.

Sister turned back. The field tried to get out of her way, backing into the woods. Clucking to Aztec, who needed no encouragement, she hit fourth gear, turned right onto the state road, staying on the edge. She never liked galloping on macadam. She could hear the field behind her but didn't turn to look. Keeping track of the hounds, whom she couldn't see, absorbed her attention. The red-shouldered hawk kept up with hounds. They were scattering mice, rabbits, gophers, and the occasional nasty mink.

Two miles down the road, hounds stopped. So did Sister.

Not a peep. Taking a deep breath, Sister and the field this Tuesday happily paused. Bishop's Gate, a difficult fixture, at best, baffled everyone. No one expected a hard run. The line had to be red hot to provoke that kind of cry and speed.

Weevil walked with his hounds, weaving his way through the loblollies, some down. He tried casting forward. Casting back. Casting in a circle. Nothing.

Sister turned around; Kasmir, Alida, Gray, Sam, Yvonne, and Ed,

Freddie, and Barry waited. Everyone wore a heavy tweed. While not bitter cold, it was cold enough.

"Come along," Weevil sang out.

He emerged sixty yards down the road. Riding up to Sister, some hounds in tow, Betty and Tootie emerged from the woods on either side.

"It's another mile down the road but if we go to Beveridge Hundred, we have more room. We'll struggle with downed trees on both sides of the road here."

"Yes, Master. They want to hunt," Weevil answered her.

"So do I." Sister smiled.

Once reaching Beveridge Hundred, Weevil cast behind the big, main house. Ribbon, Yvonne's Norfolk terrier, on the back of a wing chair, watched intently.

"Lieu in," Weevil instructed behind the main house.

Aces paused then walked deliberately due north. Soon the others followed, noses down but no music.

"Old line," Dasher noted.

"Better than nothing." Ardent caught a whiff of old skunk scent.

Audrey, behind him, giggled. *"Better let that go."*

Hounds pressed forward. A coop loomed up ahead in the old fence line between Beveridge Hundred and the back of Tattenhall Station. Hounds leapt over it. Others wiggled under the three-board fence.

"Gris," Diana called, recognizing the scent of a gray male fox they knew.

All opened at once, trotting over the back acres of Tattenhall Station, thousands of acres. Across the road was Old Paradise, five thousand acres. This part of Jefferson Hunt territory was spectacular. Hounds ran down to the burbling creek, Gris fouled his scent a bit. The trotting turned into a blazing run. The back of Tattenhall has some woods, coverts all along the creek bed. There would be breaks in the tree line but in the main the oaks, witch hazels, sycamores, and beech trees were turning high color.

Hounds then shot upward over the pastures. Sister followed, keeping close to Weevil but not too close. Gris had run in a straight line once away from the creek, so hounds didn't waver. They reached a stone jump in the rail fence. Solid, one took it seriously. Everyone made it. Bobby Franklin with two people in Second Flight headed for the gate. Fortunately, it had a kiwi latch on it, so he could lean over and open it by hand. He waited for Elise and Cameron, not jumping today, to get through.

"I'll do it," Cameron offered.

"I'll do it. There's only three of us. Let's stick together." Bobby closed the gate, slipped the latch through the U-holder, and off they ran.

Catching up to the main body meant hard running. Bobby kept his eye on Elise but she was doing great.

The field managed the stone jump, although Freddie's horse balked, an unusual event. She trotted to the back of the line, as was proper, then popped over after Gray, who had slowed down to make sure she'd make it.

On the other side they raced past Tattenhall Station, pulling up at Chapel Cross Road East. The crossroads were two football fields away. Sister looked both ways then hurried across, reaching the mud fences on the other side of the road. Those mud fences had been tended to since after the Revolution. One took them as any other jump. One mud fence then four strides to a coop. They were now on Tollbooth Farm. Hounds screamed, running to the old unused barn, roof still good.

"Come out of there." Jethro's high voice, as yet unchanged, pierced the air.

Inside the barn's plush living quarters for a fox, Vi, Gris's mate, complained. *"Why did you lead them here?"*

"I didn't." He defended himself. *"I was over at Beveridge Hundred, the pretty lady puts out treats and I wanted to bring some home. She even leaves jelly beans."*

"Come out!" the youngster squealed.

Audrey counseled, *"Jethro, give it a rest."*

"But he's in there," the young entry whined.

Dasher, deep voice, said, *"He isn't coming out but you did a good job of getting here first."*

"I did?" The good-looking tri-colored was thrilled.

"You did. Now the Huntsman is blowing 'Gone to Ground.' We need to move along."

As hounds moved off, Audrey, now alongside Dasher, moaned, *"That voice could raise the dead. We've got to shut him up."*

"It will change soon enough. He's taking longer than the others."

Gris and Vi listened as hounds left.

She turned to her mate. *"Jelly beans?"*

"Really," came the reply.

Once across the road, Sister rode up to Weevil. "Good run. We have five miles back to Bishop's Gate. Let's walk it. If we find scent, great. But not every horse is hunting fit yet, so people will lag behind. I'll keep up with you though." She grinned.

"Master, I'm the one who has to keep up with you."

"Flatterer." She loved it.

While they were walking across the hay pastures at the back of Tattenhall Station, a stiff wind came up. The temperature in the mid-fifties soon felt like high forties. Reaching the corner of the field, Sister took the coop, as did everyone else but Bobby, Cameron, and Elise. Another jump squarely faced the coop and that was in the Beveridge Hundred fence line. Again Aztec and Sister took it.

She was glad that was the last jump, as everyone had quite a run. You never want an exhausted horse to take a jump if you can help it. That's why hunt clubs actively discourage larking, taking jumps once the hunt is over. People, not realizing how tired their horses may be, have gotten killed that way.

While they were walking back, the wind put a glow in Sister's cheeks; she could have done without the glow. Twenty minutes later they reached Bishop's Gate. Everyone was relieved to dismount, loosen their horse's girth. Some took off the saddle and threw on a rug. Others threw a rug over the saddle. Everyone hung out a feed bag. A few stepped inside their trailer tack room, took off their coat, slipped on an old Carhartt or light down jacket.

Yvonne, using her key, opened the door to the church. Sam, with her, fired up the big wood-burning stove in the middle of the church; it sat on slate, which protected the floor. The potbellied stove had seen almost two centuries of service before the church was abandoned. It sat centered under the north-facing windows. This way parishioners could go up the center aisle for communion.

Sam had stacked firewood in the vestibule, also putting wood outside in a makeshift shed he built. He liked helping Yvonne with her project. After restoring the Lorillard home he proved a big help. He knew how to save money restoring old buildings.

"Works fast." Yvonne smiled.

The two of them turned around the pews in the rear so people could face one another. An old table was put in the middle. So two church pew rows faced each other as the potbellied stove warmed the room. Had the long-ago parishioners had the funds, they would have installed a stove on the opposing south wall.

The riders brought in dishes. Walter carried in a cooler of drinks. Betty carried in carafes of tea. Elise brought a thermos of hot chocolate. It was catch as catch can, somehow always the most fun. Deviled eggs, chicken sandwiches, macaroni salad, coleslaw, cookies, more sandwiches, butter, too. Sister headed straight for the mayo.

Weevil and Tootie grabbed food then walked back to the party wagon. She drove their horses back in the two-horse trailers while

Weevil drove the hounds in the party wagon. He always wanted to get the hounds back to the kennel as soon as possible. He made a rich mash for them the night before hunting. All he had to do was put it in the trough, pour some warm water over it. Hounds loved it.

Horses outside drank from their water buckets. Some riders offered them a bucket then put it back in the trailer with a lid. Others tied a long rope to the trailer, giving the horse enough room to reach the water buckets. Everyone had their own system.

Inside, people sighed as they sat in the pews, sandwiches in hand.

"That was a longer run than I anticipated," Alida confessed. "Legs feel it."

"By Opening Hunt we'll all be in shape," Kasmir promised as he, too, felt a twinge.

Cameron came in last. "Betty, Magellan untied himself. I tied him up again. He's happy with his hay."

"Thanks, Cameron." Betty felt ravenously hungry.

Cameron sat next to Barry, who sat next to Ed.

"Ed, I know you didn't steal my stamps," Barry soothingly said.

"Damnedest thing." Ed was glad Barry didn't think he stole the stamps.

Cameron interjected, "How do we know you don't buy stamps when you travel the world speaking?"

"Cameron, come on." Freddie looked at him.

"I was joking," Cameron defended himself.

"How do I know you didn't steal the stamps? You fly everywhere." Freddie was disgusted.

"Come on, Freddie, I was joking," Cameron again said.

"Well, I'm glad my stamps were recovered, although I don't have them yet. Ben still has them. Fingerprinting." Barry's sandy eyebrows rose.

"No fingerprints. Who would be that dumb?" Bobby sounded authoritative. "All you need are doctors' gloves."

Walter, sandwich in hand, replied, "Don't look at me."

"But the weird thing is, I drove down to the station, looked at the box, yes it's my stamps, but one was missing."

"Barry, do you know which one?" Sister asked.

"Actually, I do, as I had photographed my meager collection. It was a 1987 American Wildlife stamp of a box turtle, twenty-two cents." Barry impressed the group with his precision.

"How is my box turtle?" Sister asked.

"Doing great."

The story of the box turtle followed this, plus Barry informed everyone what can be done to help injured amphibians and reptiles. Although fortunately Sister's turtle was not injured, just lost, he thought.

After the hunt, all returned home. Put up their horses, all of whom deserved a bath, maybe an Absorbine Jr. rubdown, a blanket, and turnout.

Ronnie, who didn't hunt that day, came home from work. An envelope was taped to the garage door.

He opened it and pulled out the 1987 box turtle stamp. "What the hell is this?"

CHAPTER 19

October 12, 2022, Wednesday

A fire warmed the room, giving off an apple odor, in Ronnie Haslip's living room. Unlike most everyone else in Jefferson Hunt Club, Ronnie lived in a modern house, which he built. The fireplace was set in white marble, which ran floor to ceiling, with a place to sit in front of it. A brass screen was in front of the glowing fire. On the simple mantel, a large mahogany Victorian clock, ornate, provided a contrast to the surroundings.

Freddie, Ed, Gray, and Ronnie sat around the glass coffee table. The Barcelona chairs, expensive, suited the living room, which was white and beige with large teal pillows in the corners of the leather sofa. Again, modern in design.

Each person had a notebook opened, a drink on the coffee table, hoping for money-raising ideas.

"Two years," Ronnie stated.

"Two years for the grandstand repair, resurfacing the huge arena." Freddie bit the end of her pencil. "The resurfacing will cost a fortune. People well . . . point-chasers," she pinpointed those riders who lived in a certain district being part of a national equestrian organization. They needed points to qualify for the national shows. "They won't come if we don't use the new surface."

"I don't see how we can afford this." Gray was not negative but he was cautious. "Let's go back to money now. When this first came up at the breakfast, you all felt we could work out selling seeds from Elise Sabatini's farm."

"We can. Fifty-pound bags. She is harvesting milkweed, butterfly bush, huge sunflowers, and I don't know what else, but she says she has tons, literally tons of seeds."

"Did anyone know she was doing this? She had to have cleared and planted this spring?" Freddie wondered.

"No. This was her idea, an experiment, but she talked to Marty Howard. At any rate, she really did it and we can buy the seeds from her wholesale and sell them retail. We can advertise through our newsletter, and the newsletters of other clubs, that we are working to save monarch butterflies, bees, and so on." Ronnie got up to toss another apple log on the fire.

"While I'm up here can I get anyone anything?"

"No thanks," they said in unison.

Gray asked, "Where'd you get the applewood?"

"Old Dalby. Passed by and saw some old trees cut in the small orchard. Smells great, doesn't it?"

Old Dalby was a fixture, sometimes also called Little Dalby.

"Does. Okay, the seed bags. We won't know if it will make us money but we can try. As to the show ring, that really is a long haul."

"It is, but it has the possibility to make a lot of money over time. The focus is on horses. It is a natural fit. The club used to do it, up to the late nineties," Ronnie remembered. "It was a hell of a lot of work but it made money."

"Work. You hire a course designer with a big name and a judge with a big name. The grounds need to be cleaned. You can rent out space for food, for vendors, and the class fees bring in money." Gray was thinking of expenses in and out.

"Don't forget parking. Always good money," Ronnie said.

"Puts a lot of club members to work." Gray smiled. "But it is a good flow. Well, okay, that's a long-range goal. And we have to get people on the bus. Back to the seeds, where do we store them?"

"I know there's no place at the farm. Plus you all have to take care of the kennels, the outbuildings." Freddie then added, "What about the Franklins? They're central."

"Bobby has that storage building for papers. He might not want seed bags near the paper. Paper costs."

Gray pondered what Ronnie had just proposed. "We could see if he'd let us use his garage. Betty's Bronco stays there but he usually parks his truck outside. There has to be something, a place some-where. If the seeds are near moisture they might germinate. If they are near moisture and heat, they really will."

"Let's ask around." Ronnie reached for his vodka and tonic. "Someone will have a tight, dry space. Who knows, we may be out of those seeds in a month. I'm willing to bet that people will do this. We are charging, what, fifty dollars for a fifty-pound bag, that's a lot less than what's offered in seed catalogs."

Freddie put her pencil on the table. "We can also offer smaller amounts."

"Bagging the seeds will be a big job." Ronnie scribbled in his notepad, as he returned to Freddie's suggestion. "We should have smaller seed bags, too. A lower price."

Gray got up; Ronnie rose and Gray waved him down. "My turn. Anyone need anything?"

"Bourbon," Ed called out.

"Let's take a break," Ronnie suggested, to which they all agreed.

Ronnie brought out pound cake and plates. He freshened drinks.

"I didn't realize I was hungry." Freddie grabbed a piece of pound cake with vanilla icing.

"I have cold chicken. Want some?" Ronnie offered.

"No, this will do it."

Ed, grateful for the good bourbon, as Ronnie always had good bourbon, said, "Saving monarchs, zebra swallowtails, bees, a great idea. But what about having a horse or dog rescue be the club's main nonprofit? You raise money for them and take a percent. Everyone wins. Few nonprofits have enough money to keep giving parties, trips, special lectures to raise funds. Anything requiring an audience takes tons of work."

"True." Freddie ate another piece of pound cake.

"Are you sure you don't want cold chicken?" Ronnie asked.

Freddie wrinkled her nose. "No. I know I'm eating too much sugar. I'll stop. Back to money." She diverted Ronnie's attention from the pound cake.

"Nonprofits?" He picked up the subject. "Ed, what you can do is focus on animals in crisis. That naturally gets people's attention."

Gray spoke up. "How many calls do we get? Sister? Weevil? People found a lost hound and think it's ours. It's not. Turned out by people, usually men, after their particular hunt season is over, deer, bear. Weevil always goes and picks the poor animal up."

Ed said, "Skin and bones?"

"Yes, sometimes wounded. Weevil, who has a gift, gets them healthy, shots, house trains them, then finds them homes. He's dedicated to hunting hounds."

"That should rivet people. You could have a dance or a trail ride, just thoughts to raise money for abandoned hounds. Keep a small percent. Rehabilitating animals takes time, money, and medical care."

Freddie jumped in. "Who better than a foxhunting club to do that? It's good coverage as well as being necessary."

They agreed on this, came up with other thoughts, ideas for spring, as it's difficult to launch major fundraisers during hunt season.

Ronnie, bringing in another tray of cake and brownies, sank into the sofa and turned to Ed. "Any news about the stamps?"

"I had to fill out forms, answer questions. What irritated me . . ." He looked at Freddie. "Notice I didn't say 'piss me off' with a lady present when Cameron made a crack that I would sell stamps to raise money for the Wildlife Center."

Ronnie shrugged. "He can be a smart-ass sometimes."

"He has just enough money to think he's intelligent." Gray smiled.

Ronnie questioned, "This is America, right? If someone makes money we think they are special. As the CFO of the farm equipment co-op, I see a lot of people who move here assuming because they've made money in the city, they'll make money farming."

"You know everything before we do." Freddie smiled.

"What I'd better do is go over to Elise's and walk through the fields. She's excited about hunting. Good for her and good for us. We need rich members and good on her for becoming so involved in environmental matters." Ronnie smiled.

"From your mouth to God's ear." Freddie held up her glass. "We have caring people in the club. Ed Clark and the Wildlife Center. Barry and his reptiles. Weevil puts in one afternoon a week at the SPCA apart from his hound salvation project. Half the club has rescued dogs and cats."

"And some people." Gray nodded.

"What do you think?" Ronnie asked Freddie. "About the stamps?"

"I don't know what to think," she honestly answered. "What would Ed want with stamps?"

Ed laughed. "Well, I still write letters. I need stamps."

Ronnie laughed with him then asked Gray, "Has Ben said anything to Sam about the dead man?"

"He did talk to him, as Sam found the body. Ben said while Tim didn't have family, didn't marry and his parents are deceased, he had many business associates. The photographs jogged memories. It also seems that people liked Mr. Snavely. He helped a lot of people with imports and exports, which can be difficult depending on country."

"Any mention of drugs?" Ronnie wondered.

"Why?"

"Exporting and importing. Millions to be made," Ronnie filled in the question. "Maybe he was killed because of that. Some drug revenge. Overlord. I don't know, but then we have to ask: Is anyone in our club on the stuff or could be dealing?"

"No." Freddie shook her head.

Ed remarked, "If they were, you'd think we'd see some money."

"We'd know. Someone would know. How long can you hide that kind of money?" Freddie believed that.

Gray didn't. "Oh, Freddie, the really smart ones don't keep books. The money is in cash. You'd be surprised at how many upstanding citizens, including elected officials, are on the take. Turn a blind eye. They may not be dealing, some are using, but they turn a blind eye. The corruption is rampant no matter where you look: government, corporations, universities." Gray added, his voice lower, "Maybe I saw too much in D.C."

"How can people get away with it?" Freddie's eyebrows lifted.

"If someone is on the take and not using, it's easy. You stash the cash. Perhaps a corporate person in charge of transportation allows a drug dealer to use his company cars. Put the stuff in a hidden box or whatever, but deliver to wherever the company does business. That's an easy one. Then again, anyone working at a lab can cook meth. It's not all heroin, cocaine, and fentanyl. Our country is ravaged by drugs."

"You know, I never think of it," Freddie confessed.

"I don't either. Oh, I smoked weed in my teens, but that was it," Ronnie confessed. "Some people can't control the craving, I suppose."

"Those high up can hide it. The other people lose their jobs, their families, wind up on the streets. Our homeless population is huge and a portion of that, a large portion, is due to addiction and mental illness." Gray continued, "People can walk by and look down on them and they are a problem. If we had any idea how many respectable people, so to speak, were keeping this misery alive, we would be shocked. If there is a way to address this, I'm willing to work for medical help. It has to be horrifying not to be able to trust yourself."

"Yes." Ronnie had seen Sam's struggle, so he understood Gray's position.

"So it's possible our murder victim was bringing in drugs?" Freddie asked. "And if so, who was dealing? He wasn't. That would have come out by now, I would think."

Ed added, "It's not just drugs. There are so many illegal ways to make money. You pay no taxes. Think of what people will pay for zebra skins. All illegal."

"How did we get on this? I want to go back to fundraising," Freddie almost pleaded.

"Before we do that, I wanted to tell you after our meeting was over that someone put an envelope on my garage door and in it was the missing stamp, one of Barry's stamps."

"What!" Freddie's voice raised, while Gray's jaw dropped.

"An envelope taped to the door and inside was a 1987 box turtle stamp, twenty-two cents. Barry recognized it as the missing stamp, as did Ben, because Barry had provided photographs of his collection. So Ben checked against the photographs then called Barry, who drove down to the department," Ronnie informed them.

"That's crazy. That's crazy," Ed repeated. "What do you or I have to do with stamps? And you only got one. Was I the lucky person to get sheets of butterflies, reptiles, and turtles?"

"We need to get to the bottom of this before someone else gets hurt."

Freddie asked Ronnie, "You told Ben?"

He nodded yes.

Ed, voice clear, looked at the others. "This has to do with money, and maybe the dead man. Figure out the stamps and I think you've got it."

"As Ben is working with the police department in Charlotte, was the deceased a stamp collector?" Gray asked.

"That's a good question." Freddie felt a chill despite the fire.

CHAPTER 20

October 14, 2022, Friday

Fortunately, Sister was wearing her Wellies, as there were puddles everywhere at Barry Harper's. Betty, resplendent in her pair of Dubarry Galway boots, sloshed after her friend. Ronnie wore Le Chameau.

"You two sure spent money on boots." Sister eyed the boots.

"You have worn those Wellies since the earth was cooling." Betty then turned to Ronnie. "You've known her since your childhood. Are these the same rain boots?"

"Well."

"Don't weasel, Ronnie," Betty chided him.

Diplomatically, Ronnie said, "They may not be the same boots but they are the same brand. Simple Wellies."

"And you, Betty, paid about four hundred and seventy dollars for those damn Dubarry boots. Ronnie, I know Le Chameaus run for almost five hundred. I looked at a pair for Gray."

"And did you pass out?" Betty teased her.

"I did need smelling salts. Ronnie, do you like your boots?"

"I do. They're warm and when I bought them they were about four hundred and twenty. They really are close to five hundred now. They last forever."

"So do mine." Betty felt rain on her shoulders, falling harder now.

The rain canceled yesterday's hunt. It wasn't done with them yet.

"Well, my boots, which you so kindly noted are ancient, are actually twenty-five years old. Haven't got a hole in them yet."

"But they're cold. My Dubarrys are warm."

"For that you paid four hundred and seventy dollars? I wear knee-high silk socks and a pair of woolen socks over them. I'll be damned if I'm paying hundreds of dollars for rain boots. I would pay that for my husband for Christmas though."

"Well," Betty considered this, "you are generous but you can be too careful. You only live once."

"Sometimes that's too long." Sister laughed.

Ronnie, who had known Sister almost all his life, laughed, too. "Have you ever met anyone and wondered why they were born?"

"All the time." Betty giggled as they reached the door of the Amphibian and Reptile Foundation.

Ronnie stepped up and knocked. "Barry."

"Come on in." The door opened and Barry beheld the dripping group, every one of them wearing a Barbour coat. In Sister's case, her Barbour was over thirty years old.

"We'll get your floors wet." Sister stepped through the door.

"Have a mop. Here, let me hang up your coats. Is this rain ever going to stop?"

"I have three weather apps. They declare one more day of this, but each gives a different time for the rain to end. It won't be so intense all the time. Should fall back to a steady pace." Ronnie felt hopeful about that.

"Would you like us out of our boots?" Sister asked.

"Here, step on this rug. Should get the mud off." He pointed to a thick rug by the door. "Should have pointed that out."

"We should have looked. I'm afraid all I wanted to do was get out of the rain, and that mercury is dropping. Bet you we get a real freeze tonight," Sister predicted.

"This time of year we might get a freeze, then it bounces back again." Barry hung all the coats up, which did drip on the floor.

"This place is bigger than it looks from the outside." Ronnie noticed there were two rooms off the entrance. "Barry, before I forget, I'm glad you didn't think I took one stamp."

"Of course not. Ben notified me immediately. I wish I knew what this was about."

"Me too." Barry dropped the subject. "Right now it's not crowded. Come on, I'll show you around."

"Is my box turtle okay?" Sister asked.

"I was going to show you him first. He's young and enjoying food without having to look for it. Come on." Barry, smiling, led them into the next room, where there were a few small toads and salamanders in little specially built cages. The walls were lined with small living quarters, except for one wall that had runs, like small kennels. The living cages varied in size but all had solid bottoms, most had glass sides. Others had wooden sides with a glass door for those animals liking the dark.

"There's my fellow." Sister looked at a satisfied box turtle.

"He's perfectly healthy. I really believe he wanted to cross the road, got a bit confused. At any rate, he's eating a lot, sleeping, and then he walks around for his exercise." Barry grinned. "He has lots of room."

"He does." Betty admired the setup.

"Come on. I'll show you who is left. Here is an iguana. A pet. Big fellow, and the mother decided she wasn't going to take care of her son's lizard, as she put it, anymore. So here he is. Tame. You can touch him if you like. I let him run around when I'm in here alone. He can be quite energetic. He is ready to go into his big living room when he sees me carrying collard greens, parsley; he loves greens, including dandelion. He likes it warm. You can see his heat lamp, which is above his branch. He likes to rest on the branch."

"Can they take the cold?" Betty asked.

"Fifty degrees Fahrenheit is getting cold for them. This fellow loves to doze under the heat lamp. He has a little pool there and the water is warm. It's his cleaning pool. And he has his water bowl. You know, with proper care an iguana can live to twenty years. That's why it's cruel for people to buy them and not care for them. They take a bit of work."

"He seems content." Sister liked his color.

"Come on." Barry led them to the next room, perhaps fifteen feet by fifteen feet. "This is the snake room. Most of the snakes that were injured have been rehabilitated. Those left here are healed but their injuries healed too late for me to put them back in the wild. So they'll spend the winter here. I don't use a lot of light in this room, as they are bromating. So everyone is snug under a log or even an old towel. Every cage has dirt in a corner so they can not exactly dig but curl up in the dirt and again usually under something. Everyone in here is harmless. No poisonous snakes."

"Winter is less work for you?" Ronnie asked.

"In terms of my patients . . . or guests, as I think of them . . . yes. But it's when I do most of my fundraising."

"I'm glad you still have time to hunt with us," Sister remarked. "You're doing well in the First Flight."

He beamed. "Thank you. I rode with a club in Tennessee as a kid, then got out of it during college. Of course, out of college I needed a job and wound up in Atlanta. Worked out."

"Do you ever take non-reptiles or -amphibians?" Ronnie thought the place clean, well thought out.

"No, but if I find an injured animal, say a raccoon, I'll call the Wildlife Center of Virginia and wait for them. Ed does a great job."

"Are reptiles endangered?" Sister asked.

"Climate change impacts every animal, including us. Amphibians and reptiles are adjusting to the warming up better than, say, caribou, but if you think about it, we humans have only begun scientifically monitoring any species fairly recently. Do I think reptiles and amphibians are perhaps a bit better off? I do, but I don't know for how long."

"You mentioned with the iguana that you took it in from a family . . . well, Mom . . . who could no longer deal with the creature. Do you see a lot of that?"

He nodded. "Yes, like with any other pet, people realize too late it's not the pet for them or someone dies and no one in the family is willing to keep the snake or whatever. People aren't as fond of reptiles as dogs, but they can make good pets and they do know who you are. They recognize your voice and your face. They know your schedule."

"Do you think they like their owners?" Betty had never thought of a reptile having emotions.

"Oh yes." Barry became enthusiastic. "Once they trust you, you can pet them. Some like to be held, some don't. And in time if you establish that relationship, your blacksnake can follow you around the house. You'd be surprised at how versatile these animals are. We, or many of us, fear snakes, but think about it, snakes are one of your best friends in terms of pest control. They eat bugs, mice, and they usually don't eat or destroy what we harvest. We can all understand the fear of poisonous snakes, but they don't want to be around you and they aren't looking to bite you. If you step on one, chances are you'll get bitten, but how often does that happen?"

"Have you taken in poisonous snakes?" Betty tried not to shudder.

"I have. I'm very careful."

"Ever been around a cobra?" Ronnie was fascinated.

"No, they aren't North American, but I have been around them at conventions, visiting other countries. They are intelligent. You'd be surprised at how intelligent some of these creatures are, but cobras are definitely intelligent. Again, you can't violate an animal's basic nature. Accept them for what they are. Help them if possible but respect their boundaries, for lack of a better word." Realizing he'd been talking a lot, for him anyway, he offered, "Come on into the little kitchen room. Sit down and have a drink. I rarely get visitors unless they are looking for an escaped, say, bearded dragon."

They followed him into the small space with a table and four ladderback chairs, plus two more comfortable chairs against the wall. He pulled one out for Sister while Ronnie pulled one out for Betty. The ladies took the offered chairs while the men sat in the ladder-backs.

"Coffee? Tea? Perrier? I have soft drinks."

"Barry, we're fine."

"Well, I'm going to have a Perrier with lime."

"Okay. Me too." Betty thought if her host was going to take a drink she should.

"Anyone else? Something to prepare you for walking through the rain."

"Oh, I'll have tea. You know how I love tea," Sister responded.

"Me too," Ronnie chimed in.

As the small stove was right there, a pot on it, Barry flicked on the flame then fetched a Perrier for Betty and himself. He put ice cubes in a crystal glass, surprisingly nice for the setting. The water boiled in no time.

Once everyone had their drinks, they chatted, compared hunting notes.

Ronnie's curiosity got the better of him. "Barry, you've been with us for two years and I regret I never asked you much about your life before moving here."

"Well, I came up from Atlanta." He crossed one leg over the other. "Atlanta was good to me. But I couldn't take the city anymore. Any city, I think. Traffic, noise, endless housing developments."

"Has some good museums." Betty loved museums.

"Yes, it does. It has cultural resources it didn't even have forty years ago, thirty years ago. Emory University has grown and with it more people coming into the city with, shall we say, broader views, new views. I think it's good but sometimes I just got tired."

"Think we all do," Sister agreed.

Ronnie laughed. "I'm all for change as long as someone else is doing it. You practiced law there?"

"I did, and I never ran out of clients, as I am a defense lawyer. I believe in our legal system. I believe every citizen deserves representation in the courtroom, a good lawyer, and I represented people who needed a lawyer, and I might add they could pay for it."

"Ah," escaped Ronnie's lips.

"This is part of the backbone of our system but I'll tell you, if you're a defense lawyer you know most of your clients, at least the ones who came to me, were guilty. Perhaps not to the degree that they were accused, but fraud, for one example, is easy to commit if one is intelligent. Millions can be siphoned out of corporations, nonprofits, and our federal government is ever ready to hand out money without properly vetting the recipients. I learned so much. And I learned high-end criminals are very intelligent. Even those who get caught are generally intelligent. Crime pays. Nonviolent criminals often don't serve long terms."

"Fascinating." Sister's eyes widened. "I bet they think they won't get caught."

"Exactly." Barry squeezed his lime into the cold Perrier. "Now, Cameron, and we've known each other since undergraduate school, he wanted his own business. Cameron learned to fly, started with one small airplane, and now has four twin-engine planes. He flies people in the United States and Canada. He'll fly cargo, too. Sorry, I got on that because he says I'm cynical. But he never represented some of the people I did."

"Where did you two go to school?" Betty asked.

"Georgia. It was a lot tougher than I thought it would be. I got a job in Atlanta and stayed, Cameron moved to D.C. We stayed in touch, as both of us started riding to relieve stress. I swore I would never play golf even though it is good for business. He found wherever he delivered cargo if he ran into another foxhunter or looked up a club, he'd meet people. His business grew." Barry paused.

"Well, I'm talking too much, but once I saw central Virginia, which I did at Cameron's invitation to come up for the Shenandoah Apple Blossom Festival. Was a good excuse to get out of the big city, and the countryside, the beauty of the Blue Ridge Mountains dazzled me. A couple of years later, wanting to retire early, I started looking in central Virginia. I liked Northern Virginia, but it was too close to D.C., too much development there, too. Had seen enough of that in Atlanta. Anyway, I wound up here. That's pretty much it."

"Do you still get called to represent people?" Ronnie wondered.

"I do. I'll take an odd job but it has to interest me. I don't just do it for the bucks anymore. Growing up in Tennessee somewhat prepared me for Virginia. I don't think anything could have prepared me for Atlanta."

"Really?" Sister was happy to sit and listen.

"It was a big city when I arrived there as a fresh graduate, but it exploded, just exploded. Maynard Jackson and Andrew Young as well as Mr. Hartsfield were really the keys to all that. Practical visionaries and now it is one of the most vibrant cities we have, but it just keeps growing, thanks to them. I don't know where all the people are coming from. Guess, like me, they got a job."

"Did you hunt there?" Sister asked.

"The clubs were too far away for me, and my schedule was hectic, but I'd try to get out twice a month."

When they left, rain pelting them, Ronnie got into his car, while Betty and Sister slid into the seats of Gray's Toyota Land Cruiser.

Sometimes Sister would borrow what she called The Beast, because it was big and could go through anything.

"I guess if you're a turtle or snake or big lizard, Barry's is a great place to be." Betty listened to the rain pelt the Land Cruiser.

"My turtle looked happy." Sister hit the high swish on the windshield wipers.

Betty, arms across her chest, for she knew her friend well, intoned, "You are going to take that turtle, aren't you?"

"I don't know."

"Sister."

"Well, we found him. How much trouble can a turtle be? I'm curious about him and I have plenty to feed him."

"And how are you going to break this to your husband?"

"I haven't figured out that part yet."

This sent them both into peals of laughter.

Ronnie pulled into his garage, door up. He didn't put it down. He picked up his mail, which he'd thrown into the backseat of his Mustang. He loved his Mustang, which was hardly practical for where and how he lived. He stood up to carry his mail into the house, and someone stepped from behind, hitting him on the side of his head.

He fell, mail scattering onto the concrete floor. His attacker didn't strike a second blow, as the FedEx truck pulled up behind the garage. The driver, seeing Ronnie on the floor, for his lights were on him, also saw a figure running away. He rushed to the fallen man.

"Mr. Haslip."

Blood ran down the side of Ronnie's head. He'd been hit with a blunt weapon and very hard.

The FedEx driver called 911. He wisely did not try to move Ronnie at all but he held his hand and absentmindedly rubbed it. The blood frightened him.

CHAPTER 21

October 14, 2022, Ten PM

Sister sat on one side of Ronnie's hospital bed with Gray next to her. Betty sat on the other side. The room was dim, the sounds filtering in were that of nurses and nurses' aides walking along the polished corridor. Occasionally a phone would ring.

Ronnie, asleep, fidgeted from time to time.

Fortunately, an emergency crew had reached him within fifteen minutes once the FedEx driver called. Sister was contacted at around six in the evening. Gray was home. They immediately drove to UVA hospital. She called Betty along the way. Bobby stayed home to get everything ready for tomorrow's hunt.

Sitting there listening to ragged breathing, no one said much. Sister was listed as the person to call in case of emergency. Fortunately, Ronnie carried that information in his wallet.

Once there, Sister, Gray, then Betty were spared the blood. Ronnie had been cleaned, an Xray taken. Further tests, an MRI, would need to wait. He suffered a cracked skull, his bone above the eyebrow was crushed, plus he had a concussion. As the blow was near his eye, there was the possibility of eye damage. This might take some time to develop. His eye wasn't wounded but it was possible there was damage behind the eye. Until he was awake, some decisions couldn't be made. His head was cleaned, his hair shaved off, he was bandaged. The attacker didn't get a chance for a second blow. It was bad enough, but that might have killed him.

Betty nervously kept checking his pulse, her thumb in the inside of his wrist. "Steady."

Sister smiled slightly, whispering back, "He's tough."

Gray nodded. "Struck from behind. It sure was done with purpose."

The three knew that Ronnie's mother had died when she was thirty-six. She suffered from cervical cancer, which took her quickly. Today, with more treatments, advances, she might have lasted longer. He loved his mother. His father . . . once Beatrice, his mother, died . . . berated Ronnie mercilessly. Beatrice could stand between father and son. Without her Bruce Haslip turned on his son. He loathed that Ronnie was gay. Beatrice softened that somewhat. Ronnie, finally tired of Bruce's hatefulness, severed all contact with him. Sister knew the father now lived in Tempe, Arizona. She would make no effort to find him. He'd done enough damage to his son, a good man and a loyal friend.

They leaned forward. Ronnie's eyes fluttered. He opened them, closed, then opened again.

"Sister," he whispered.

"You'll be fine, Ronnie. Gray, Betty, and I are here."

His eyes opened wide. "I saw RayRay."

This was Sister's deceased son, dying at age fourteen.

She didn't know what to say so she picked up his hand and held it.

He repeated, "I walked along a corridor and saw a bright light. I wanted to go to the light but RayRay came from the light and told me to go back. Go back to you."

Gray put his hand on his wife's shoulder. Tears silently slid down her face.

"I'm glad you saw him, Ronnie. I'm glad you came back."

He sighed, deeply, clearly exhausted. "My left eye is blurred. I'm so tired."

No one knew what to say.

Betty, voice reassuring, told him, "Sleep if you can. Once you're stronger, the doctors will give you tests."

He closed his eyes, opened them again, and squeezed Sister's hand.

She smiled at him. "I have Atlas, don't worry."

He smiled again, falling asleep.

"Let me get the nurse. Or the doctor. They need to know he regained consciousness. There wasn't time to call for them." Gray stood up. "I hope he doesn't lose his vision."

"Concussions, injuries to the skull, hard to say. People can regain their functions. Others don't. Why don't you two go home? I'll stay with him tonight," Betty offered. "Sister, you need to lead the field."

"Kasmir can do it. I don't want to leave him either."

"We can take turns," Gray advised as he left the room. Betty searched her friend's face. Ronnie seeing RayRay was extraordinary. "You okay?"

Sister nodded, tears falling again. "People tell similar stories about dying. Seeing a light. Some turn back. They remember. I believe he did see RayRay. I want to believe it."

Betty started to cry as well. "I hope so. I truly hope so."

"Go on home, Betty. I'll stay here. I can sleep in a chair."

"I'll stay with you. If you text Gray, he'll come back early in the morning. He can go feed everyone. I'll text Bobby. I don't think we should leave Ronnie alone. He's bound to be confused."

"Someone tried to kill him. He shouldn't be left alone."

Betty's face registered the thought. "Right. While you text Gray, I'll text Ben."

Soon the sound of footsteps stopped at the door. Ben Sidell quietly stepped inside. He'd been on his way long before Betty texted.

"Any perp?" Betty thought she was using police language.

He shook his head. "In the rain, footprints were washed away. We closed up his house. Have an officer in the house, sleeping on the sofa, just in case the attacker comes back, which is doubtful."

Their voices were low.

"He woke up briefly," Sister told Ben. "Said a few words, vision blurry in the left eye. Went back to sleep."

"You two go home. Jackie has been at the nurses' station. Jude is covering the stairway door. I'll move Jackie in here and tomorrow there will be another crew, one more for the nurses' station, too. We can't take any chances."

"But we can come back, can't we?" Betty asked.

"Of course."

"Are you going to sit with him for a while?" Sister didn't want Ronnie alone either. "He doesn't know Jackie. Well, he's seen her."

"She'll soothe him if he wakes up again. Don't worry. You will come back tomorrow. With luck, he'll be fully conscious. And hopefully not in great pain."

"Ben, Ronnie never did anything to anybody." Sister's voice stayed low.

"Someone would disagree with you. If that FedEx driver hadn't come by, Ronnie could have been taken out with a second blow. He is a target. I hope we find out in time, which is why I want someone with him, including when he's discharged."

Once home, Sister felt exhausted. She took a shower then

joined Gray in the bedroom. He had tucked everyone in for the night. He had gone to Ronnie's to pick up Atlas. Ben called his man there and told him it was okay. The door to the bedroom was closed, as Atlas was there, a little frightened but he had a case filled with a towel, water bowl and food bowl outside of it. He didn't want to be in a nice case, he wanted on the bed. Sister picked him up.

Trembling a little, he wiggled under her arm. Gray smiled, putting his arm around his wife.

"Ronnie did have a vision." Gray leaned back on the pillows. "People describe that type of thing often."

"I believe he did." She smoothed Atlas's thin fur as he snuggled closer. "You'll be fine, little fellow."

"I want Daddy," he whimpered.

She petted him.

"How do you feel?" Gray wasn't sure how to phrase the question.

She leaned her head on his shoulder. "Frightened. Why would anyone try to kill Ronnie?"

"Right. I meant, how do you feel about what he said?"

"About my son?"

Gray said, "Yes."

"I believe it. I believe when my time comes RayRay will be there and everyone I loved or loved me, including Archie, the great hound that started the A line; my horses; my cats. Love. I know people will say it's wish fulfillment. There is no heaven. There is no God. You know, honey, there are people who would look down on us because we go to church."

"They'll look down on us until they need help. Until they're on their deathbed. If someone wants to be an atheist, fine. But don't belittle the rest of us. Nor should we push them to believe. I do hope you see RayRay. I hope I see Mother. Even if it's not true, it's a comfort and reminds me to be grateful for the people in my life."

"Yes. I am grateful, too. And I thank God Ronnie was not killed or further injured. I expect it will take some time to ascertain if there is brain damage or ocular damage. He will work hard to come back. If whoever did this had broken his bones, Ronnie would be in rehab next week."

"He's faced a lot in his life, like Mercer. Neither of them ever seemed bitter. Angry sometimes, but not really bitter. If a man wants to love another man, whose damn business is it?" A flash of irritation crossed Gray's face, as he'd witnessed much of what his cousin had endured.

"Gray, people need to stay out of other people's business. Look at some of the hornets who flew out of the nest when we started dating."

He laughed. "A lot of jealous white men out there because I won this beautiful, elegant, athletic bombshell. All mine." He kissed her on the cheek as she turned her face up to him.

"*Loving vs. Virginia.* Supreme Court decided that case in 1967. Thank God. Doesn't mean it wiped out prejudice, but at least we won't serve jail terms like they did. You know what I think?"

"I'm ready to hear it."

"People need a vertical scale. Someone is on top. Someone is on the bottom. That will never change. Never. The people on the top and bottom change. I don't like it but it is what we are. We're like a pack of hounds. We create hierarchies."

"Aunt Daniella is at the top." He grinned. "Just her."

Sister felt a tiny little snore escape from Atlas. "Seeing Atlas will make Ronnie happier than just about anything." She paused. "I do believe in an afterlife. And like I said, I think it's all about love."

"Let's make a promise." He lifted her free hand and kissed it. "Let's live long enough to be a trial to everyone."

"Honey, we may have already achieved that."

CHAPTER 22

October 16, 2022, Sunday

The organist played a sprightly tune as parishioners walked down the aisle to be greeted by Rev. Sally Taliaferro of Emmanuel Episcopal Church. Sister couldn't place the piece of music. Usually if it was Bach she could, but so many wonderful hymns had been written since Martin Luther nailed his thesis to the door of Wittenberg Cathedral on October 31, 1517, that she couldn't identify each one. Soon it would be the five hundred fifth year since that world-changing day, at least world-changing for Christians. She thought he picked October 31 because the next day was All Saints' Day. The ecclesiastical calendar, far more important then, meant he would have paid special attention to the symbolism of the day. Modern man, if there is such a thing as modern man, paid little attention to saints' days, seasons of the church, although everyone did follow Christmas Day and Easter. Her mind wandered as Betty and Reverend Taliaferro chatted, then Bobby stepped up. Finally, Sister reached for the reverend's outstretched hand.

"Sister." The younger woman greeted Sister warmly. "I called on

Ronnie yesterday. Thank you for informing me. I'll be going over this evening after Vespers."

"He will be glad to see you. I checked in briefly yesterday. His mind seems clear in those brief moments when he is awake," Sister said.

"Yes. He forgets things." She noticed the line piling up. "I will call on you, too, if you don't mind."

"I would be grateful." Sister squeezed her hand.

Outside, a light wind, tousling carefully combed hair, promised stronger winds to come. The sky was darkening.

"I just wish I could depend on the weather forecast."

"Ha." Sister put her arm around Betty's waist. "We're right by the mountains. If the forecasts are correct for Richmond, doesn't mean they are for us."

Bobby agreed with her as he turned to his wife. "You watch the weather on the TV. You watch The Weather Channel like some people watch football. You have three weather apps on your phone. You could be a meteorologist."

"Well." Betty thought about this. "Lots of science. I still think I'll depend on my bones. Which reminds me. When I dropped in on Ronnie, his doctor was there and said he had no broken bones except for the part over his eyebrow and a crack in his skull."

"Means a heavy object. Maybe a hammer or something like that." Bobby had visited Ronnie along with his wife. He was deeply disturbed.

"Little Atlas is doing as well as can be expected. My dogs are sweet to him. Golly is not, of course. She gets huffy. Poor little guy." Sister loved her animals, most animals.

"Sister, who was with Ronnie when you were there?" Bobby asked.

"One of the young officers. I don't know this woman but she was quiet, efficient, and armed."

"The doctor informed us that the guards are changed every four hours, which seems terribly frequent to me," Bobby mentioned.

"It is. I spoke to Ben on the phone. He said sitting there can be tiring. Your senses flatten. He wants the guards to be sharp. Ronnie's near miss better stay a near miss."

"That's an awful thought." Betty put her fingers together as if in prayer.

"We've all had it," Sister truthfully confessed. "The other thing was . . ." Bobby guided the "girls," as he thought of them, to the car. "He has had a Jefferson Hunt Club member constantly with him throughout this. The hardcore. At least that's how I think of us. When we stopped by, Freddie was there, and Barry left just as Freddie came on."

"Barry. That was good of a fairly new member." Sister switched her handbag, which she hated carrying, to her other arm.

"Barry said he felt terrible that this happened after you all visited his foundation." Bobby added, "Whoever did this lay in wait for Ronnie. I truly don't believe this was an impulse attack."

"Yes, but Bobby, someone could lay in wait because they felt Ronnie had expensive items to steal. His house is a showplace. No one could mistake Ronnie for poor, not that he throws his money around, but the house is quite something."

Betty nodded. "It is. He put so much into it but I still can't stand modern architecture."

"Well, don't tell him that." Sister slid into the backseat of the car.

Betty, sliding into the front, turned around. "You know I would never do that."

"I know, but the older I get, I swear the more I have to guard against myself. So many things come to the tip of my tongue," Sister confessed.

"Like me saying to you you're twenty-some years older than I am so I don't have that problem yet?"

"Of course you don't, sweetheart. You have no edit button."

"Unfair." Betty reached back to swat at her friend.

Bobby, now behind the wheel, said, "What is wrong with you two?"

"Don't look at me," Betty purred.

"You should look at her. She was mocking her elders." Sister flopped back in the seat. "Hey, don't drive yet. Give me a minute. How about I call Gray and see if they would mind if we all gathered at the Lorillard place?"

"Sam will worry about the food."

"There will be enough. When Gray cooks, he always makes too much. We should be together." She punched the circle on her phone containing her husband's number. "Honey, we just left church. Would you and Sam mind if we all came over there? We can stop and bring anything you need."

"Hold on." She heard him put his hand over the phone, call something to his brother, then as he came back on the phone, she heard Aunt Daniella in the background say, "Do we have enough bourbon?"

Sister, laughing, replied, "Tell Aunt Dan we are bringing more bourbon."

Off they drove.

"The liquor stores aren't open yet."

"I know. Bobby, swing by the farm and I'll grab one of our Woodford Reserve bottles. She likes that and Blanton's."

"Too far. I've got Blanton's. Let's go."

"Bobby, really I don't mind."

"Neither do I, but you know someday we should all put our money together and get her a bottle of Pappy Van Winkle. A twenty-year-old bottle is about four thousand dollars. Twenty-five years old is about sixty thousand," Bobby told them.

"That's insane," Betty pronounced. "Insane. Why spend that for something that will disappear. Really?"

"True. What goes in must come out," Sister agreed. "It's a status thing. More a male thing. Pardon me, Bobby, I'm being sexist. You know one man ups another by bringing out a sixty thousand dollar bottle of bourbon."

"I believe Aunt Daniella is more than capable of it." Betty grinned.

"True." Sister smiled.

Cocked Hat, the Franklin farm, was somewhat on the way, so after picking up the bottle it only took the three friends twenty minutes to arrive at the Lorillard place.

The front door opened to calls, embraces, and a bottle handed to Gray. Yvonne was there, too, as she came from her Catholic service. Her reason was she adored Aunt Dan and the Lorillard family. The Lorillard family was hoping she would be adoring Sam, although he still dared not.

"Sit out here by the fire. I'll bring a light drink. We're almost ready," Gray offered.

Once settled in, Yvonne now with the group, they reviewed the shocking events of Friday, swapped tidbits from each preacher's sermon. Sam called them to the table.

Gray had experimented with a pork loin, coating it in lemon juice, which sounded awful but turned out delightful.

After this sumptuous midday meal, Uncle Yancy, in his hideaway over the mudroom door, hoped the humans would shortly be filling up a garbage can. It was easy to pry off the lid.

The group gathered in the living room.

"How was Ronnie when you saw him?" Sister asked Sam.

"Asleep. I was there with Jude. He loves working with Ben. It's good when people find out what they should be doing in life."

"We're all sitting here. Why don't we compare notes and thoughts? I wish I had a better idea, more insight, but I wonder if these odd events couldn't be connected." Sister threw that out there.

"You mean, the corpse in the chair could be connected to this?" Yvonne, startled at the thought, took a drink for good measure.

"I don't know. He was meant for us to see him," Sister reminded her.

"That is creepy," Betty acknowledged.

"What do we know? I mean, that we all have seen or experienced?" Bobby, ever logical, started thinking. "Ed had stamps in his trailer. Ronnie had one on his garage door."

"And then someone tried to kill Ronnie," Gray stated.

"We know someone stole Barry Harper's stamps. But just some of them." Yvonne was fascinated. "He didn't have any idea why anyone would want a few of his stamps."

"What do we know about the dead man?" Bobby asked. "Didn't Ben, once the man was identified, say he was a respected businessman? They couldn't run photos, as his face was disfigured, plus the vulture got his eye. Would be too awful for people. But the Charlotte police had photos of him from conferences. Business stuff."

"Right. No police record," Gray added. "No one has come forth for whatever he owned. Sam told me that. Ben informed him since he made the grisly discovery."

"Well, I say let's think about the stamps." Aunt Daniella had been carefully listening. "Gray, you asked me if I still have Mercer's stamp collection. I do. The stamps interested you."

"My first thought was they had value. They do, but not a lot. They were mostly from 1987. Not a lot of value," Gray replied.

"Out of curiosity I checked my son's collection, looking for snakes, turtles, frogs. I found a few sheets when stamps were thirty-seven cents but not much before that. As he had quite a few books I didn't go through everything." Aunt Daniella then added, "There was one gorgeous stamp but it wasn't reptiles or frogs. It was a mountain ram, black sky against a blood moon. Stunning."

"So you did go through stamps." Yvonne smiled at her.

"Some." Aunt Dan nodded. "He really had more than I realized. Some of the stamps, none postmarked, of course, are little works of art, like the mountain goat, you know those ram horns that curl around their faces."

"Ammon." Sister nodded.

Aunt Daniella, who knew her mythology, lifted her head a bit. "Yes, exactly."

"Aunt Dan, I need reminding about Ammon," prodded Yvonne.

"Here's my version of the story. Simple. Zeus needed to hide from probably his father, who wanted to kill him, but someone else also wanted to kill him. He assumed the shape of a ram, hence the horns. Some mythologists say he went to Egypt, and an old god there was Ammon, I don't know. At any rate, the horns, being a ram, hid him."

"Are we getting off track here?" Betty had no interest in mythology.

"Maybe not." Sister rested her glass on the old coffee table. "Disguise. Maybe someone or something is in disguise. When you think about it, what do stamps have to do with anything? And yet one was missing and put on Ronnie's garage door. A box turtle stamp."

"There is another path. Actually, Ronnie brought this up at the hunt breakfast. Remember? He asked what happened in 1987?" Yvonne recalled. "As I remember, the subject more or less died."

A silence followed this.

"A few people recalled the year," Sam spoke. "That was the year

President Reagan in Berlin called out for Gorbachev to 'tear down this wall.'"

"I remember that." Aunt Daniella raised her voice. "Electrified the world."

"Right." Sam brightened. "It did electrify the world. And that was the year August Wilson's play *Fences* was a big hit. Won awards."

Gray, less enthusiastic about 1987, stated, "It was also Black Monday. The stock market dropped 22.6% on October 19. October is not a good month for the market, so it appears. But that was a real jolt."

"And *Fatal Attraction* had everyone talking. What a scary movie. I thought so anyway." Betty found movies that could happen far more frightening than monster movies.

"So it was eventful." Sam looked at the fire, deciding it didn't need another log yet.

"I guess they all are," Yvonne posited.

"So it could be that 1987, the year of the stolen stamps, means something." Sister was trying to figure out something, anything.

"Maybe the pictures on the stamps are important. The amphibians. Or that the stamps celebrate the National Wildlife Federation. You know, sort of like all this interest in monarch butterflies." Aunt Daniella lifted her glass for another drink. "Your Blanton's is excellent, Bobby. Even though my beloved nephews have bourbon here, I wanted to try yours. I do like Blanton's."

Gray fixed her another drink. Looked around. No one indicated they wanted a freshener.

"The stamp left on Ronnie's door was of a box turtle," Gray mentioned.

"The only thing we know about amphibians and reptiles is of course Barry would have stamps of them. That's his passion." Yvonne pushed up the sleeves of her teal sweater, her Saint Hubert's ring catching the light.

"Is that it?" Betty asked.

"You mean is that all we remember or could be of importance?" Sam asked her.

"Yes. So it's a year. The stamps themselves. The pictures on them. And someone in hiding . . . well, hiding in front of us."

"The stock market crash might mean someone is desperate for money or an investment should be sold." Sam considered that. "But that's a stretch."

"It all is, and yet . . ." Bobby trailed off then picked up his thought. "And yet it's close. Whatever this is, it's here."

"I hope we aren't grasping at straws." Betty sighed.

CHAPTER 23

October 17, 2022, Monday

Heavy clouds hung over Roughneck Farm and central Virginia. The temperature was dropping, with a few snowflakes predicted for later in the afternoon.

Sister rode Matador, a flea-bitten gray, who needed some light work. Reverend Taliaferro rode Lafayette, Sister's older, tried and true horse. Sister invited her to ride, as the reverend said she wanted to visit. Both needed a light ride and the horses needed it, too. Like people, they can get stiff. Light exercise is often best.

"No wonder you like to lead the field on this guy." Reverend Taliaferro felt how smooth he was, such a long stride.

"We've been partners for close to fifteen years."

"Where did you find him?"

"Jane Winegardner, the other Jane." Sister smiled, as both their names were Jane, but as Sister was the older, she called Jane *O.J.* "She's got a great eye for a horse, especially the horse's mind. Sooner or later most riders can recognize a good-looking horse. It's the mind that needs your attention."

"Like people." Reverend Taliaferro pulled her wool scarf up higher on her neck. "You know, it might really snow a bit later."

"Feels like it. Thought if we squeezed in a brief ride we'd be glad we did. No telling if we will hunt tomorrow. One of my apps predicts three inches of snow. Another app declared steady rain, and the third app, the one up on Wintergreen mountain, so far predicts no precipitation. Gives me a headache."

"I don't have to worry about that. The good Lord never said anything about weather other than Noah's Ark." She smiled.

"You're right. How about if we ride through the wildflower field, the narrow path? I'll tell you what I've been planting and nurturing for next year. I'm on a monarch butterfly kick and so many of our friends are starting to create areas for butterflies, bees. Of course, Marty Howard leads the charge as well. We were all surprised to hear of the work Elise Sabatini is doing. Elise has ridden a few times now and she's doing pretty good."

"I like her. Father Mancusco tells me they are regular churchgoers." Reverend Taliaferro mentioned the Catholic priest, who also hunted.

"I always feel better when you and Father Mancusco are in the field. Surely our Heavenly Father will take care of his servants."

Reverend Taliaferro laughed. "I tell Father Mancusco that he cheats because he calls on the Blessed Virgin Mother as much as the Heavenly Father."

"How do you know?"

The reverend laughed even harder. "Because I am either in front of him or behind him at a jump."

"I can't wait to tell him." Sister laughed with Reverend Taliaferro. "Having the two of you hunt, besides being a bonus upstairs," she pointed to the lowering sky, "is fun. Great fun."

"Thank you."

The two rode through the field, where Sister pointed out what she had planted, what she had hoped for with sanctuary and food for next year's insect population.

The two women discussed habitat, wildlife habitat, and the current status of the fox population. Good.

Once back at the stables, both women stripped their mounts of tack, hung it up on the tack hooks, then wiped down Lafayette and Matador, who had not gotten sweaty because all they did was walk. Often when people are loaned a horse, they volunteer to clean up after the ride. Half the time Sister would rather do it herself. She could do it faster than telling the guest. Reverend Taliaferro knew her way around a horse, as she had a beloved Appendix horse, so she easily cleaned Lafayette, threw a blanket on him, and put him in his stall.

Once the horses were attended to the women repaired to the comfortable tack room. Following Sister's lead, Reverend Taliaferro hung her coat on a tack hook. The room stayed pleasant at seventy degrees. On a bitter cold day, Sister might bump the temperature up to seventy-two or even seventy-five, because bitter cold had a way of sneaking into any and all available crevices. Tight as the tack room was, Mother Nature could still bite you.

"How about tea?" Sister turned on the hotplate.

"You can't live without tea," Reverend Taliaferro said, then added, "Neither can I."

"Love the smell of coffee but the drink itself makes me jittery. Gray can almost drink a full pot. Doesn't affect him."

Tea ready, both women sat in the small but comfortable chairs, a bit of padding and pillows for your back if you wished.

"Thank you so much for Lafayette. I needed that ride."

"Lots going on at church?"

She nodded. "There always is. You can't be part of a church

that's over two hundred years old without something needing a fix. And the grounds are considerable, which is one of the attractions of Emmanuel. I mean, apart from being Episcopal." She smiled.

"Well, yes. When I was a kid, all the higher-ups were Episcopalian. Some Lutherans and a few Catholics. It was just the way it was, a kind of social order of faith, I guess."

"Was for me, too." She drank more tea. "This is good."

"It's an Irish tea. I'll give you some," Sister offered.

"I'll take it." Reverend Taliaferro inhaled the odor of the tea, strong. "Do you remember being in Sunday School, learning about Jesus at the temple asking questions? He was supposed to be traveling with his parents on their way back to Nazareth. They thought he was along. Well, anyway, they realized he wasn't and traveled back to find him."

"I remember. His father was upset. Jesus said to him, my paraphrase, 'I am in my Father's house.' "

"It's one of those stories that hits you when you're young. A kind of affirmation of your developing mind. At least that's how I take it." She held her cup up for a moment. "I told you I've been visiting Ronnie."

"The club has been diligent about seeing him." Sister was proud of them.

"This morning he was pretty good. We prayed. He wants to pray. And he wanted to tell me about seeing your son. This is the second time he has mentioned it, only this time it was more fully. His mind is becoming more clear."

"He was radiant when he told me. Not able to continue, as he was so beat up, so tired, and I am sure so drugged," Sister replied.

"He cried."

"Reverend Taliaferro, I cried. Gray fought back the tears. He was wonderful, but then he always is. My husband is a loving man."

"He is. I am here if you ever want to talk to me about something like Ronnie's vision or your son. I never knew him, of course, but Ronnie loved him."

"Like brothers."

"You had catechism?"

"I did. And our priest, Father Jocelyn, made us study the Protestant Reformation, the ensuing fractures into many ideologies . . . you know, Methodist, Presbyterian, Baptist. He was thorough but he always came back to the Episcopal outlook. He used to say to be an Episcopalian, you have to think."

"True." Reverend Taliaferro nodded.

"But you know," Sister leaned forward, "I really liked Martin Luther's concept of by the grace of God. God's grace is love and we are saved by that as well as our faith. And we don't have to buy indulgences."

Reverend Taliaferro, early forties, dark hair, a warm smile, replied, "No, but there are times when the budget gets low when I do consider reviving indulgences."

They both laughed at that.

"Maybe money is the root of all evil. I don't know."

"I don't either. I just know there is never enough of it. Which brings me to Ronnie. I assume he is well off, good insurance. If not, between you and me, we can round up some help."

"Ronnie is very smart." A long pause followed this. "I am beginning to wonder if that isn't what got him into trouble. I'm not sure this was a random act." Sister slightly grimaced.

"It could be." The reverend almost sounded hopeful. "Theft?"

"It could be, but I have this little gargoyle nipping at my heels. He either stumbled on something or scared someone without knowing he was getting too close."

"But close to what?"

"He likes puzzles. The puzzle of the corpse in a chair. Mostly it's gross but I can see where Ronnie would wonder. Perhaps he thought of something we all missed, including Ben. Or what have stamps to do with anything and why were they put into Ed's boot box? And why was one taped to Ronnie's door? All seeming so petty. All pointing, I think now, to someone having it in for Barry Harper, since those are his stolen stamps."

"They were his stamps," echoed Reverend Taliaferro.

"But whatever could he do to provoke stamps being stolen? I don't see how any of this connects to the corpse."

Reverend Taliaferro waved her hand. "Probably doesn't."

"Well, I trust my husband on things like this. Given his work in D.C., he has insight into the political process, as in who is getting money under the table and from whence it comes."

"A different form of indulgence." The reverend lifted one eyebrow. "But what does the murdered man have to do with any of that?"

Sister added, "The murdered man's ears were popped. Eardrums pierced. Sam said the vultures got his face, one eye, and something nibbled on his hands. Plus his tongue was split. Maybe this is political. Maybe he knew too much, but why dump him here?"

"It's some bizarre coincidence." The reverend couldn't imagine any connection at all, especially to stamps and Ronnie.

Looking at the clock, Reverend Taliaferro said, "I'd better head back. Thank you again for Lafayette." She stood up and Sister rose with her. "You know, a split tongue. Like a reptile." She paused. "Too strange."

Both women looked out the window in the tack room door to the outside; snowflakes twirled down.

Sister grabbed the reverend's coat. "Guess you'll need this."

Pausing at the door, the younger woman thought a moment. "Sister, for what it is worth, I believe your son could have come to Ronnie in his hour of need, told him to return to the living. The Lord moves in mysterious and wondrous ways."

Sister kissed her on the cheek as she opened the door. "Thank you."

CHAPTER 24

October 18, 2022, Tuesday

Ared fox gave hounds a terrific run at an old fixture, Mouse-hold Heath. Comprising two hundred acres and a formerly run-down Virginia farmhouse, all had been restored by the owners, a young couple, Lisa and Jim Jardine. Not having much money, they did all the work themselves. There wasn't a fence post on the property that the husband and wife hadn't dug in.

Today, both at work, they missed the hunt but gladly allowed Jefferson Hunt access to what had been an old fixture. The club, thankful, built jumps, helped with gates and manpower. The Bancrofts donated logs, having them carried to the big sawmill on west Route 250. The Jardines then had to carry back the fence boards, which they did in shifts.

The fox appreciated the work, as did a few other foxes. Tidy pastures usually had higher grasses along the edge outside the pasture. This provided cover and habitat for rabbits especially. Some birds like the taller grasses; although the fox wasn't averse to eating a bird, finches weren't their first thought.

This fox, walking now, as he had left hounds far behind, climbed up a fence post to sit on it. Gave him a good view. He'd lost the hounds back by the four-foot waterfall. He'd hurried to the waterfall, got his feet wet, then moved away from it. Scent remained, but it was confusing since the line was clear to the four-foot drop, then hounds would smell a few feet of scent then none. Smart fellow kept dipping his paws in and out of the water until he found a thick tree trunk traversing the creek. Scrambling over it, he hit the afterburners on the other side. Sitting now he could hear hounds, searching. No point waiting until someone crossed the fallen tree. He left off the fence post, trotted through the back pasture, then began to run. A large outcropping, two stories high, had some scrubs on it. The fellow scrambled to the top of the rocks. Picked his way down, slipped into a narrow walkway and then into a large den. The rocks kept the wind out. He had grasses, some old towels in there. The rehabilitation of Mousehold Heath gave him the pick of materials thrown out. Old towels were the best but remnants of pillow could be comfortable. Took time to drag stuff back to the den but he did.

A half hour later hounds finally made it to the rock outcropping. Barmaid, a young entry, stood on top of the huge rocks.

Looking down, she spied the crevice, a narrow walkway. She could smell the fox.

Dasher, now next to her, looked down. *"We'll never get down there."*

"Are all dens this narrow?"

"No. Most of them are in the ground or hidden by logs. There is one other rock den over at Old Paradise. I'll bet this fox's den is actually big."

The youngster asked, *"Have you ever been in a fox den?"*

"Had my head in one once, trying to dig out the fox. Didn't work, as he had tunnels to other dens. They're pretty smart. Lots of entrances and exits and lot of times the den is hidden. There are more places to sleep. Those tunnels led to different places."

Barmaid soaked all this up. Weevil, slowed by debris on the path, finally got there. He praised his hounds, called Dasher and Barmaid down, blew "Gone to Ground," then moved off.

Barmaid found one of her B litter, Bachelor, and relayed what Dasher had told her. Both were learning that foxes are more clever than they could have imagined.

Weevil turned back. Reaching the trunk over the creek, he dipped down to the wide crossing. Hojo, water running fast as high as his knees, pushed through. The horses in the field evidenced less enthusiasm but everyone got through the creek because no horse wanted to be left behind.

Weevil pushed along the creek, hoping for scent close to the water. Hounds tried. After a half hour of this, he moved away from the creek, finding a path around the edge of a newly fenced pasture. Having been out for close to three hours, he lifted the hounds. He hadn't realized they'd been hunting that long. He so often lost track of time.

Back at the kennels, Sister walked in as hounds, the males, were eating. The girls would follow. The reason for this was that it was best to get the boys in and out. Often they could sense a female going into season before the humans noticed it. Their concentration would wander and sometimes there might be a fight.

Simple rule. Boys first. Girls second.

Once in the draw yard, Weevil and Tootie called the girls, each by name, to her side of the kennel. They went in and waited for the boys to eat, which never took long. The boys followed Tootie down the corridor to their side of the kennel. All the runs opened to larger areas, where condos provided more housing. Hounds could pick whether they wanted to sleep in a condo or sleep inside the kennels on raised beds. The inside kennels had a door, a big flap, hounds could push to enter or leave. Same with the condos, but instead of flaps they had double canvas, one canvas covering the inside of the door large enough to enter and one outside. There were no rubber flaps large enough for those doors.

As the girls gratefully ate, Sister, who observed the boys first, remarked, "Doesn't look as though anyone is footsore."

Weevil replied as Tootie came back into the large area, "No. I worry when there are rocky places, little caves. That and dryness. When the ground gets hard in Virginia, it's like brick."

She smiled. "That's why so many of the early homes are made of brick, it lasts. For centuries. Then again, most of the clapboard homes have lasted, too. But the boys looked good; so did the girls."

"Long day out there." Tootie pointed to Barmaid. "She did well."

"Our B's and J's are coming along." Sister smiled. "I'm tired. Guess I rode harder and longer than I realized."

Weevil agreed. "Think we all did."

"Let me get back to the barn. I left Betty with all the work."

Betty, in the tack room, cleaning the bridles, grinned as Sister exclaimed, "You've done most of the work."

"Did. Left your bridle for you."

Sister removed her jacket, dipping a sponge into the small water bucket. The two worked in silence, Betty humming, so it wasn't one hundred percent silent.

"My version of 'Before the Parade Passes By.'"

"Funny how much wisdom is in songs. Musicals. I loved *Hello, Dolly!*" Sister replied.

"Think everyone did. Rough hunt today. The territory is rougher at Mousehold Heath than I remember, or maybe I started tired."

"There is that." Sister washed the bit. "Stopped by Ronnie's last night. Reverend Taliaferro was there in the morning. We rode, chatted, then I cleaned up and checked in on him. He still has a guard."

"Good. His head is getting better. Was when I saw him."

"Better than it looks. His vision is still blurred. The eyebrow bone hurts but he is clearheaded. He can't remember picking up his mail or driving into the garage. He can't even remember the rain, but he can remember stuff before that."

"So it just seems to be, what, a few hours that he can't remember?"

"I think so." Sister grabbed a small washrag and dried the bit, a simple D snaffle. "I wonder if he caught a glimpse of who hit him. Or sensed it."

"Given where the wounds are, probably not," Betty answered. "Whoever it is is still out there."

"All the more reason for a guard."

"Too bad you can't sneak Atlas in." Betty hung up her bridle, making the figure eight with the throat latch over the noseband up to the headband.

"I go every day to give him the Atlas report. Even if only for a minute. He doesn't need rehab. He can walk, his arms are fine. Of course, they'll give him some more tests, but I bet he could come home by the end of the week. He wants to go to the symphony."

"Well, maybe he can." Betty thought if anyone bumped his head, though, it would be awful. "He'll look like a holy man with the bandage wrapped around his head."

"I told him to grow a beard. Will divert people's attention from his head and left eye."

"Sister, it won't."

"Doesn't mean he can't try. He is planning the seed order. Really, he was sitting up in bed with his notebook, thinking how to raise money. As always, he comes up with good ideas. He said we can put on our website that we can ship anywhere, but if someone is in a hurry we can fly the seeds to them."

"They would have to be in a big hurry."

"Maine, New Hampshire, Vermont. They're about to run out of

planting time. Snowstorms in October are not that rare. Same with upstate New York, but his idea is worth thinking about it, Cameron could fly stuff."

"Boy, that would be expensive." Betty sat down, having hung up her bridle. "Expensive."

"Yes, but if the person paid the gas, maybe Cameron would do it for free. His labor, I mean." Sister finished her bridle. "It's a thought. A long shot, but the point is, Ronnie is on the mend. Then he had ideas about stationery."

Betty sat up straight. "Yes."

"You don't need to buy anything. His idea is that you and Bobby create stationery for our club. Regular-sized paper, correspondence-sized, fold-over cards. Use our logo, the fox mask with the two tails underneath. They can pick the color for their paper and the color of the ink."

"We could probably do that, but Sister, there is no way Bobby and I can afford to give away expensive paper for free."

"He knows that, and so do I. But maybe you could do the actual printing for free. Or at a nice discount. Like twenty-five percent."

"I'll talk to Bobby about it. A discount is more realistic than free printing. You'd be surprised what it takes to keep a big press like ours in shape. In essence, it's like a car. Okay, not quite as complicated, but it's a big press."

"I've seen it. You know whatever you all come up with is fine. But if you go talk to Ronnie about it, that will keep him focused."

"Is he worried?" Betty frowned.

"He's not talking about it, but he'd have to be an idiot not to be worried. Ronnie is not an idiot."

"Right." Betty let out a long stream of air. "If only we had an idea what this is about. Does Ben say anything?"

"No. The most likely cause would be robbery."

"I don't know. I have a terrible feeling that's not the case." Betty reached over for Sister's hand as she had sat down. "We've got to do something."

"The only thing we can do is make sure someone is in the house with him, sticks with him. The department can only afford protection for so long."

"Well, they can damn well afford surveillance. I pay enough taxes."

"If we received the full benefits of our taxes, Albemarle County would be the wonder of the nation." Sister laughed. "But I'm with you. If a few of us talk to Ben I think we can convince Ronnie to hire security until we know more. That isn't cheap but we can't protect him. I mean, we can be with him, but we aren't professionals."

"Right. I'll keep my .38 close."

"I've got my gun in my glove compartment. I've always had a gun there, because if an animal is run over, people just leave it there to suffer. At least I can put an end to its misery."

"Saint Hubert said when he heard the voice of God in the eighth century that we should allow no animal to suffer nor should we kill a mother with children. We should take care of wildlife, animals, God's gifts." Betty liked the story of Saint Hubert. "If you think about it, his teaching is the basis for Western culture's relationship with animals."

"It's a wonderful story about the cross of gold between the stag's antlers." Sister smiled. "Oh, the other thing is Ronnie insists the stamps mean something. He thinks it's the year, 1987."

"I'll visit tomorrow," Betty promised. "Today got too crazy. I can't carry my gun into the hospital but I am going to carry it elsewhere. I believe someone wants to kill Ronnie. I don't think the attack is motivated by robbery, wanting his stuff."

Sister hated the idea but she couldn't refute it. "We don't know enough."

"We know enough that we have to protect him."

CHAPTER 25

October 19, 2022, Wednesday

"He can't do it. I understand." Sister sat in the clean office in the kennel.

In the corner a fireplace blazed. The kennels, built in the early part of the twentieth century, had fallen into disrepair. Sister's first husband's uncle, a passionate foxhunter, bought the estate, remodeling the kennels but keeping the good features. The office's corner fireplace remained, as did the crown molding. The beautiful brick archways fanned off the center of the building, which contained the office, draw pen living quarters, and medical rooms. These walkways, in front of the huge fenced-in yards, added symmetry. The central building itself was larger than one noticed until walking inside and realizing the structure was about forty feet. What you saw standing in front of the kennel was the door to the office. A door to the right opened to the feed room. The draw room to the side of that had a door opening to the outside. So three doors faced you. Once inside, the living quarters impressed with their size, a large overhead fan centered in the high ceiling turned in both the boys' side and the girls'. The ceiling fan pushed the warm air down in winter, reversed in summers. The aisle from the feed room to either side of the hounds' quarters was wide. One could easily push a wheelbarrow down for cleaning. High windows, opened by a crank, allowed air to circulate. Low windows invited a dog to crash through.

After feeding, cleaning, assisting any hound in the medical room should one need help, the humans could sit down in the office.

Behind the Louis XV desk, out of place but fabulous, Sister had stud books in front of her.

Weevil and Tootie faced her in the wing chairs.

"You really don't know about a hound until you see him hunt if you can." She looked up. "You know the great names like Orange County Melody 1999, gone now but I was fortunate enough to hunt with Orange when she was in her glory. Other hounds I know only by reputation."

"Meaning today or generations back?" Weevil, keenly interested in breeding, asked.

"Both. If I have seen a hound hunt, I check the pedigree, and say she goes back to Bull Run Dawson, a great hound from 1981, even though that's far back, I'd try that."

"But don't you think it's best if you have hunted behind hounds or seen them hunt?" Tootie asked.

"I do, but there are only so many hours in the day. I wish I could go over to Tennessee and Kentucky more often. Or hike all the way to upstate New York to hunt with Genesee Valley. The older I get it seems the more I have to do. People talk about retirement. I have no idea what they're talking about. I have less time now than I ever had."

"You can get to Piedmont, Orange, or Middleburg. Warrenton. Old Dominion. Even Blue Ridge up there on the border," Weevil mentioned.

"Sometimes. Over the years I have hunted with those hunts.

Had a cracking good time, too. And don't forget Green Spring Valley or Radnor or Elkridge Hartford. Those hunts have long histories, often beautiful grounds, and kennels plus lots of terrific staff. I know I'm getting old but I still learn. And why am I babbling about this? We need to find the right girl for Giorgio."

"Ah." Weevil nodded. "He isn't the fastest."

"No. But we don't need blazing speed in our territory. Far better to have terrific stamina with a great nose and cry. Not that I'm against speed, but if hounds are too fast and your territory isn't flat, you leave the field behind. And people will sooner or later go to other hunts."

"Do you think people would really leave Jefferson Hunt?" Tootie was surprised.

"We have a hardcore group but you can't expect people to be loyal to you. If you have a bad year, or two, they'll go somewhere else. Everyone generally thinks they are a better rider than they really are." Sister laughed. "So they want to go to a fast hunt and brag about it."

"Do they ever come back?" Tootie asked.

"Actually, some do. They realize the grass is always greener until you're there for a time. I believe it is in every hunt's best interest for other hunts to flourish. I have no desire to take members from another hunt. I'm happy for anyone to ride with us, cap, or even join if they can afford more than one hunt. But lure people? Pretty low, I think." She had a strong sense of ethics about clubs supporting one another.

"You mean like Crawford stealing our members." Tootie was trying to piece together the past.

"Well, that was a special case. He thought if he had a pack of Penn-Marydels he couldn't lose. He'd heard how good their noses are. He had no idea how to train a pack of hounds. He'd hire people, infuriate them, and they'd stalk out. Eventually he found Cynthia Skiff Cane. She endured. He has Sam, too. Marty eventually talked some sense into him. His pack is pretty good now. Took a few years of hard work. Did he try to steal my members? No. It all worked out but he made it hard on himself."

"It's interesting, when we have joint meets, to watch his hounds work. Skiff is good." Tootie liked Crawford's huntsman.

"She is. Which brings me to Shaker. He can't be our wheel whip because of working with Skiff. I asked him, knowing he couldn't do it. I didn't want him to think I've forgotten him. As Saturday is every-one's biggest day, she needs him. I have asked Kathleen Sixt Dunbar if she would be interested. We'd pay her a stipend plus gas and she said she'd love it. No stipend. Just the gas. Of course, Aunt Daniella will be with her, and who knows the territory better than Aunt Dan? So now we have to buy the new Garmin Alpha 200i. I'll face the crisis later. First the wheel whip." She smiled. "Next, finding Giorgio the right girl."

"I can help. I'd like to go to other hunts, on Mondays or Wednes-days or Fridays, days we don't hunt. I can watch their hounds. Get ideas, and we can always have joint meets." Weevil brightened.

"We can, and we should. Covid screwed that up for a few years. I'm finishing a fixture card. I'll pop in a few joint meets. Always fun." She smiled. "Anything I need to know? Someone need vitamins? Spe-cial foods?"

"We're good."

Her phone rang as they walked out the door, a brief blast of air coming inside.

"Ben. How are you?"

"Good and yourself?"

"Trying to get ready for formal hunting. We have our Opening Hunt the first Sunday in November."

"I know. I've already hired a braider for my Nonni." He took a breath. "Sister, I called because I've been texting the Charlotte police. They've been working on the Timothy Snavely case. They are finding him a source of some fascination."

"Really?"

"He had bank accounts offshore, as well as accounts in Charlotte. He had quite a bit of money but not a lot to show for it. You know, no fancy cars, or a young wife needing jewelry." Ben chuckled. "He was a member of the big country club in Charlotte as well as having an out-of-state membership in a club in Atlanta. But here's the thing. He had a stamp collection. It was valuable, but he also had many stamps of reptiles and insects. He had everything that was printed for 1987. Also stamps from 1996, 2002. All amphibians, reptiles, and butterflies. They were not with his major collection."

"His corpse, as you told me . . . we didn't really discuss it . . . had a slit tongue." Sister, apart from the violence of it, thought it weird.

"Like a reptile."

"There's some connection. Absurd as it seems." Sister listened to the wood crackle.

"I'm going to call on Barry. But first, do you know anyone in the hunt club or among your friends who is a serious collector?"

"I'm sure there may be a few people, but I don't know about it. Mercer Laprade was a collector but he's been gone for a few years. I can send an email to the club."

"No. Don't do that. Just in case." Ben paused for a long time. "The good news is, Ronnie will be home tomorrow."

"Yes, we were talking about that. I'm going to see if I can convince him to hire a security service until some of these oddities become clear."

"That would be a big help. If he's willing, I can recommend the better companies. As long as you don't say I did."

"Of course."

"What can you do with a stamp if you don't collect it or use it to mail a letter?" Ben wondered.

"What if it's a sign," Sister suggested. "Something like a bill is due. I don't know. It has to mean something."

CHAPTER 26

October 20, 2022, Thursday

"Beautiful photo of a monarch butterfly." Gray studied the flat of stamps in one of Mercer's stamp books.

Mercer had book upon book. Gray, Sister, Yvonne, and Aunt Daniella pulled out the more recent ones. Mercer organized his collections by year.

"That was made by a Maryland photographer." Sister studied the old twenty-two-cent stamp. "I remember because it made the news."

Yvonne, flipping through her book, which was more beat-up, remarked, "Here's one from 2010. Sixty-four cents. Another beautiful representation."

"Well, we've pored over insects, reptiles, and amphibians." Aunt Daniella exhaled, tired. "We've gone back fifty years. Granted, we only stopped when encountering bugs or frogs or whatever. I don't see why any of this matters. I take that back. Yes, two people have had collections. The dead man and Barry. Anyone collecting stamps could have these stamps."

"True, Aunt Dan," Gray agreed. "But the stolen stamps now returned to Barry match some of the stamps Mercer has. And what the Charlotte police told Ben about Timothy Snavely."

"If Mercer has monarch butterfly stamps, stamps of frogs, and toads, and turtles, why wouldn't most stamp collectors?" Yvonne felt her eyes getting blurry. "They are beautiful."

"I'm sure plenty do." Sister closed the stamp book she was reading. "The stamps for the most part really are beautiful, little works of art. This one I just looked up on the computer, a butterfly, was twenty-two cents and is now worth a dollar forty. You can buy this stuff online."

"You can buy anything online." Yvonne sighed. "And given the beauty of particularly the butterfly stamps over the years, I bet millions of collectors bought them."

"Oh look. Here's a butterfly stamp from New Zealand," Aunt Daniella exclaimed. "And another one from Mexico. Mercer mostly collected U.S. stamps but I guess he thought these were especially gorgeous."

"Bet Mexico has monarch stamps over the years because that's where the butterflies migrate to." Sister paused. "Not so much the reptile stamps. I mean, I don't think reptiles migrate to Mexico. They just sleep in people's basements and sheds." She smiled.

"Let's think about money." Gray unrolled his sleeves, as he had rolled them up. "Mercer's collection, just what we've looked through, the last fifty years, is considerable. He began collecting as a child."

Aunt Daniella interrupted. "Seven. Second grade."

"As he grew, made more money, he bought more stamps." Yvonne eyed the books they had now placed on the coffee table. "Many of these books precede fifty years."

"Yes. He focused on stamps from the nineteenth century once he became successful. He would always buy what our postal service released each year, say a flat or however you describe a sheet of stamps. He put his real money, as he would say, in tracking down stamps from the mid-nineteenth century. Mercer said our country didn't issue stamps until about 1847. Think that's what he said. I would listen to him but I don't share the passion." Aunt Daniella was truthful.

"What did we do before that?" Yvonne wondered.

"Hand stamps, you know, use a carved wooden block or something and stamp the envelope." Aunt Daniella then added, "I only know that because my son would rattle on as he would put his purchases in the books, which you see. He'd use tweezers and carefully put them under protected cellophane and later clear plastic. He said you had to be careful because not all paper or plastic is the same. And also no humidity. That's tough in Virginia."

"He kept his stuff in a safe in the back room and once he put air-conditioning in his house . . . next to Aunt Dan's, as you know . . . he swore he never worried about anything getting stuck. He was a little bit obsessive. That was why he was so good at Thoroughbred bloodline research." Gray had loved his cousin. "He could also be fussy about clothing."

"Taste," Aunt Daniella simply said.

"We've paged through later books. What have we found?" Yvonne felt defeated.

"That stamps truly are works of art. That some are worth a great deal of money, and I expect my cousin's collection is. He had a healthy discretionary income. That's what we know."

"Back to money." Sister smiled at her husband. "Stamps are worth money."

He nodded. "Yes."

"What if the stamps we know about were payment?"

"Really?" Yvonne's eyebrows shot up. "But the ones we've focused on are 1987, a 2010 monarch for sixty-six cents and some worth thirty-seven cents. They might be worth a bit more now, thanks to the passage of time, but what, a dollar? Two dollars?"

"Barry and the Snavely fellow would have to have large amounts of these stamps for there to be some kind of payout." Gray stroked his chin, feeling somehow they were getting close but yet not close enough. "No one has that many stamps."

"You mean instead of cash, let's say Barry was paid in stamps?" Yvonne puzzled. "He couldn't have done much. Not enough money. Plus pay Barry for what?"

"True." Gray folded his hands in a steeple. "There would have to be cartons of stamps. Okay, here's a stretch. Monarch butterflies. If someone was sent stamps of the butterflies, maybe it would mean there's something in Mexico or coming from Mexico."

"Like drugs?" Yvonne stated the obvious as Sam came in the back door.

"Sugar threw a shoe. Sorry I'm late. The boss paid a lot of money for that mare so I stayed, waited for the blacksmith. Looks like I missed a party."

"Not exactly." Sister waved at him as he sat down. "Your cousin has some of the same stamps that were stolen from Barry. Anyway, since those stamps were also found in Charlotte—"

He nodded. "The dead man."

"Exactly," she replied. "We've been trying to think of what it could mean, if anything. Could be coincidence."

"I don't think it is. Too many of the same stamps and no other stamps." Yvonne was starting to get it, clicking upstairs. "Go back to monarchs wintering in Mexico. It could be a signal."

"Could." Sam thought that reasonable.

"We were trying to figure out if the stamps were payment but there would have to be carloads of them. They aren't super valuable." Sister continued the line of reasoning. "This started when we thought maybe stamps were substituted for cash."

"Well, that's not so far-fetched, just the wrong stamps." Sam was glad to be in a comfortable chair.

"You know, I think we're on the right track but in the wrong lane. Go back to monarchs wintering in Mexico. Maybe it really is a signal something is coming up from Mexico."

"Drugs. Obvious, I know." Gray rolled his sleeves back up. He couldn't make up his mind.

"Well, what else can we get from Mexico that would bring profit, especially if no one knew?" Yvonne asked.

"Silver," Aunt Daniella immediately replied.

"That would be easier to get into our country than petroleum or cars. Big exports from Mexico," Gray added to silver.

"Food?" Sister asked.

"Too difficult to hide . . . say, avocados." Sam was getting into this. "Do you all know Mexico is the largest Spanish-speaking country in the world? It's important internationally. We see it through the prism of our border but it is sophisticated. Mexico invented the color TV."

"I didn't know that." Yvonne was surprised.

"Has a strong infrastructure. Its credit markets aren't great but I think will be." Gray thought as an accountant who dealt with world issues when in D.C. "Americans are ignorant about the country for the most part. I think it's a good investment, especially in electronics. But I am not a stockbroker. Anyway, there are all manner of things that could be smuggled into our nation from Mexico. However, wouldn't we know if someone in the hunt club was doing this? I mean, what would Barry Harper smuggle into Virginia? I name him because he has these stamps."

"True." Yvonne couldn't imagine anything. "But those stamps have to mean something. And why put them in Ed Clark's boot box? Or one on Ronnie's door?" She looked at Sister.

"Okay. They aren't payment. They probably are some kind of signal." Gray glanced over at his brother, who usually was on his wavelength. "What do you think?"

"I think you're right. They mean something. It may have nothing to do with money but most things do. We are, what is the old expression, 'close but no cigar.' "

"Yes." Aunt Daniella smiled.

"Yes, but my fear is Ronnie got close. If something illegal is going on, I believe he tripped a wire." Sister knew they had to talk to Ronnie once he got home and convince him to hire bodyguards, convince him in capital letters.

"He seems far away from whatever this is." Aunt Daniella couldn't see a connection. "And, as to the dead man from Charlotte, why is he connected?"

"We don't know. He, too, had stamps," Sam reminded her.

"And he was in the import-export business. He could have been importing illegal items. It is a stretch." Sister felt a gnawing worry about Ronnie.

"We can't assume there isn't danger." Gray felt his wife's unease. "If someone slips, or gets close, I guess we'll find out."

CHAPTER 27

October 21, 2022, Friday

"*Daddy!*" Atlas screamed as Sister put him on the floor.

"My baby." Ronnie wiped tears from his eye, for on the left he wore a pirate's patch on it, as the little dog leapt onto his lap.

"He was a good boy."

"*I love you. I love you. I love you.*" The chihuahua licked Ronnie's tears, put his little paws on either side of his owner's face.

Not that Atlas thought of Ronnie as his owner, more his best friend.

Sister sat next to the bandaged man, having pulled up a light chair since Ronnie was folded into a big club chair in what he called his workroom.

Sister noticed the fire, got up, and threw a log on. "Needs another one."

"Thanks. I can walk. I actually can throw a log in the fire."

"You can, but I can do it better." She leaned over to kiss his cheek before sitting back down, having gotten her cheek kissed by Atlas. "We were all worried about you. You are dear to me. You're my second son."

He teared up again. "Sister, we have been through a lot. You stood by me no matter what."

"It's funny how you learn about people. I saw you with RayRay, boy stuff, baseball, riding, water balloon fights in the summer. And sometimes eating me out of house and home. As you entered your teens. My God, boys can eat." She beamed at him. "When we lost RayRay, you and your mother helped me so much. At fourteen you somehow knew what to do. And then when your mother passed away, I took you in. Big Ray always thought your father couldn't handle a son, any son. Without Beatrice it was as though all his worst qualities came out, which he took out on you."

"I was hardly the son he wanted."

"He was the immature one. Having you around was fun. And you were already out of high school, so I didn't get to see you as much as I liked. Not that I was ever glad your mother passed away but I was glad she didn't do so when you were still in high school, under your father's roof. Life plays tricks on all of us. Anyway, I'm rattling on here but I am so glad you're home."

"Me too." He kissed Atlas again and the dog finally settled down in his lap.

"I'm also here to give you an order. We aren't going to discuss this."

"Oh." He knew that tone of voice.

"You are hiring a security service. The sheriff's department can't protect you twenty-four hours a day and neither can your friends, plus we aren't professionals, honey."

"I've seen you shoot." He smiled at her.

"Blowing clays out of the sky is not the same as shooting to protect someone. Whoever did this to you is still out there. I'd bet on that."

He stroked Atlas, lifted his feet up on a fat hassock, which she'd pushed toward him, positioning it under his feet.

"Sister, sit down. You don't have to do all this."

"If I do you'll eventually feel guilty and do what I tell you."

He grinned at her, as always, feeling she had mothered him when he needed her. She never once said a word about him being gay. Not one. He knew it wasn't that she was unable to discuss it, only that she loved him and didn't need explanations. Mercer Laprade had helped him understand, as did Aunt Daniella in her own way. Sister simply loved him. She only wanted him to be happy. He was mostly happy but he hadn't found a partner and he was cruising into his early forties.

"The fellow from the police is out front in a car. I told him he could come in but he said he was told to watch from the car. This is the damnedest thing," Ronnie muttered.

"I suppose Ben grilled you once you were up to it."

"He did. He wasn't bearing down on me but he asked so many questions I really got a headache." Ronnie paused. "But I think I would have gotten one anyway."

"What about now?"

"My left eye hurts, obviously, and I feel the little broken blood vessels. You know how someone's eyes are red when they're hung-over? Well, if I take this patch off my eye, it's bloodred."

"Does it hurt a lot?"

"No, but when I look right or left, I really feel it. Plus the patch. I suppose it helps, no bright lights, but I don't like the eye in the dark all the time."

"When do you see the doctor again?"

"Next week, but an RN comes every day now. And you've come every day since the beginning. Most of the time I've been sleeping. I'd wake up and find what you left for me. I like the little keychain with the leather fox on it. Liked the batch of Micron 08 felt-tip pens you left me."

"You are fussy about your pens." She smiled.

"I am. But I always knew you'd been there. So many people stopped by. Most of them I didn't see the first days in the hospital, but I bounced back pretty fast. Well, I had no organ damage. I think that would have been a real drag. No broken bones except for the eyebrow bone. I am not using the proper name."

"No need. Can I get you anything?"

"No thanks. Reverend Taliaferro will be here in about a half hour and she's bringing a cook. She's been terrific, too."

"There was such a fuss before hiring her. Some of the congregation didn't want a woman. Everyone seems to have gotten over it." Sister watched Atlas lie on his back and reach up to Ronnie's face with his paw.

Ronnie held the paw, rubbing the pad.

A knock on the door got Sister up.

"Sister, I can get up."

"Stay there." She walked to the front door, opening it. The officer was there with Barry Harper. "I called the sheriff and he cleared Mr. Harper. Thought I'd better knock."

"Fine." She opened the door wider for Barry. "We're all getting checked in until the full-time security force arrives."

"No kidding." Barry's eyes widened.

Sister thanked the officer then led Barry back to Ronnie.

"See you've got your dog." Barry sat down across from Ronnie. "Is your eye still blurred?"

"Yes, hence the patch. I guess I do better with the patch. I bump into things a little bit on my left side."

"Makes you look dangerous," Barry teased him. "That and the bandaged head. If you put a tricorne on, you'd look like a pirate."

"Anybody need anything?" Sister asked.

"No. No. I was on my way to town and thought I'd stop by since Ronnie's been home, what?"

"A day. You can't count the day they release you. It's an entire day of paperwork." He grimaced. "Fortunately, I didn't have to do all of it since I am one-eyed. The nurse did it for me. Why is everything so complicated?"

"To create jobs. Especially accountability jobs."

"Sister," Barry answered this, "corporations have proven they will give you shoddy products or charge you exorbitant fees. Someone has to hold them to account."

She nodded. "I agree, but Barry, who watches the watchers? Where does it stop?"

"Speaking of hospitals. I dread the bill." Ronnie jumped as a log popped in the fire, followed by a crackle.

"You have good insurance, I'm sure." Barry sounded soothing.

"I guess I'll find out. I don't think you ever know about your insurance until you actually need it. I will give the hospital credit, they took good care of me and my doctor was terrific. He spelled it out once I could focus. So I will essentially be monitored in one form or another for about one year. The eye, obviously, and the concussion."

"Do what he tells you." Barry sounded forceful.

"Oh, I will, but that doesn't mean I won't bitch and moan about it," Ronnie replied. "And I am determined to be in good enough shape to go to the Waynesboro Symphony concert."

"Take it a day at a time," Sister advised. "Something like that could give you a headache. You don't know."

"I'm going. And if it affects me, someone can take me home." His lower jaw jutted out. "Those concerts are such fun besides the music. It's hard to believe that an orchestra from a small town can be so good. Wins national awards."

"Does. It's like so many things. If people have passion, discipline, they can pretty much do anything. And here is a group of people who have it together." Sister then added, "I told you my husband sponsored a chair. The tuba."

"What?" Barry laughed.

"Tuba," Sister repeated. "He says the tuba doesn't get enough attention."

"He has a point. Can you imagine holding that big thing up . . . or worse, marching with it and swinging it right and left?" Barry figured he'd fall over.

"Has to be, I don't know, has to be fun, different. And when the light hits that big horn it glows. I never thought about it until Gray said there are pieces of music written especially for the tuba. Anyway, he sent it in, so I will be focusing on the tuba player."

"Kettledrums," Ronnie said.

"Bassoon," Barry rejoined. "I like all the woodwinds."

"To change the subject," Sister checked the clock on the wall, "Barry, Aunt Daniella, Yvonne, Sam, Gray, and I went through some of Mercer's stamp books. You never met Mercer. He was Aunt Dan's son. He had quite a big collection. We found the same stamps you had or were taken from you. Pretty."

"I think a lot of people have those stamps. Anything with flowers or animals attracts people, even serious collectors," Barry replied.

"Curiosity?" Ronnie wondered.

"Yes, we surmised they are pretty. We tried to figure out if they had any significance other than that but didn't come to a clear conclusion. Gray thought maybe stamps were a form of payment."

"Would take a lot of stamps," Barry replied.

"We all also came to that conclusion. You'd need wheelbarrows full."

Ronnie, listening intently, offered a thought. "They could still be payment. Maybe promise of cash. Stamps have been used for so many things over time."

"Wouldn't it be easier to just write a check?" Barry posited.

"Depends on the size of the check. But it's not such an outlandish idea that they represent money." Ronnie's mind was working just fine.

"I doubt I'll ever know." Barry shrugged.

"Before I forget. I would like to take back my box turtle."

Barry turned to face Sister. "He is in the pink."

"Ah, there's the door again." Sister rose to go to the front door.

Barry stood up. "I should be going, too. Take it easy."

"I will. It's good of you to come by. The head nurse told me you had stopped by at the hospital. I was mostly asleep."

"Sleep is healing." Barry patted Ronnie's shoulder.

As he walked to the door, Sister was letting in Reverend Taliaferro and a cook. "Good to see you, Barry."

"We can work out a time for you to pick up your turtle." He smiled.

"Probably Monday. But I'll call." She watched him walk to his car then joined Reverend Taliaferro and the young woman who would be cooking.

Ronnie looked up as Sister again sat down, the other two women also sitting. "This young woman says she studied nutrition at University of Virginia."

"I did." The slight woman, maybe late twenties, smiled at Sister.

"He'll need it. Protein, I would think." Sister liked to cook but she didn't think of it as a nutritionist would.

"Her name is Dorcas," Reverend Taliaferro informed Sister, as Ronnie had been introduced while Sister was still at the front door.

"The woman in the Bible known for her charitable deeds." Sister still remembered her catechism. "Greek, Dorcas."

"The Aramaic is Tabitha," Reverend Taliaferro added. "Both are so lovely but you rarely hear them anymore."

"Names go in and out of fashion like hemlines." Sister smiled. "How often do you hear *Mildred*?"

"Mildred Pierce." Ronnie felt a little sleepy. "Wasn't Joan Crawford perfect? Oh, do I have to come up with menus?" He switched back to the cook.

"I'll make them and you can give me your approval," Dorcas suggested.

"Excuse me, you all, but I need to head out. New water heater arriving." Sister paused. "Shouldn't take too long to install. And Ronnie, I am leaving a list of security firms right here on your table. Atlas wants to make sure you read them."

"I think it's a little extreme." Ronnie chafed at the thought.

Reverend Taliaferro said sternly, "Ronnie, your situation is extreme. If you don't do this, all your friends will arrange times to be with you, including nighttime. I'm sure one of us in an old nightgown could frighten your assailant if he returns."

"What about me?" Ronnie laughed.

"That's a thought." Sister laughed, bidding them goodbye.

Atlas opened one eye. *"Thank you."*

CHAPTER 28

October 22, 2022, Saturday

Soft rolling hills with one five-hundred-foot ridge announced that Jefferson Hunt was on its easternmost territory. The land, gentle and generous, invited long gallops should hounds pick up scent. Sister, Weevil, and Tootie thought the youngsters should go to this type of terrain at least once before Opening Hunt. Jefferson's terrain, beautiful in its views, had some open pastures, places for brief gallops but much of the land was hilly to really steep, criss-crossed with deep fast running creeks as well as a few welcome shallow meandering ones. The estates, some impressive, taught riders history whether they wanted to know it or not. Some still had slave quarters kept in good condition, and as most were built with chestnut logs, an extraordinary work.

Sister wondered about both the big estates and the sturdy chestnut cabins. Who lived there? Did they have loving families, free or enslaved? What skills did people possess and how tough were they to live before electricity, refrigeration, and power tools? Compared to our ancestors, regardless of status, we are candy-asses. She kept this to herself except for Betty and Gray, who never failed to fascinate her, Sam and Aunt Daniella. Over the years one learns to whom one can truly speak and to whom one should shut up.

Walking along the back one thousand acres of old Kingswood, originally named in honor of King George, she marveled at the temperature, already in the sixties, as well as floods of sunshine. Chances of a good run or runs faded under these conditions but you never knew.

Behind her on a slight rise, the home built immediately before the Revolution indicated brave people or people who couldn't absorb current events. Whatever, they prevailed. Kingswood was now owned by a couple fleeing the long bitter winters of Vermont. Thrilled to be in Virginia's four distinct seasons of equal length, they were also respectful of history. Then again, Virginia, one of the Original Thirteen, was deep in history.

She tried not to let her mind wander but sometimes when hounds pushed hard with little result she did look around, think of the past; she spied raptors spying on her, saw herds of deer, large herds, contentedly grazing, and joy washed over her. To be outside, in good health, amidst such beauty, what could be better? Perhaps for another person it would be a huge apartment on the ninetieth floor overlooking Central Park. She could enjoy being in Central Park, but she had no desire to look at it. Sister truly was a country girl.

Dreamboat, a hound who had improved dramatically with age, nosed around the old deep well used to store foods in summer. Ice prevailed down there longer than the more shallow wells up by the main house, a large painted brick home, unadorned yet impressive. The original roof, slate, still held. Dreamboat, while not interested in human expenditure, did realize through his nose what humans built that attracted wildlife. He inhaled the unmistakable odor of skunk, a nice home, ten yards from him. A pair of beady black eyes looked out at him from a pile of small brush dragged over the entrance. Wisely, he kept going as she complained.

"You come near me and you'll stink for days. You won't be able to see either!" She left her home, standing right outside, flicking her lush tail for emphasis.

Dreamboat didn't reply.

Jethro, to Dreamboat's right, voice a bit high, asked, *"Can she blind us?"*

"For a minute or two. Best to give skunks a wide berth. Not only will she let fly, the Huntsman will be upset. We'll stink for days and we won't be able to go out because we will ruin the scent."

"Oh." The skunk's powers were sinking in. *"Is there anyone else out there that can keep us in the kennel?"* Jinks, just behind her brother, asked.

"No. Not like a skunk, but if you roll in a dead animal, that grosses the humans out, too, and in truth the odor does linger. We have to focus exclusively on fox scent or coyote. Even if something smells glorious, not a fox, pass it by," Dreamboat advised. *"This might be a hard day, so let's keep our noses down and our mouths shut."*

The two J's did as told.

The open pasture, maybe thirty acres although it looked larger just because you could see all of it, remained rich green. Those riding who farmed or at least tried to grow hay marveled at how long this year's growing season was. Just the best, really, and it made up somewhat for the last two years of beastly, destructive weather, the results of which could be encountered in the forests, so many trees down, including gigantic ones. You never know about the health of root systems until it's too late.

Hounds reached the woods, cleaned up, no undergrowth. Looks pretty but gives no habitat for rabbits, underground nesters. Foxes will move through it and keep moving, despite temptation. Hounds, walking briskly, hurried through the woods, coming out on the other side where things were more natural. As this was out of the sightline, humans couldn't see it and be disturbed by things like milkweeds, pampas grasses, those plants given via bird droppings. Even black gum trees can start out as a seed dropped by a bird.

Once in rougher territory, wafts of scent filled noses despite the temperature.

"Gray," Aero announced.

The others went to him, now all searching for scent, which was faint. Dreamboat, reversing direction, kept pushing.

Dasher joined him. The two littermates' tails swished.

"Got it," Dasher called out.

Hounds ran to the spot. Yes, scent heated up. Trotting, the pack moved toward lower ground, where a strong creek ran. They didn't reach the water because the scent now zigzagged. Foxes, like cats, could reverse direction, walk in circles, baffle others.

Weevil, behind his hounds, remained silent. They needed no encouragement. He didn't know this fixture, having only hunted it once and that was in a light snow.

Hounds opened all at once, tearing toward the south.

Sister, on Rickyroo, dropped her hand on his neck and they shot off, the large field behind them. The land undulating even in woods opened to another back pasture. Ahead the field could see the hounds running as one, a thrilling sight as was the music. A stout coop in the fence line demanded concentration. Kingswood's new owner had put in new jumps. Nothing yet sagged, an always welcome sight, a jump with a bit of a sag.

Looking to the other side of the jump, Sister let Rickyroo pick his spot. Many people, especially show jumpers, decided where their takeoff spot was and they were probably right, as they knew their horses. Sister, full confidence in Rickyroo, let him pick it. She concentrated on keeping her weight over his center of gravity.

On the other side they took off, as the hounds had gained real estate. Sister could see Tootie on her left but had no idea where Betty was.

Bobby Franklin had to find a gate. He did, but opening it always took time. The last person stayed to close it so the closest horse wouldn't take off. Bobby had ground to make up.

Tinsel and Trinity, neck and neck, moved to the front of the pack. Young. Fast, they stretched out to their fullest with most of the D's behind them. The pack wasn't strung out but there was a bit of distance between the leaders and the others.

The gentle pastures encouraged speed. On the other side of this large pasture, fifty acres and mowed, another jump awaited them. Hounds crawled under the fence or jumped up, scrambling with their hind legs to get over the obstacle. This jump was three solid logs tied together. Big logs. Fat.

Rickyroo took off two feet from the jump, a tiny bit close given his size but not so close he'd pop straight up. Others behind Sister did pop straight up, which means some popped off. Walter stayed back to help anyone who might need it. No injuries, but hearing the music, seeing other horses run away, it took time to calm some of the mounts. Walter had to get side by side and hold the animal's reins. Clemson was a saint. Once everyone was up, Walter realized they were now far behind. Going flat out after being tossed might not be the best approach for a few of these riders. Walter, having learned throughout the years, broke into an easy canter.

"Follow me. They'll slow down up ahead. Get your leg under you."

Most of the riders were grateful. One or two thought they were above the suggestion but you don't pass a master, so they rode behind Walter, upset that no one realized how good they were. Egos never die but they especially flourish in the hunt field for some characters.

Dreamboat, right behind the T's, caught something moving out of his left eye. It was not the fox. He didn't swerve toward it, the scent line didn't go there but two youngsters in the back, smelling bobcat, and seeing one, broke away. Tootie, on that side, cut them off.

"Jeeter, Jerry. No."

Seeing Tootie right alongside them, her crop in her hand, the two stopped.

"Go to him," Tootie commanded.

The young hounds did as they were told and she didn't need to crack her whip. Given the speed that they were moving, she would have had an easy time of cracking her whip. She was pleased they listened to her voice and the sounds of their names.

A small country store at a crossroads came into view. Weevil knew he couldn't let the hounds reach the crossroads. He spurred Hojo, who hit the afterburners. Coming up right behind his pack, he slowed slightly so as not to overrun anyone should a hound stop.

"Hold hard," he bellowed.

"What?" Trident slowed.

"Hold hard," Zorro repeated the command without enthusiasm.

"But we're right behind the fox!" Jethro wailed.

Betty, who charged on the right, reached the front of the pack and began to turn in toward them, swinging her whip, not cracking it, but hounds could see the whip was unfurled.

They stopped, crestfallen.

Tootie just reached the front from the left side and Sister stopped twenty yards back.

"Good hounds. Good hounds," Weevil praised them.

No huntsman or whipper-in ever wants to turn a hound from a red-hot line, which this was, despite the air's warmth. No staff member ever wants their pack to charge into a highway. They were perilously close. Weevil patted Hojo's neck, as he was excited.

Waiting, breathing hard, horses and humans watched as Weevil talked quietly to his pack, their faces still registering disappointment.

"Let's turn back," Weevil told his two whippers-in. "Sure glad you're on fast horses." He smiled.

The two whippers-in with Weevil in the front turned back the pack, hounds moved in front of their huntsman. He liked having the pack in front of him.

The field, catching their breath, turned with Sister, who wondered about the mysteries of scent. This should have been a so-so day. Warming into the sixties with a slight breeze and a high pressure system.

She leaned closer to Rickyroo's ears. "You never know."

"True." He snorted.

Horses have larger vocabularies than people give them credit for but Sister felt her horses understood her even if they didn't understand every word. She rarely underestimated another animal's intelligence, although she was a bit surprised when Barry told her turtles recognize a person. Then again, why not? We are different heights, genders, ages, colors, and we each throw off our own scent as well as having individual voices.

Gray, riding back with Sam and Yvonne, remarked to his brother, "This is when I'm glad I bought Cardinal Wolsey."

"He was expensive but he's worth every penny. He has that big Thoroughbred heart," Sam agreed.

Old Buster, not as fast as Cardinal Wolsey, rode at the back of First Flight but moved up once they were walking back, a wise decision on Weevil's part as well as Sister's. Jefferson Hunt so rarely encountered flat or undulating pastures. Their horses were more tired than they realized and even the staff horses breathed heavily, now slowing down.

"How'd you like that?" Cardinal Wolsey asked the older fellow.

"Great fun and my lady never wavered. I listen to them talk. She's try-ing to buy me."

"What do you think?" Trocadero joined the conversation.

"I like her. She takes me places. I hope she does."

"Sam will try hard for you," Cardinal Wolsey said.

As they rode to the trailers, Audrey fell back to walk with Ricky-roo and Sister.

"You all right?" the elegant Thoroughbred asked the hound.

"I am. Cut my front leg back in the woods. I'll be okay," Audrey an-swered Rickyroo.

Sister looked down, saw a trickle of blood. As Audrey was limp-ing slightly but not a lot, she didn't call Betty back to pick her up. Once at the trailers she would point out the cut. Given all that was out there in the woods, nails protruding from fences, it was amazing there weren't more injuries.

Freddie Thomas rode with Barry and Cameron back to the trail-ers.

"Saw Ronnie yesterday," Barry informed her.

"I haven't checked in since the last day at the hospital. Ava-lanche of work. How is he?" she asked.

"Pretty good. Has to wear an eyepatch on the left eye. He said his vision is still blurred."

Cameron joined in. "He's lucky that's it."

"Well, he is," Freddie agreed. "Sister told me he was in the hos-pital coming up with more ideas to make money for the club."

"I guess we'd all better come up with ideas," Barry suggested.

"You can get people to start stamp collections." Cameron laughed at him.

"Thanks."

"Cameron, I don't think there's a lot of money there but we could encourage people to buy lottery tickets and if they win give half to the hunt club." Freddie let the reins lag loose in her hands, having no contact with her horse's mouth. There was no need.

"That's such a scam." Barry frowned.

"Scam or not, if you win you get money." Cameron smiled at Freddie.

"And what are the odds. Nine million to one?" Barry shook his head.

"What are the odds for anything?" Freddie didn't mind someone not liking her idea. "Think of Ronnie. What are the odds that he would be attacked in his own garage?"

Both men said nothing and then Cameron did. "For what? He's not poor but why hit him over the head? There has to be a better way to steal."

"Not if you're stupid. Think of the bulk of crimes, Cameron. Most of them are spur of the moment. Some idiot thinking if you just grab that purse you'll get away with it, and some do."

"I guess. Not that I am promoting crime but you have to be impressed by those well-thought-out crimes like armed robbery or the big scams like Enron."

"How many people did that man ruin? How many people lost everything with Enron? Maybe you get caught eventually," Freddie wondered.

"No. You only know the people who got caught. None of us know the people who got away with it," Barry forcefully replied.

Back at the trailers, this and other discussions flourished once people sat at the card table and director's chairs, which people carried in their tack rooms.

Sister was still over at the party wagon with Weevil, Betty, and Tootie. "It doesn't look bad. The blood makes it look more serious than it is."

"Audrey stopped bleeding but she's not going to hunt until she is one hundred percent healed," Weevil announced.

"She's so keen. She'll be upset." Tootie loved the hound.

From inside the party wagon they heard, *"I am upset."*

Betty smiled. "She knows we're talking about her. Anything else to do here?"

"We've got it. They have water and cookies to hold them until we get back to the kennel." Weevil liked to reward the hounds as soon as they came in.

"I'm starved. Let's go eat. And let's hope Alida made her magic deviled eggs." Betty was already walking toward the large group. Sister, following her, remarked, "She really does make great deviled eggs."

The breakfast, wonderful, had everyone in a good mood because of the food plus the terrific run.

Aunt Daniella and Kathleen Sixt Dunbar served hot sausages to those passing their table.

"I didn't know you were here." Betty eyed a pile of sausages.

"We wheel-whipped for the first time. We were on the other side of the farm. I need to learn to read the radar screen better. That's why we were late to the crossroads," Kathleen confessed.

"You'll get it." Walter, behind Betty, inhaled the sausage smell, which made him ravenous.

"Wasn't it something to get a run on a warm day?" Alida actually sweated out there as they were running.

"Unusual but terrific," Cameron, reaching for another sandwich, agreed.

"Do you have your symphony ticket?" she asked.

"I do. You all have done a great job selling tickets." Cameron bought only one ticket; in case he didn't enjoy himself, he could slip out without offending a date who wanted to stay.

"Sister," Barry called to her. "How about I bring over your turtle tomorrow? I'll be passing nearby as I head to town."

"Sure."

"Barry, are you giving away turtles?" Cameron grabbed yet another sandwich.

"I'm giving back the turtle she saved. Betty, too. He's fine. Why, do you want one?"

"No."

"If I run out of turtles, you'll be the first to know." Barry laughed.

CHAPTER 29

October 23, 2022, Sunday

Old as the sofa was, the springs held up, no sag. Kathleen Sixt Dunbar and Sister sat side by side with maps of Jefferson Hunt fixtures. Ronnie, bored beyond belief, had drawn lines on U.S. Geological Survey maps, duplicating what he had done for the board meeting.

"This is easy to read." Kathleen held the map for Old Paradise.

"And he did it with one eye." Sister pointed to the main stable. "If you wind up there, and you well might, as there is a fox with a den in the main stable as well as the Carriage House, sit and wait. Best to not move."

"Will he run out?"

"No, usually he stays put and his den system is extensive. Hounds get frustrated. It takes coaxing to lure them out."

"I know Old Paradise is a huge fixture but seeing the topographical maps," she pointed to the maps placed together, as Old Paradise comprised more than one, "makes me realize how big it is."

"In the beginning it was more acres, but Sophie sold some to those who would make good neighbors. Like Beveridge Hundred."

"Tattenhall Station?"

"No. The land east of the crossroads had been owned by the Yancey family. Their fourth-generation son sold it to the railroads. Made a bundle and headed west, and the west was opening, so the story was he bought thousands of acres in northern Colorado."

"Okay. Here. This road climbs up, then nothing."

"Kathleen, you'll notice any road heading up the mountains diminishes to a trail. Building roads, especially back then, proved close to impossible. Three Chopt Road made it over the mountains and then was paved finally. But even today there are few roads, even farm roads, that surmount the difficulties. If a road is cleared, leveled, no ruts, that sort of thing, all it takes is a gully washer to make it impassable until more work."

"Yes, I can see that." Kathleen looked up, as there was a knock on the door.

"Come in," Sister called.

The door opened, Barry opened it wide, bent down to pick up a fancy cage, lifted it, stepped in, and closed the door. "Your turtle."

"Barry, we would have helped."

He waved that thought away. "Easy. And I made a special cage for him. Where would you like your fellow? House? Here?"

"Here. He'll be warm and he won't have to endure Raleigh and Rooster poking their heads to see him. Golly won't be friendly either. Here he'll have his own living quarters and see me every day and usually Weevil, Tootie, and Betty. But much of the time it will be peaceful. No other animals. Well, occasionally my dogs come in."

"Where would you like him?"

"How about here on one side of the desk? That way I can look down at him and he can look up if he pops his head out."

"He will." Barry glanced down at the fellow shut tight in his shell.

Kathleen watched Barry place the living quarters by the desk. "He has everything. Food, water, a place to burrow down under a small log. How big will he get?"

"A little bit bigger. He's not quite mature but close."

"Have you ever worked with the giant turtles?" Kathleen was interested.

"I've seen them but no, I have never worked with them. They really are huge. Would take two people to lift one if needed. Turtles live a long time."

Sister looked down at the fellow now opening his shell. "J. Edgar."

"Like J. Edgar Hoover?" Barry asked.

"Right. I always thought he looked like a turtle." Sister laughed.

Kathleen, also looking down at the little fellow, asked Barry, "Did you get your stamps back?"

"Did. No crime was committed other than they were taken then showed up elsewhere. Ben gave them back to me."

"Will you still keep collecting?" she wondered.

"Yes. My system is unconventional but I like to look at them."

Sister realized she hadn't asked Barry to sit down. "Forgive me. I was so enchanted with my little rescue. Please sit down. And I have a hotplate should anyone want anything."

"Thank you, no." He sat in the worn but enveloping chair facing the sofa. "This has seen years."

"And so have I." Sister laughed. "Old furniture was often so well made. Wing chairs, club chairs. Now they cost a fortune, especially if covered in leather."

"One thing I have learned in life, prices go up. They rarely come down." Barry rested his arms on the massive armrests. "Which reminds me, Sister. J. Edgar likes greens and vegetables, which you know. Don't give him sugar. He'll lick it but it isn't good for him. Isn't good for us either. He likes to eat. If his swimming bowl is warm, he'll get in the water. If not, he won't. I change his drinking water daily."

"Does he like to be picked up?" Kathleen was fascinated.

"Not so much. But in time he'll follow Sister around once he trusts her, and sometimes he might chirp."

"Chirp?" Sister smiled.

"Turtles aren't talkers but they can snort, chirp, grunt, and even click. I don't know what it all means and he can go days without saying anything."

"Does he need a friend? Another turtle?" Kathleen wanted to hear a click.

"Not especially, but if you want to give him a friend, make it a female. Males don't always get along, especially if a female is present. So if you had two males, no female, they would coexist but not necessarily be friends. He'll learn to recognize your voice. Amphibians and reptiles are more intelligent than we give them credit for. Remember when people thought birds were stupid and now they are realizing they are highly intelligent? Someday research will prove fellows like J. Edgar are smart in their fashion." He stopped. "Well, Sister, think how dumb most people believe hounds to be? They rarely win at AKC shows."

"True."

"Have people at those shows ever watched foxhounds hunt?" Kathleen was surprised.

"No. Then again, many people at the dog shows never have those animals do what they were bred to do. I'm not opposed to shows, don't get me wrong, but I do think it's unwise to breed an animal away from its primary function to become what you think is pretty," Sister replied.

"Hear. Hear." Barry nodded. "Do you all need anything in town?"

"A winning lottery ticket." Kathleen grinned.

"I'll be sure to do it. How is biz, by the way?"

"Fortunately, my late husband left me a thriving, high-end antiques business. I'm doing okay. It isn't steady. I'll have periods when every day someone buys something or dealers come down from Washington. Thanks to Buddy Cadwalder, I am getting customers from Philadelphia and that area. I was surprised to learn how many people and interior decorators in the area really know their stuff. Remarkable taste and, fortunately, the money to utilize it."

"That's always the rub." Barry stood up. "Luckily in my work people don't necessarily need taste but they do need to care about the environment."

"More and more people do." Sister stood up also and walked him to the door. "Thank you for taking care of my turtle."

"My pleasure. See you Thursday. I have a fundraiser in Milwaukee but I'll be home in time for the hunt and for the symphony. Look forward to it."

"Thank you," Sister remarked as he stepped outside.

Returning to the sofa, Sister stopped for a moment to look at her new responsibility.

Kathleen giggled. "Has Gray seen him?"

"When Betty and I found him by the side of the road I had him in the kitchen for one day before going to Barry's. Have you ever been there?"

"No."

"It's interesting. He said it's cyclical. Animals come in in the spring and summer then by fall most of the ones restored to health are back outside. Barry finds places for them where he thinks they'll be safe, can find dens and such. I'm surprised he doesn't need more help. Well, I guess he does in spring and summer, but keeping some-one on in late fall and winter would be an expense."

"One of the costs of a hunt club." Kathleen returned to her map.

"We are lucky to be able to afford a paid huntsman and one whipper-in. Many clubs rely on volunteers and those people are often as good as the paid whippers-in, but they can miss days, their private lives come first. With an employee, that's not the case, and with hounds and horses you need dependable people."

"Help always is the problem. I could use a true bookkeeper but I'm fearful to hire someone. What if I hit a dry spell? I only make money if I sell what I have." Kathleen wrinkled her brows.

"It's a conundrum. Especially in a seasonal business, which yours isn't but I would expect spring loosens people's purse strings as much as it does in other businesses."

"Does. Didn't mean to get off the subject. We were looking at Old Paradise topography maps."

"Right."

"As long as you can read the radar screen you can get to the right place." Sister put her finger on the border with Tattenhall Sta-tion, which was across the road. "Two big fixtures and Beveridge Hundred abutting Tattenhall Station on the west. That's a lot of ground to cover but all have farm roads."

"What's amazing is the radar gives me property boundaries and owners' names. Shaker and Skiff helped me learn to read the radar. Aunt Dan can read it, too."

"Aunt Dan can do anything. She had interesting ideas about the stamps. Her son was a stamp collector. She, Sam, Gray, and then Yvonne thought the stamps were payment. Then everyone realized you'd need wagonloads. But it would appear those stamps mean something."

"Maybe it's a warning." Kathleen considered this. "What do Ed, Ronnie, and you all have in common?"

"They're hunt club members and all can ride. Ride well."

"Everyone deals with money. This has to be tied to money."

"I can't see what those three have to do with paying someone for services or items."

"Somebody is paying someone." Kathleen, shrewd about money, then added, "Those three probably aren't paying anyone but I would be willing to bet that Louis XV desk right there that they might be able to figure it out first."

"I hope not."

"Whatever this is, it's probably right under our noses. Successful crimes or hidden profits so often are. You'd be surprised how easy it is to cheat in the antiques business. Falsify authenticity. Stuff like that. Really, Sister, this has to be under our noses."

CHAPTER 30

October 27, 2022, Thursday

As if announcing November lurked around the corner this morning, heavy frost silvered the pastures, those leaves still hanging on trees glimmered silver. The announcement reached fingers and toes, too.

Matador, a flea-bitten gray, looked lovely against the frosted fields. Sister, wearing bye-day boots, kept her feet relatively warm with a pair of silk socks and then a pair of cashmere socks over that.

As she and the large field followed the hounds, puffs of breath looked like cartoon balloons. The nip in the air energized hounds, horses, and most humans.

Old Paradise, beautiful in any season, took on an almost melancholy air, the scotch pines, Douglas firs, other evergreens provided the only color as most of the outbuildings, brick, painted, shone with frost.

Earl, snug in his den in the Carriage House, too much commotion in the main barn, listened to the horn far away. The only thing that could disturb his living conditions would be if a human opened the door to the Carriage House. His den was by the place where the carriages were lined. Crawford paid big money for those phaetons and one extraordinary coach-in-four. The traces hung in the large tack room, a second den. The carriages themselves, spotless, had piles of blankets either in them or on benches by the side of the wall. Carriages were not heated so foot warmers helped, as well as blankets. People would wrap up. Earl used the blankets, wool. He could burrow into the warm fabric. By the wall to the outside was one of his den entrances. Once he was in the Carriage House, he felt everything was his. Sometimes he would use the tack room. A few wool blankets sat on a bench; horse blankets, neatly piled on the wooden floor, were old. He liked the wool better. The best thing about the large tack room was sometimes people left food. They'd come in to wipe down carriages even though the vehicles had not been used, leave half a sandwich or a candy bar. Earl felt this was an additional benefit.

The horn sounded closer. Hounds were tedious. From time to time they would mass at the outside entrance and shout for him to come out. The older hounds knew he wouldn't stick his snout out. The younger ones stood there and barked until blown back. Those voices gave him a headache.

The horn was loud now. Earl roused himself, leapt into the two-seater, the summer carriage. From the driver's position, he could see out the large windows as the pack was coming for the Carriage House. He also saw Sarge, a young red fox, ahead of them running flat out, his tail straight behind him. The fellow had enough room that he should be safe, but then again, a stumble or an unseen obstacle could stop that. Sarge headed right for the Carriage House; within four minutes Earl heard the noise in his den entrance.

Sarge popped up. *"Dammit."*

Hounds soon crowded the entrance, carrying on.

"That's a nice greeting." Earl stared at the hard-breathing fellow.

"I found a silver bracelet up in the graveyard. A visitor must have dropped it. It's new and shiny. I tarried."

"And you underestimated hound speed." Earl finished his sentence for him.

Dreamboat, at the outside entrance, knowing Earl, hollered, *"You are harboring a fugitive."*

"Dreamboat, you're mental," Earl shot back.

"He knows your name." Aero, surprised, emitted a high bark.

"That's Earl. We weren't chasing Earl. Yes, he knows my name. We've known each other for years. Earl fully uses Old Paradise. Talk about living high."

"I heard that," Earl called back.

Both foxes then heard Weevil call to his hounds to "Come Away." They then heard hounds turn as well as hoofbeats going in the opposite direction.

"Should be good scenting. Maybe they'll pick up Mr. Nash or Gris. Gris usually marauds at Beveridge Hundred. He doesn't come here too often but Mr. Nash has made a den in that old toolshed. It's not as splendid as here or the main stable but it's good. All the buildings at Old Paradise are tight."

"They are, but too many people, especially now that people found slave graveyards and Monocan graves, too many people. And what I don't understand is why do people leave flowers in the warm season and wreaths in the cold? The dead don't know." Sarge found this illogical.

"Look at the graveyard at Chapel Cross Church. Those big tombstones, how about the one with the angel then the other one with the sleeping lamb with a cross between its hooves, leaning against its shoulder. That cost money and people are hysterical about money." Earl had studied the species.

Sarge sat on an adjoining blanket, warm. *"How do they know who is who?"*

"Names. They leave names. That's what's carved into those tombstones and monuments. So they know. Even if it goes back far, they know." This fascinated Earl.

They heard the horn now distant.

Sarge guessed, *"Going toward Beveridge Hundred."*

"Sounds like it. They'll pick up some of Gris's scent. You know he hangs over there. Jelly beans. Now, I don't mean to sound judgmental but grays are only so bright. His partner is smarter than he is. She sticks close to home. Those humans throw out enough food for litters of foxes."

"Good for us." Sarge smiled.

"In the meantime, you'd better realize that American foxhounds are fast. Don't wait too long when you hear the horn. Go home or find a den to duck into. They also have good noses. If there's a shred of your scent they'll pick it up."

Ruefully, Sarge admitted, *"I know. I know. I was stupid. I don't know why I like shiny things."*

"You and the crows." Earl grimaced.

Sarge did not reply as he, too, hated crows.

They listened to the horn recede.

"Did you hear about the human body tied to a chair?" Sarge curled up on the blanket. *"Target told Grenville who I guess told that old crab James at Mill Ruins. Think I left out a few foxes on the way. But you were talking about humans and their dead. Well, here was a human left out."*

"Gris mentioned it. I didn't pay much mind except that they bury or burn their dead. So this means one human killed another. They do that, you know?"

"Odd. Odd. To pay so much attention to the dead and then leave a body to the elements." Sarge pondered this.

Earl observed Sarge luxuriating on the blanket. *"You can stay if you like. We might even get a little snow tonight. Warmer here than your den."*

"It is. I've got some old coats and towels. I can usually snuggle up and no one knows I'm there. Humans, I mean. Maybe some of the foxhunters do, as hounds have been there, but it's quiet. I need quiet."

"I'm older than you. Not many years but older. Back to graves. Any time

humans do something out of character it means trouble. Either among them or trouble for us eventually. Wreaths on graves or flowers, that's natural for them. Digging up a grave is not. Leaving a body out is not. That's why I watch them."

"That makes sense. I like that the lady who hunts the hounds here, the black and tan hounds, she'll leave food throughout the winter. It helps."

"Does." Earl thought again. *"Far away now. Good. Watching people on horses is interesting. Then watch them on their own. They are unsteady. Must be hard to walk on two legs. Unbalanced. Well, how did I get off on that?"*

Sarge laughed. *"We started out talking about dead people. Leaving presents."*

Earl laughed, too. *"We did, didn't we?"*

"Thank you for letting me spend the night. It's fabulous here."

"It's nice to have company."

Moving through Beveridge Hundred, a large field for Thursday, hounds feathered but no one opened. They'd been working hard, wanted another run. That first long run bolstered everyone, especially the field, since all got a view.

Sister felt a view was worth a twenty-minute run. In this case they had both. Matador noticed the fox, too. Seeing quarry, then running behind hounds at full throttle, ginned him right up.

Now, on the other side of the old house as well as at Yvonne's small house, hounds pushed harder, tails swishing harder. Yvonne was again on Old Buster. She was realizing your feet got cold first. She may have grown up in Chicago but that's not the same as riding, your feet above the ground. Next time she'd do better in the sock department.

Sam, on Czapka, Crawford's main horse, stayed with her. All the diehards rode today except for Ronnie, who fretted at home. He wanted to ride with Kathleen and Aunt Daniella but they suggested he wait another week just to be sure, as they were bound to hit bumps in the road. Why jostle his head?

Creeping along, radar in view, Kathleen recognized the pack was together. The details discussed at breakfast now made sense to her. She could see when hounds were out of eyesight thanks to the eight-inch screen.

Tattoo, moving through the back pasture, could hear Ribbon, Yvonne's Norfolk terrier, barking in the house. *"Worm?"* he thought.

Taz, nose also down, whispered, *"When you're that little what else can you do but bark?"*

Not a bark but a low moan almost, Angle with his sister, Audrey, uttered, *"Coyote."*

All hounds moved to the spot, and realizing this was good, off they roared. Coyote was better than nothing.

Weevil doubled his notes on the horn then screamed at the top of his lungs.

Then he blew again, *"All on."*

What could be better?

Sister cleared the simple coop in the old fence line, almost flinging herself to move ahead, for the pace was electrifying. Coyotes can fly and they usually run in a straight line. This fellow was no exception.

He was far enough ahead not to worry, but as his scent was stronger than a fox's, hounds could stick.

As the animal slid into the woods, the field had to get on a decent path, but they weren't far from the action. Hounds, single file, threaded through the woods, then as the topography opened to another fenced field, still Beveridge Hundred's back acres, they fanned out again but ran close together. The old jump there, logs, had the top log broken, so it sagged in the middle, making for a small obstacle. Up ahead a trail snaked into the back woods. A tree had fallen,

Sister could elude the branches but had to jump the trunk, very thick. She did, but she hoped she would not have to do that on return. The footing, good, as the frost was melting, helped. Some people's horses balked at the trunk. They had to fall back to Second Flight, where Bobby had his hands full keeping everyone together and finding ways around the obstacles. He knew they were on coyote; falling behind would mean far behind.

Dreamboat, Dasher, and Dragon surged to the front. Barreling through more woods they again came out in a clearing, an abandoned pasture from years ago. The brush and stickers had died in the cold, but one still had to force through them. This slowed everyone.

Betty cursed, realized she was cursing loudly so she shut up. Weevil did the best he could to stick with his roaring pack. Tootie was running along a narrow creek, which made going easier, but she soon saw she was going to have to climb up as the creek path disappeared, fallen trees everywhere.

On and on they ran, stopping at a large rock outcropping. The coyote's den was there. He leapt to the top of the rocks, dropping down into a large crevice, and slipped into his den. Dragon reached it first and dropped down.

Sister could hear the terrible fight.

Weevil jumped off Gunpowder without handing his reins to anyone. Fortunately, Gunpowder knew the game. He stood still. Weevil had grabbed his gun in a holster on the right back side of his saddle. He clambered up the rocks. Betty reached him first. She, too, dismounted, grabbed her pistol, and climbed up. It was slippery.

"Dragon!" Weevil called as the hound fought the coyote.

Dragon heard his huntsman's voice but his blood was up. He wanted to kill the coyote, but the wily animal was getting the better of him.

"Leave it." Weevil fired in the air, which scared some of the horses in the field unaccustomed to gunfire.

Betty, gun in hand, was going to let herself down into the crevice.

"Betty, don't. For God's sake, don't. He'll turn on you." Weevil felt sweat trickle down his back.

Sister stayed put. She would only add to the confusion. Tootie was crawling up on the rocks.

Weevil fired at the coyote but not directly. Enough for the bullet to crease the rock. He knew the two animals were so entangled that he could as easily hit Dragon as not.

"Tootie, go back down and hold the hounds. The last thing we need is for the pack to get into this," Weevil ordered.

Tootie immediately clambered down to stand in front of the pack, excited by the fight.

Weevil again fired. This time the coyote slunk back into his den.

"Dragon, no!" Weevil shouted for the hound. Arrogant as always, Dragon started to go inside the opening, a little small for him. "Betty, I'm going down. I'll lift Dragon up but if he turns on me, I'll probably drop him."

"Right." Betty knew once an animal is enraged, many things can happen, none of them good. Dragon might go for Weevil's throat. A tear on the arm or leg is one thing. A large canine can kill you in short order if he or she grabs your throat. Betty was not foolish enough to say "Be careful."

Sister, Gray now next to her, watched, both knowing this could get a lot worse.

"Dragon. Dragon. Good boy." Weevil's voice was now calm.

Dragon, blood flowing from deep bite wounds, stopped a moment. He was a little shaky. The coyote had done a lot of damage.

"Come on. Come on. Brave boy. Good hound."

The handsome, large animal looked directly into Weevil's eyes. Weevil thought he could calm him enough to lift him.

Betty, seeing all this, called over her shoulder, "Gray, help me. I don't know if I can lift Dragon up."

Gray dismounted, Sister taking Cardinal Wolsey's reins. Once up on the boulders, standing next to Betty, Gray knew this would be dicey. Dragon was hurt. Hauling him up might hurt him more. There was a good chance he would bite.

"Good boy. Good boy." Weevil was on it.

He wasn't a huntsman for nothing. He petted the hound with one hand as he unbuckled his stretch belt with the other. Rapidly he wrapped the bright green belt around Dragon's mouth, which had to hurt, for the hound's mouth was bloody, but this was so Dragon couldn't bite. In seconds he tightened that belt, knotted it, knelt down, and lifted Dragon's hind end.

Dragon reached up on the rocks with his forepaws; Gray bent down to grab him. As the tall man steadied the hound, Weevil stood up under him, so now half of Dragon was above the top of the rocks.

Betty knelt down to put her hands under his chest.

"One. Two. Three," Gray counted.

On three, Gray and Betty pulled Dragon up.

Weevil struggled a bit to find his own way up. His white breeches and scarlet jacket were covered in blood. He knelt down, petting Dragon's head.

Betty also was down.

Gray, blood on his hands and also his breeches, took a deep breath.

He turned and shouted to Sister, "Call Kathleen. We'll need to get him in the car."

Sister, who hated carrying a cellphone in the field except for those times when she knew how useful it was, did that.

She then shouted up, "They'll be here in a minute."

Weevil knelt down over Dragon. He did not remove his belt. "You'll be okay, buddy."

Dasher, no fan of his littermate, turned to Dreamboat. *"He has guts."*

The youngster observed all this, too upset to speak until finally Jethro quietly whimpered, *"Was he wrong?"*

Giorgio, not whispering, replied, *"No. We are within our rights to attack a coyote but it's never wise to attack a cornered animal, any animal. Even a squirrel can tear you up a bit. Anything with teeth can hurt you."*

Kathleen and Aunt Daniella drove onto the field.

Sam dismounted, running to the SUV. "Kathleen, do you have an old blanket, anything?"

"Actually, I do. Lift up the back and you'll see it. I keep it for Abdul."

Sam then called to Gray, "Can you bring him down?" He then shouted to Sister, "Can you call Dr. Ligon?"

Gray hit the ground along with Weevil. Gray took Dragon's hind end as Weevil took the front. They carried the injured hound to the back of Kathleen's car.

Gray and Weevil carefully slid Dragon onto the old blanket and Weevil, after thinking about it, did remove his blood-soaked belt. Dragon might bite but his mouth was torn up, his tongue bleeding. He needed to open his mouth to breathe. He was going into shock. Weevil removed his coat, placing it over the bleeding animal. He didn't think twice about it. Hounds first.

Sister rode over. "She'll meet you at the clinic and Chris Baker will be there also."

"Thank God. Thank God," Weevil repeated himself, for he knew how difficult it is for vets to clear their schedule.

Kathleen turned around. She'd make it to the clinic in twenty minutes if there was no traffic. Thirty if there was. They were all thankful this was not a football weekend.

The field remained silent, unusual, but they were well trained.

Sister announced to them that the hunt was over. They would ride back to the trailers. Gray mounted up on Cardinal Wolsey as Sam easily vaulted up on Czapka.

"Honey, thank you for that. You could have gotten chewed up."

Gray turned to his wife. "Weevil knows what he's doing, but what a hell of a fight. I didn't get a good look at the coyote. Don't know whether he'll live or die."

As they rode back, a half hour ride at a walk, Yvonne asked Sam what he thought.

Sam felt the cold seep into his bones.

"I have never seen a fight, two animals like that. Once I saw a pack take down a coyote, years ago, but not one on one."

"I hope Dragon makes it." Yvonne patted Old Buster.

"I do, too. He's hardheaded but has a great nose," Sam replied.

He took her hand as she reached for his, the first time she ever really touched him. He squeezed her hand then let it go.

The trailers, parked at Tattenhall Station, proved a welcome sight. Once horses were attended to, they repaired to the train station, grateful for the warmth. Kasmir immediately pulled a chair in front of the fireplace and insisted Weevil get warm, as he was shivering.

Although Tattenhall Station was not the day's fixture, it was in the middle of everything. Kasmir and Alida offered parking and a breakfast afterward.

People crowded around the food. Gray, bloody, stayed back.

"Honey, I'll get you a dish. Sit down."

"Thanks," he said to Sister. "I don't want to drip on the table or anyone else."

She piled up a plate with the usual scrumptious feast offered by Kasmir Barbhaiya and Alida Dalzell. As Sister plucked deviled eggs for Gray, she wondered how long before it would be the Barbhaiyas. Kasmir was head over heels with Alida. They were a good team.

"Here."

"Thanks, honey."

Barry came over after bringing Weevil a plate of food and a hot drink. "Gray, let me get you a scotch."

"Thanks. On the rocks."

"Of course." He left for the bar.

Cameron, plate in hand, chose to sit with Freddie, whom he liked. He had paid some attention to Elise, who was there today, but once he got a good look at her husband, he decided that was not a wise path.

Gigi Sabatini was there; he didn't ride. His wife was excitedly telling him what had transpired.

It impressed Cameron how muscular Gigi was, muscular and rich.

"Can I get you anything else?" Cameron offered Freddie.

She appreciated his offer, thought him reasonably attractive but not her type.

They chatted and she mentioned it was good of Barry to fetch a drink for Gray. "You two have known each other for years, right?"

Cameron nodded. "I'm not happy with him right now but we'll work it out. He owes me money."

"Does he usually not pay his debts? I've never heard that."

"Oh, he'll pay." Cameron didn't sound malicious, just tired. "We have a different time frame. Know what I mean? I like my money now. He thinks later is better."

"What can you expect of a man who loves bearded dragons?" She laughed.

This made Cameron laugh.

Kasmir insisted Weevil take a down jacket from the station closet. He had clothes, bootjacks, and scarves stashed inside.

Once hounds were put up, Weevil took a hot shower. He sat in a chair by the old stone fireplace. Tootie wrapped a fleece-lined throw tighter around him.

"Finally warm?"

"I'm getting there." He smiled. "I'm lucky I didn't get bitten. What a hell of a fight."

"It's amazing what animals will do when cornered. Even humans." She sat on a hassock and rubbed his feet, still cold even after the warm shower.

CHAPTER 31

October 28, 2022, Friday

Voice low, Sister leaned up toward her husband's ear. "Have I ever told you how much I hate heels?"

"Many times." He guided her to the stairway, his hand under her elbow.

She could walk well enough but she had never found a pair of heels that were comfortable. At six feet, although shrinking, she often towered over men. She didn't mind that. She minded the pinch.

Gray, taller than his wife, listened to the swish of the long skirt of the emerald green cocktail dress. She could have worn it at twenty-four and she could wear it at seventy-four. If nothing else, Sister remained a testament to the athletic life. In his evening scarlet, Gray, like the other men in evening scarlet, dazzled.

Finally, at the top of the stairs Gray handed their tickets to the usher, passing through.

"Honey, do you want a drink before we go to our seats?"

"No. I want to sit down. I can find my way if you want something."

"Actually, the bar is mobbed. I'm fine."

They reached another opened door, showed their tickets, and were guided to front-row seats in the balcony. This area, great views, had been reserved for Jefferson Hunt Club. The seats were filling up with members.

"Do you recognize everyone with their clothes on?" Sister again leaned toward Gray's ear.

He laughed. "In a manner of speaking, no."

They were so accustomed to seeing members in hunt kit. Viewing hard riders in evening attire or even work clothing caused a moment's hesitation. Is that who I think it is?

Add exotic hairstyles, divine earrings, impressive cleavage, which could befuddle many a man.

Betty and Bobby, seats next to Sister and Gray, followed them. They chattered and all four gratefully sat down.

Everybody was showing up wanting to get inside before the lights dimmed. This meant a few chugged their drinks.

Freddie, Alida, and Kasmir sat in the row behind Sister. Aunt Daniella was in the same row as the Master but farther down, her date being her nephew and Yvonne. Aunt Daniella had engineered the seating.

Tootie, Weevil, Barry, and the Bancrofts sat behind this front row also. Ed Clark; Kim, his wife; Skiff; and Shaker filled out the second row. Across the narrow aisle, Cameron sat with the Sabatinis, as he was the one who had encouraged them to attend, even buying their tickets. As he had no date he could leave early if he wanted to; they probably wouldn't mind.

Sister noticed that Cameron understood that evening scarlet was actually white tie. He was in black tails. Other men wore black tie but no one said anything. Dress codes, no matter the event, had been relaxing for decades. While it certainly made dressing less stressful, it did not add to the beauty of any occasion.

The women were particularly happy because at a hunt ball, they could only wear white or black. To this they could wear a colored cocktail dress or an evening gown if inspired to do so. Everyone looked wonderful. Tootie so resembled her mother, once in finery, that people couldn't help but comment on it.

The sheriff sat with Margaret DuCharme, MD, thrilled to have a night off work for both of them. They got along but rarely had open schedules. Both were highly intelligent people, dedicated to their jobs, which they enjoyed. In a true sense they both saved lives.

As Ben had won his colors, he, too, was in evening scarlet, but unlike the other men he had a .38 tucked inside his red tails. Unless you were looking for it, you would miss the bulge. However, if a woman hugged him tightly, they noticed and he simply explained this by saying he had learned to be prepared regardless of the occasion.

Cameron stood up, waving to Sister, who couldn't have been ten feet away. "How is Dragon?"

As everyone heard him, they shut up, looking toward their Master.

She turned around, as she was in the front row, then realized she needed to stand up.

As she did so, Gray held her hand, steadying her, for the space was quite narrow.

"He will live but he will never hunt again." Noting the silence and expressions, she added, "He'll walk out once he's able and he can be a stud hound as needs be. One thing we all know, his get will have drive and courage." Then she looked at Cameron and said, "Thank you for asking."

She sat back down and everyone buzzed at once. Those who had been on that incredible hunt informed those who had not, relishing every detail.

Barry leaned down. "Sister, how is J. Edgar?"

"Very happy." She smiled.

This gave Barry the opportunity to describe the box turtle, with such a lovely pattern on his back, which American box turtles have. Turtles can be beautiful.

The lights flickered. Conversation did, too.

The president of the Waynesboro Symphony Orchestra, Charles Salembier, came out to applause, as many in the audience recognized him. Those under the balcony were people who loved music. They were not necessarily hunt club members, those paying for the privilege of being upstairs. Also young people filled the seats below, as the program was affordable. The place was packed. Not one empty seat, a testimony to the appeal of the orchestra to both those loving serious music and those willing to learn. But the orchestra, wisely, added popular pieces. No one understands those big pieces all at once. And music like film soundtracks often led people to more difficult pieces.

Sister glanced down. "Gray, I have never seen the Paramount this jammed."

She named the theater, a restored movie house that opened in 1931. The moldings, brass chandeliers, tapestries, and golden touches took one back to an earlier time. As she looked around, the lack of adornment in so-called modern architecture became vividly apparent. Sister thought of gilding or fancy plaster moldings as a form of exuberance. Then she wondered if so much had happened since this theater was built, depression, wars, mass death, maybe there wasn't much exuberance left in the human race.

As President Salembier finished, more applause. Then the house lights dimmed and the music director and conductor, Peter

Wilson, came out. A little shift in the seats as people readied for the first piece of music, Aaron Copland's *Appalachian Spring Suite,* the orchestral version.

Sister never liked this piece of music but she settled in to listen. As the orchestra played it, she felt she was in the middle of the orchestra itself. Every note hit her ears, every shift in tone, a delay until the next push. She had never recognized how difficult this piece of music was to play. Leaning forward, she became enraptured. How could this orchestra, started in 1996 in a small town, not even famous among Virginians, always thought of as a Dupont town, how could this group become so extraordinary? WSO, as it was called, took on difficult pieces of music. They didn't shy from Mahler's First Symphony or Shostakovich or Tchaikovsky.

She came back to passion. Does anyone or anything really succeed without it? Her passion, not earth-shattering but all hers, was hounds and horses.

After the suite was finished the audience went wild. They finally settled down to hear music from *Legends of the Fall,* "Ashokan Farewell," and *The Magnificent Seven,* which thrilled everybody.

Intermission followed this. People ran out to get another drink or go to the bathroom or marvel with friends as to how exciting the night was turning out to be.

It was going to get even more exciting. They could feel it.

Betty, a Perrier in hand, listened as Alida and Kasmir raved about the music. One could pick up other conversations as the upstairs room, with its long bar and tables with food, was jammed. People stood back to back or shoulder to shoulder.

Ed, Barry, Kim Clark, Cameron, and the Sabatinis stood at a small round table discussing the program.

"What an interesting mix of pieces," Elise enthused.

"Each year," Ed filled in, "WSO comes up with a theme. Like tonight is *American Frontier.* You think it won't work, and yet it does."

"It sure is a big fundraiser," Cameron said admiringly, then added, "Barry, maybe you can organize a string quartet for your amphibian foundation."

Before Barry could reply, Ed suggested, "Barry, get in touch with the National Wildlife Foundation. The statistics they have, say, of garter snakes can actually help raise money. Ronnie and I were talking about fads in wildlife. Maybe you're due for a boost."

"That would be good news," Cameron said a touch acidly.

Barry ignored him.

Everyone went back in, settled down. The second half of the program contained more film music with pictures behind the orchestra of America, whether it was the gorgeous valleys and Blue Ridge Mountains, the Grand Canyon, endless plains, wheat swaying in the wind. One extraordinary picture after another accentuated the music.

Dances With Wolves received a murmur of recognition. When the lights came back on and Peter Wilson with the orchestra took a bow, the applause deafened. No one would stop. So members played an encore.

Finally, reluctantly, the audience let the players stop. The balcony audience filed out, some already going downstairs.

Sam walked on one side of Aunt Daniella, Yvonne on the other. Barry walked behind them, Alida and Kasmir immediately behind them.

Cameron shoved his way up to Barry. "If you don't pay up, I'll blow your career."

"I'd be careful if I were you. People who push for more than they are worth come to bad ends," Barry coldly said.

"You wouldn't have a cent without me." Cameron's rage built. "You need my shipping, my contacts. Who else would carry your cargo?"

"Don't get greedy. You are well rewarded."

Cameron hit him. "Liar."

Barry, realizing he was now jeopardized, stepped next to Yvonne as he pulled a penknife out of his pocket. He grabbed her arm, pulling it behind her, putting the knife to her throat.

Cameron bellowed, "He'll hurt her. Stop him."

Yvonne, coolheaded, did not struggle. Sam jumped down two steps. He was now next to Barry. "Touch her and I'll kill you!"

"Idiot. I'll kill her first."

Sam knew if he reached for Yvonne, Barry would plunge the knife into her throat. He kept as close as he could.

At the bottom of the steps, no ushers, Barry dragged Yvonne into the theater's main seating. Most people were out in the lobby already, as there was still food there.

Barry hoped he could get backstage, where he could dump Yvonne and shoot out the back doors into darkness. Either he could steal a car or hide downtown until he figured out an escape route.

Cameron tagged along, not helping Sam but thinking he could attack Barry if the right moment presented itself. He'd get his money or he'd get revenge.

Sister and Gray had turned back up the balcony stairway when Barry pulled his knife. They reached the upstairs lobby.

"Ben!" Gray shouted.

Standing at the bar, five dollars in hand, Ben dropped the money, said to Gray, "Come with me."

Then he ran with Gray as they thundered down the steps.

Sister followed.

Hearing the commotion behind the downstairs doors, Gray and Ben hit those doors, ran inside, saw Barry pushing Yvonne, Sam dodging around him.

"Sam, I will jab this knife into her jugular. Don't get near me," Barry threatened, now hauling Yvonne up the side steps to the stage.

Cameron ran to the steps on the other side of the stage. Sam stayed close to Yvonne.

Barry knocked chairs over as he propelled the endangered woman to the back curtain, his escape route.

Ben, also now on the stage, Gray beside him, pointed his gun at Barry.

Barry laughed. "I'll have her blood all over the floor by the time you pull the trigger."

Ben would not risk Yvonne's life, but like Sam, he kept following the man.

Given the size of his instrument, the principal tuba player was at that stage corner. He stepped back as though to let Barry pass, then lifted his gleaming tuba, swinging the horn. It caught Barry's elbow, throwing his arm away from Yvonne's throat.

Sam, lightning fast, grabbed Barry's arm. He could feel the tuba on his back. The player couldn't move, the space was tight.

Yvonne eluded the knife, but Barry still held her with his other arm.

Ben rushed up. "Drop her, Barry, drop her."

"The hell I will." Barry felt Sam grab his knife arm, bring his knee up, then smash Barry's arm onto his knee.

The pain made Barry release Yvonne.

Gray ran over to her as Sam prepared to hit Barry, who was raving. He turned on Sam. Ben yanked his collar. Barry turned on Ben, tried to get the gun from Ben's hand. He was as wild as yesterday's coyote.

He thrashed at the two men then launched himself at Yvonne. Gray stepped in front. He turned again to get Ben's gun. In the struggle, Ben fired.

Barry dropped on his knees, keeled over. Dead.

Everyone stopped.

The tuba player hoisted up his tuba to go.

Sam put his arms around Yvonne. Then he touched her neck. A

little trickle of blood. He pulled out a handkerchief and held it to her neck.

He was crying. She was crying. She took his hand and kissed it. Then she put her head on his shoulder.

By now, half the hunt club was at the front of the stage.

Ben, seeing the tuba player, gently said, "Good work, man. I'll get a statement later. Don't worry. I'll find you."

Sister, Betty, Tootie, and Aunt Daniella, at the foot of the stage, noticed Weevil, who emerged from behind the curtain at the other end, Bobby with him.

Yvonne turned and touched Sam's hand. Then she took Tootie's hand with her other hand, as Tootie had rushed up the steps.

"I thought I was going to die." Yvonne's voice sounded scratchy. "Just when I realized I have everything to live for. Sam, I owe you my life."

"Yvonne, you don't owe me anything."

She put her arms around him, her head on his shoulder, and she cried.

Tootie cried as Sam held them both. Tears spilled from his eyes. Weevil came up, stood by Tootie, her mother, and Sam.

Aunt Daniella, next to Sister, now reached for her friend's hand. "A miracle. Thank the Lord."

People were so moved, relieved, most everyone felt tears welling up. As Tootie released her mother, Weevil embraced her, then walked her down the narrow steps.

Sam preceded Yvonne, reaching up for her hand, steadying her descent.

She broke into a smile, more tears. "Sam Lorillard, I am never letting you go. Just try to get rid of me."

As she reached the last step, he lifted her up, put her down, and kissed her.

"Finally!" Aunt Daniella exalted.

Sister, laughing, kissed the nonagenarian on the cheek. "Romantic. You are a hopeless romantic."

As they were laughing, Ben, still on the stage with Gray, realized Cameron had disappeared.

CHAPTER 32

October 29, 2022, Saturday

Lazy snowflakes twirled down outside Sister's living room window. Hunting canceled the day after the Waynesboro Symphony Orchestra, a tradition, meant the club members could gather at Roughneck Farm.

Aunt Daniella, Yvonne, Sam, Ronnie, Betty, Bobby, Alida, Kasmir, Ed, Weevil, Tootie, and Freddie squeezed together. Weevil and Tootie sat on pillows on the floor. The fire, that wood smell, always seems to draw people together.

Ben Sidell stood by the fireplace while Margaret DuCharme, about as tired as he was from last night's events, sat in a chair Gray had carried in from the library. Golly stretched on the back of the sofa while the two dogs, no room on the floor, sat across from Ben at the fireplace.

Despite all, Yvonne was glowing, thanks to realizing she loved Sam. Plus he had finally gotten Marty to sell her Old Buster.

"I can't believe you all didn't let me go to the symphony," Ronnie complained. "I missed everything."

"And what would have happened if you'd been pushed in the crowd? Got worse once the shouting started." Betty gave him her tough mom look.

"Maybe. But I missed the best symphony ever on all counts. No one else will ever be shot at a performance."

"No," Bobby agreed. "But perhaps they should be."

"Is this a critique?" Freddie fiddled with the gold ring on her finger.

"Only for counter-sopranos," he replied.

"Not fair." Kasmir leaned toward Bobby, whom he much liked. "But there never will be a night like last night."

"Let's hope so." Ben liked the warmth on his legs, as he'd pulled his calf muscle in last night's chase.

"Can you talk about it or do we have to wait?" Ronnie was dying for details.

"What is the truth? Well, I don't know exactly but I can tell you what Cameron said once we caught him. As Barry is dead, we will never hear his side of the story and I would like to know, too."

"But why would someone in Barry's position take such a risk? He wasn't poor." Freddie could still hear the shot when Ben's gun had fired. "He just lost it."

"Never underestimate greed," Aunt Daniella answered that. "My father used to say, 'Never underestimate the greed of the rich.' There's a lot of truth in that. How rich was Barry?"

"He'd made a great deal of money representing high-powered criminals. A conservative estimate, I'd say thirty million. Some from his work but most from poaching."

"Representing criminals, he must have learned from the best," Alida piped up.

"You may be right. He has in his bank account only a million. He had more in stocks and bonds. Obviously he had millions stashed outside of the United States. And a chunk of cash to pay off his helpers, for lack of a better word. Much of our work is in front of us. I'm sure he had offshore accounts. The huge infusions of cash he was making would guarantee he wouldn't bank in our country."

"But aren't places like Switzerland and the islands supposed to report this stuff?" Weevil, usually quiet, was curious and had a very good mind.

"Yes," Gray spoke. "I can answer that. Legally, yes. But that's not the way the world works. The laws for transparency, to follow money, are easily subverted. Hiding money is not difficult if you understand banking. Why do you think dictators look, on paper, like regular people? They have to look like one of the people. They rise on populism. Their hidden bank accounts are worth millions. Obviously, Barry was astute about money. Was Cameron?"

"Not as clever as he would like to have been." Ben smiled furtively. "Running down and finding a man in white tie on a cold night in Charlottesville's downtown was an event almost as odd as Barry's threatening Yvonne. He ran over to Water Street, hid in a parking lot, the big parking lot, waited for someone, a lone person, to get into their car. He jumped in the passenger side. Had no gun but offered money. And you know what, that guy drove him to James Monroe's place, leaving him at the gate, which was locked. The minute he dropped him he called us. We got to Highland, fanned out, and found him curled up by the basement. I actually think he was glad to see us, he was so cold."

"He's in jail now?" Ronnie asked.

"He is. He's safe. He told us a lot. Verifying it all will take time. The condensed version, the only version we currently know, is that Cameron and Barry were in business together but Barry hid huge profits. Cameron didn't really notice it until he began to question some of the people with whom they did business. Not all of those people were forthcoming. That took a few years. He was making so much money it didn't occur to him that Barry was keeping some of his profits."

Frustrated, Aunt Daniella asked, "What was their business? Drugs?"

"Much more clever. They sold amphibians and reptiles to Asian countries. A box turtle, a simple American box turtle, can fetch thousands. Cameron said once they smuggled in fifteen hundred turtles to a Chinese dealer and made two-point-two million dollars. That's one deal. Cameron flew the turtles and salamanders, other animals, to Charlotte, where Timothy Snavely shipped them out on large planes. We've shut down this end of the network, but it still exists overseas. There's more we need to know."

"So the man in the chair was in on it?" Kasmir asked.

"He was. Cameron saw more of him than Barry did. Barry was the person who collected the goods. He paid a variety of people to trap turtles, and snakes, and he paid what to them was good money. They had no idea what these creatures bring in Asia. That's another avenue we have to explore. We have to nail each of the trappers. We have a list, thanks to Cameron. He knew where many of Barry's trappers were. He never thought to examine them. Barry falsified their payments, skewing Cameron's grasp on the true profits.

"But Timothy's death was the alarm that it was meant to be. Fog spoiled it, but like the rest of us, Cameron eventually learned who the man in the chair was."

"Why kill him?" Sister wondered.

"He was pushing for a greater percent of the take. He threatened to expose Barry. That was Cameron's first hint that Barry was not dividing the money as he swore he was. Barry killed Snavely as a signal to Cameron not to try the same thing. He presented it as protecting both of them from a man so greedy he would jeopardize them. But it was a warning nonetheless."

"Did Cameron describe how he killed the man?" Tootie thought sitting a corpse in a chair macabre.

"As best we knew, because the only thing Barry ever said once

Cameron confronted him was that Timothy had it coming. Barry flew him up here to discuss payout. And he picked him up at the airport, drove him somewhere on one of the back roads, a farm road where we hunt, but Cameron wasn't sure. He told him to leave the car. He forced him to shoot up pure heroin. Then punctured his ears and slit his tongue. This made it look like a crazy person killed an addict. Cameron also flew drops for people. Barry had them, too. Some people he paid in drugs."

"Well, he was right." Sam would ever remember finding the body.

"Why haven't we heard of this reptile underground? Given the money in it, you'd think we would." Freddie thought it strange not to have some idea.

"I called Ed Clark, of course. He said it is one of the biggest problems now for wildlife people. The Wildlife Center of Virginia deals with all manner of wildlife, so Ed was aware of the profits being illegally made. It never occurred to him that Barry was reaping the benefits."

"Why do these people want turtles? Don't they have turtles in China?" Freddie thought the profits were absolutely nuts.

"According to Cameron, as I asked the same thing," Ben answered, "they love the geometric patterns on our different kinds of turtles. Same with some of our snakes. Their colors are beautiful to them. Having a reptile or an amphibian for a pet is easier than a dog."

"Some of those countries, people eat dogs." Betty shivered.

Ed piped up. "If there are trade penalties for that, it will slow it down."

"Ugh" was all Yvonne could say.

"When Ronnie, Sister, and I visited Barry's foundation, it was clean. The few creatures in there looked healthy." Betty stopped for a moment. "He did take care of them."

"But he seemed to love amphibians and snakes." Sister was thinking of her J. Edgar.

"Maybe he did but he loved millions more. Some of my team are at the foundation now, removing what's left there, which isn't much. I sent Jude over to help, to catalog what animals are there. Ed said it was mostly empty, so Barry must have shipped out a large number of creatures as the cold closed in. Cameron again emphasized how much money is in poaching. My late-night research, I couldn't get to sleep, uncovered thirty major smuggling cases in fifteen states. This really is big business." Ben turned to Ed. "Thank you for taking these critters."

Ed replied, "Of course. They'll be fine. We'll find them homes in the spring and those that can't be homed will live with us."

"What about the stamps?" Ronnie wanted to know.

"Clever." Ben nodded to him. "When a shipment was ready to go out, Barry would send stamps of what was coming. That's why so many of the stamps were the same. No phone calls. Stamps, FedExed to Timothy. Cameron was close, so the stamps were often delivered by a local service. The stamp year indicated the number of turtles or snakes. And if the number didn't correspond with the stamp year, the stamp would be affixed to an envelope, the correct number written under the stamp. No cash. No calls. No emails. The recipient knew where to meet the plane. The number of reptiles, their cages, determined the size of the plane. They used airports, where they paid off people, very easy to do at the smaller ones."

"Who would have ever thought of that?" Yvonne was astonished.

"Exactly." Ben exhaled. "If it hadn't been for greed, who knows if it would have been uncovered. Thanks to the National Wildlife Foundation people who talked to me, I now know poaching is a huge business, not just reptiles. Billions. Billions in trapped and sold animals or animals like rhinos killed for their horn."

"It's really cruel," Gray simply stated.

Ben responded, "It's possible other people were in on the take, including vets. Loaders on the tarmac at Charlotte's airport, for instance. The planes flying to Asia. Did the pilots know? Many went out on large jets, according to Cameron."

"This is hard to believe." Betty shook her head. "You know, if people this clever can think of ways to make money illegally, why can't they think of ways to make money honestly?"

"We'll never know," Gray answered.

"Do you think it's the thrill of getting away with something?" Yvonne asked.

"I'm sure there's a thrill in not paying taxes." Ronnie looked at Yvonne.

"How can this be stopped?" Tootie asked.

"We have to list protected species once legislatures identify them as protected." Gray knew the ropes. "That takes time and argument. For instance, North Carolina needs to list box turtles. That's their state reptile. Musk turtles? Maybe they'd list all turtles in their state. If every state would agree on a specific list, that's step one. Then the penalties need to be spelled out and enforced. Enforcement is difficult and markets such as exist in Hong Kong and other Asian markets would have to see a severe drop in their supply. Drive them out of business. They won't respond to our laws. Look how many countries violate our copyright laws. Without pain on the other end, the poaching won't stop."

"They might respond to international laws, even if they ignore ours," Kasmir thought out loud.

"Yes, I think most would especially if they were penalized elsewhere, say, in their gas supply. There are a lot of ways to hold people's feet to the fire." Gray sometimes enjoyed watching people squirm over this. "But we have to form coalitions with those countries also dealing with killing or stealing animals."

"You're right, but don't you think, given the problems in today's world, that this will be low on our country's priority list, as well as other countries'?" Freddie was a realistic woman.

"The only way to realize this ban is to affix it to a larger piece of legislation. That often works." Gray then continued, "And like the work for monarch butterflies, if people can come up with diminishing numbers and what that means to the environment. It's a beginning."

Listening to all this with fascination, Sister asked Ben, "How much is J. Edgar worth?"

He shook his head. "I don't know. If you're in Hong Kong or Singapore, maybe one to two thousand dollars?"

"I'll never look at a box turtle the same again." Betty laughed.

"Did Cameron ever suggest who hit me?" Ronnie asked.

"No. Barry was at the foundation when you were attacked, but Cameron did make a revealing statement. Barry feared you because you figured out that the stamps were payment or perhaps a signal. You were on the right track." Ben paused. "He could have paid someone to whack you over the head, or Cameron could have done it. It will take time to get everything out of Cameron, and sometimes you can't, even with a tempting plea bargain. They never tell all. Everything Cameron told me and the team clears him of murder. Could he have waited for Ronnie? Possibly. Could Barry have hired someone? Yes. But all we know now of Cameron's confession is he will be charged with illegal transport, risking rare species as well as common ones. Jail time? Depends on the court, but if he hires a very good lawyer, he will get a reduced sentence. Money again. And Cameron has the money to hire the best."

"Did Cameron have an idea why stamps were put in my trailer and one lone stamp on Ronnie's door?" Ed asked.

"Cameron thought Barry was unraveling. The threat from Snavely to expose him if Barry didn't pay him more money hit a nerve. Putting stamps in your trailer was a way to deflect attention from shipping out illegal animals. It made him look like an odd victim. Who steals his own stamps? But no one even thought about it. Barry opened that door a crack himself. He feared Ed because of his work here and internationally. Ed might have put two and two together. But Ronnie, Ronnie was getting close, thinking the stamps might be some kind of payment or promise of payment. Barry was seeing threats everywhere." Ben shifted his weight from one foot to the other.

"He wasn't too far off." Alida nodded in agreement with fearing threats. "Cameron was threatening him. He sort of betrayed himself."

"He did," Ben agreed.

"You put in a long day and night." Sam smiled at Ben.

"My team did. Calling them late Friday night. They all came to help, I have a great team. Young."

Sister, absorbing all this, asked Ben, "Do we even know the half of what goes on in our country? The theft? The fraud? The damage? The greed? Plus how those criminals are protected?"

"No, Sister, we don't. But I don't think they know any more in any other country either."

"You know, this gives me an idea." Ronnie grinned. "We're thinking of ways to make money for the club, right?"

Everyone, including Ben, looked at him and said, "Yes."

"This would make a great movie. We should write a screenplay and sell it."

Sister spoke, all heads turned toward her. "As your Master, I think that is an excellent idea, but only if J. Edgar is the star."

They laughed, the laughter of friends and the laughter of relief. Ronnie had been severely injured. Yvonne could have been killed. It was as Sister's mother used to say, and probably everyone else's mother: You never know from one day to the next.

ACKNOWLEDGMENTS

Ed Clark gave me the idea for this novel. I had no idea something like this was going on, endangering our wildlife. We hunt together and after hunts, there are often breakfasts, potlucks. One has a chance to sit and chat, for foxhunting is a most companionable sport. One could write many novels based on what Ed knows, works with, the politics of environmental, wildlife issues.

Rachel Moody, my stable manager, rides with me many mornings. An hour on my kind mare, Kali, gives me peace, new thoughts. Hunting on Kali makes me realize she takes care of me, for which I am grateful.

As always, Marion Maggiolo of Horse Country bursts with ideas. Her creativity is not limited to plots and characters. Her visual sense is astounding. Those of you who have walked into Horse Country know this. I have never spent a dull moment in her company.

Donna Gamache in northern Michigan, near Traverse City, sends treats for my hounds and comes up with ideas. From a Virginia viewpoint, this is a unique area, one that fosters creativity.

I thank my agents, Emma Patterson and Emily Forland, often, but not in print enough.

The same goes for Anne Speyer, my editor, who being much younger alerts me to current sensitivities. They astound me. Remember, I'm a foxhunter. Shut up and get over the fence.

Lisa Feuer as always makes my books look great.

Lee Gildea, a true hound man, gives us all those drawings, so true to life.

Lastly, whenever I needed a pickup I reread *Dreyer's English*. It's a tonic for those of us who love language.

Rita Mae Brown is the bestselling author of the Sneaky Pie Brown series; the Sister Jane series; the Runnymede novels, including *Six of One* and *Cakewalk; A Nose for Justice* and *Murder Unleashed; Rubyfruit Jungle; In Her Day;* and many other books. An Emmy-nominated screenwriter and poet, Brown lives in Afton, Virginia, and is a Master of Foxhounds.

ritamaebrownbooks.com

To inquire about booking Rita Mae Brown
for a speaking engagement, please contact the
Penguin Random House Speakers Bureau at
speakers@penguinrandomhouse.com.

ABOUT THE TYPE

This book was set in Baskerville, a typeface designed by John Baskerville (1706–75), an amateur printer and typefounder, and cut for him by John Handy in 1750. The type became popular again when the Lanston Monotype Corporation of London revived the classic roman face in 1923. The Mergenthaler Linotype Company in England and the United States cut a version of Baskerville in 1931, making it one of the most widely used typefaces today.